HARKNESS

A High Desert Mystery

---

by Michael Bigham

Published by Muskrat Press, LLC

This is a work of fiction. All of the characters, organizations and events portrayed in this novel are products of the author's imagination or are used fictitiously.

For Roxanne and Maria

Table of Contents

Grim-visag'd War hath smooth'd his wrinkled front,
And now, instead of mounting barbed steeds
To fight the souls of fearful adversaries,
He capers nimbly in a lady's chamber
To the lascivious pleasing of a lute.

Richard III

Chapter 1

Oregon High Desert

August, 1952

A hot summer breeze puffed my curtains, and dust motes sparkled in the light around Kate's hair as she traced the straight scar beneath my ribs. "Where'd you get this one?"

"Japs attacked our line. Someone tossed a grenade in my direction."

"Hurt?"

"Not at the time," I said. Sometimes I didn't know how bad I'd been hurt until the shootin' stopped.

"Why—" The ringing of the phone interrupted her train of thought, and she picked up the phone and handed me the receiver.

"Sheriff Harkness," I said.

"Harkness," Judge Barnes responded. "Where the hell are you? It's past ten in the a.m." Being sheriff in these parts meant that folks expected me to be on duty all the time. Judge Barnes expected more from me than most.

"I was up late last night," I explained. "Payday for the falling crews. I had to ride herd on the boys down at the Spur." Drunken loggers had packed the roadhouse and stumbled around like dancing bears, slapping each other up alongside the head with meaty fists and grunting "motherfucker." My duty had been to make sure they didn't break the furniture or kill each other. What I didn't bother to tell Barnes was that after helping Jeanie, the bartender, close down the joint, she and I had sat at the bar downing shots of rye and shooting the breeze until the wee hours of the morning.

"Get your ass down to the courthouse," Barnes said. "The McIntyre boy has gone missing, and his old man is frantic." He went on a bit about how the kid hadn't been seen in a couple of days, and how I had better hop right on this one. The old man, Jeff McIntyre, was the town dentist, city council member, and a community mover and shaker, just the person to get special treatment from Barnes. While he talked, I juggled the phone and signaled for Kate to light me a cigarette.

"Right," I said when he'd wound down. "Shit, shower, and shave, and I'll be on my way."

I handed the dead phone to Kate. "That was your husband." The whine of the big mill saw drifted down the valley.

"So I gathered." Kate wasn't an especially pretty woman, but more than handsome with Hepburn cheekbones and the rough hands of someone who grew up working on a farm. We'd been lovers for close to a year, but I still hadn't figured out her relationship with her husband.

"Joey McIntyre has disappeared." I lit a cigarette.

"Little Joey?"

"He ain't little anymore," I corrected. "He's sixteen and big as an ox. Over the Fourth of July, I caught him and the Kelly girl making whoopee in the back seat of his daddy's Oldsmobile up on Camp Creek Road. He's probably holed up with her or passed out drunk up in the gravel pit."

"Virginia's only fourteen," Kate said. "You didn't tell their parents?"

"Old enough," I said. "'Sides, upper-crust kid and an Okie girl who lives in a shack? We both know who would get the shitty end of that stick."

"Matthew, you are a cynic." She smiled, and the crow's feet crinkled at the corners of her eyes. I thought she was more beautiful now than when we were kids. She pulled on her panties and searched under the bed.

"Fortunes of war," I quipped. "Come here." I grabbed her hand and pulled her back onto the bed. "Have I ever told you I love you?"

She laughed, and her gray eyes warmed. "You're so full of shit."

"Believe it or not."

"Not," she said. "You've got to go. Joey McIntyre, remember? And I've got to get down to school." Kate did some part-time secretarial work at the high school.

"We've got time," I took her in my arms.

"The judge," she said.

"Fuck the judge." I nuzzled the soft spot where her neck met her shoulder.

"I have." She pushed me away. Her eyes cooled.

"You win." I sat up. "Let's hit the trail."

*

Barnestown was a fair little burg. We had one paved road, an official U.S. highway running through the middle of town. Every other street was dirt, dusty in summer, swampy for those few days in the spring when we got rain. I cruised down the main drag. Frank Flehardy, the town maintenance man, glanced up and nodded as I passed. Half of his time seemed to be spent replacing pine boards in the sidewalk in what served as the business district. I swerved to avoid the milk delivery wagon. There were as many horses on the road as automobiles, though the horse traffic had thinned as the pioneer generation died out.

Gravel crunched under my tires as I stopped in the county parking lot. The county courthouse was the largest human construction in our town, with a granite clock tower built by the faithful at the turn of the century when Barnestown had been the hub of central Oregon. People may not change, but times did, and Barnestown had slipped into the back eddies of commerce, still hanging on as a cow town, but mostly the postwar boom had eluded it.

Judge Barnes's office was on the top floor of the courthouse, just under the clock tower. Hotter than hell in August, freezing in December, it had a grandiose view of rimrock and river. The sheriff's office was in the basement, cool and dingy, a year-round dungeon. Barnes rarely ventured down there, which was fine with me.

Judge Barnes sat in his leather chair, cowboy boots propped on the windowsill. He smoked a fat green cigar that matched his suit. In Ochoco County, the county judge had no judicial responsibilities, but instead was elected by the people to run the county.

He swiveled away from the window and clomped his boots on the floor. "Cigar?" He knew full well I'd refuse. I lit a Camel instead and stood watching our smoke drift out the window while he told me about Joey McIntyre—didn't come home last night, always a good student, star tailback on the football team. I knew all of that already, but let him have his say. "You need to get on this right away," he added.

"We'll find him soon enough." I explained about Virginia, Joey, and his daddy's Oldsmobile.

"You're keeping secrets," Barnes said as he stood. He was a squat, broad man, long past bald, with Popeye arms and a perpetual five o'clock shadow. A jarhead, he'd stormed the beaches at Okinawa; I had been a G.I in the jungles of New Guinea. He rubbed me raw, and I suspected I did the same for him. I tried not to speculate on how things would turn out if we tangled.

"I keep secrets," I responded.

"Don't."

"Yes, sir." I always 'sir' a man when I'm handing him a speeding ticket or fucking his wife. I thought about asking him what Kate was up to today, but decided not to push my luck. "Where's Dr. McIntyre? I'll start with him."

"At his office," Barnes said. "Told me he had appointments to keep."

"Now he's got another."

*

I stepped over a black and tan wiener dog named Addison and entered my domain. George, my deputy, pecked at an ancient Remington typewriter with thick, blunt fingers while Miriam filed papers in the back.

"Speedy devil, aren't you?" I said to George.

"Barn door's open, Slim," he said.

I glanced down, then zipped up my fly. "Can't we do something about this damned dog?" I asked. Addison's tail thumped on the pitted linoleum floor, and I swore to Christ, the son of a bitch smiled up at me.

"You put his mistress in the hoosegow for kiting checks," George said. "Guess he's yours now."

"Take him home," Miriam said. "He adores you."

"Isn't there enough business for you up in the tax assessor's office?" I asked.

"You need me more down here," she said. Miriam was on the far side of fifty-five and was rumored to have been quite a hellion in her day. Now, she had four grandkids and wore her hair like a silver battle helmet. Though assigned to work in the assessor's office, she spent most of her time helping out down here. That suited both of us.

"Okay, fine." Addison leaned up against my leg as if I were a fencepost.

"Joey McIntyre's missing," George said, still intent on his typing.

"Fuckin' duh." I grabbed my coffee mug. "I'm talking with his old man after I get a cup of coffee." A moan drifted from one of the cells in the back. "Who we got in lockup?"

"Sam Gearhart," George answered.

"Drunk in public or beating his wife?"

"A little of both."

"Can't we do something about him?" Miriam asked.

"I'm cogitating on it," I said. Our esteemed district attorney didn't seem to think that wife beating was much of a crime. Sooner or later, I'd figure out a way to lock him away for a long while. Sam moaned again from the back. "Feeling pretty poorly is he?"

George looked up. "Yup."

"Let's keep him another night," I said. "Miriam, order up a nice batch of liver and onions for Mr. Gearhart from the café. I'm sure he'll appreciate it, him being hung over and all." Addison yipped. "And have 'em boil some kidneys for the dog."

*

Dr. Jeff McIntyre didn't seem as frantic as Barnes had made him out to be. I offered to interview him in private, but he claimed to be booked solid for the day and seemed more interested on having Mrs. Flehardy spit with accuracy in the round porcelain bowl. McIntyre wore a starched white coat with an "I Like IKE" button pinned on his breast. Nominally a Democrat, I figured I'd vote for Ike like everybody else on this side of the mountains.

I asked when he had last seen his son, and he told me he'd dropped Joey off at football practice late yesterday afternoon, but that he'd never made it home. "He's been pooped all week from daily doubles," McIntyre added. "Not like him to disappear like this."

"So he doesn't stay out all night?"

"Not during football season." He had Mrs. Flehardy spit again.

"If you were so concerned, why didn't you call last night?"

The woman in the chair squeaked high in her throat. "I'm almost done, Agnes." McIntyre twisted something inside of her mouth. "We'll have that lovely smile back in operation in a jiffy." Poor Mrs. Flehardy squeaked again, and I resolved to drive the thirty miles to Prineville to have my teeth cleaned.

"So why didn't you call?" I pushed.

"Boys will be boys," he said without looking at me. "They have to blow off steam. You know how it is."

"First twenty-four hours are the most important in finding a missing person," I explained. "We've lost valuable time." McIntyre glanced up, looking apprehensive for the first time, and I twisted the knife a little. "This could be serious."

He nodded.

"Tell me what you know about Joey and Virginia Kelly," I said.

McIntyre twisted something again, causing Mrs. Flehardy to

squeal and flap her hands. “I don’t know the person to whom you’re referring,” he said. “This is a delicate procedure. You must leave so I can concentrate.”

I told him we’d talk later and headed for the door. Behind me, I overheard him telling his patient, “Now this won’t hurt a bit, my dear.”

Back on the street, I sat in my ’39 Chevy pickup and cranked down the windows to let the afternoon breeze blow through. I wrote up a list of people I’d need to interview. My hope was that Joey had shacked up with the Kelly girl somewhere, but my gut told me that neither of them was that horny or that stupid. I’d start at the Kelly house down in Okie town. Her ma, Esther, would be there, but I wasn’t so sure about her dad, Ethan. Last I heard, he’d been shingling roofs up near The Dalles. Brutal work that, black roofs and yellow-white sun, but some folks ‘round here have to take what work they can get.

I hoped that Virginia was home and would know Joey’s whereabouts. If so, then another case would be solved, and I’d celebrate with a cold beer. If not, I’d have to start chasing down folks and interviewing them, maybe Joey’s mother, then his teammates, coach, and friends.

*

My pickup was giving me grief about starting when Anthony Giovanni, our local state trooper stationed out of Bend, pulled up in his ’52 Ford Coupe. “Hey, Sherlock,” he said. “Want me to spin the crank on that Chevy for you?”

“Give a wop a new car, and it goes to his head.”

“Get in,” he said. “We’ll swing by Grimes Flat and blow the carbon out of this baby.” I wouldn’t admit it to Tony, but he had a great-looking car. I didn’t covet the fancy new V-8, the black-over-white paint job, the growler siren, or even the beefed-up suspension. Hell, my old Hoopie—that was what I called my truck—worked just fine around this country, but goddamn, I sure would have appreciated his two-way radio set. Life could get a little nervous for a cop out here, especially walking into a logger bar fight all by my lonesome or handling a couple of liquored-up cowboys on some dirt road up on Grizzly Mountain. Sometimes a cop’s best weapon was his ability to bullshit.

“Can’t,” I said. “The McIntyre kid took it on the lam, and I’m stuck looking for him.”

"The football star?" Tony asked.

"One in the same. Seen him recently?"

Tony told me he hadn't and offered his help. I told him I'd let him know if I needed it. We dickered a bit about getting together later that evening. We concluded we'd both be off duty at eight o'clock. We'd discover if his Ford could really top out at one-thirty. He'd bring the Ford. I'd bring the whiskey.

"And bring some Cokes," he added.

I cranked the starter on my Chevy one more time, and her engine caught. "You are a dago barbarian," I said, and we both laughed.

*

Shacks in Okie town jumbled together in a warren of unmarked rutted roads on the backside of the stockyards just to the west of the main town. Shirtless boys played in the dust with makeshift toys and stared at me with vacant distrust as I passed. The Kelly house was no different from the rest, just another tumbledown, tiny one-room house with an outhouse in the back. Barnes might use a place that size as a garden shed or for a kid's playhouse someday. Kate still had a hankering for kids. I was still working up to taking in a fucking wiener dog named Addison.

The Kelly place reminded me of my childhood home—a couple of chickens and a hardscrabble garden out back, almost enough to feed the family, too many people living crammed into a single room, folks always bumping into each other, walls pushing in on us, our greatest dream a moment of privacy.

Virginia's older sister, sixteen and already out of school, opened the door. I fumbled for her name, Hope or Charity maybe, so I just called her "Sis" and asked to see her ma. She didn't seem surprised to see me, just told me to wait on the stoop, yelled for her ma, then disappeared into the house. Her ma, Esther, a burned-out woman, came outside. A husk of corn clung to her patched apron. She wiped her hands on the apron and told me she hadn't seen Virginia since yesterday morning.

"Why didn't you call us?" I asked.

"You wouldn't do anything for us folks."

"I might surprise you." I asked about Virginia's whereabouts just before she disappeared.

"She went over to Marybeth Oja's place," Esther said. "Mrs. Oja said she left around dinner time, maybe six. I was going to give her the dickens for missing dinner, but Virginia never came home that night. Never came home." Tears pooled in her eyes. She looked back into the house as if ashamed to have me witness her crying. I wanted to console her, lay a hand on her shoulder, but instead I waited until she turned back.

"You have a picture of Virginia I could borrow?" I asked. "It'll help in finding her." Esther nodded and went off to find one.

While I waited, Virginia's younger sister, a little blond-haired girl of about seven, peeked out from behind the door. "You the sheriff?"

"I am, indeed," I said.

"How'd you get that scar on your forehead? Cattle rustlers?" She pointed to the jagged scar that ran from my right eyebrow to my hairline.

"Fighting Japs in the war." Not exactly the truth—being sloppy drunk in Brisbane, I had fallen down a flight of stairs. They'd rotated me to Australia from New Guinea after getting shot for the second time. Saved my life, getting shot and rotated out. Falling down the stairs was just fucking stupid.

"Kill anyone in the war?" she asked.

"What's your name?"

"Sue Ann." She took me by the hand and pulled me into the house. As I expected, it was a one-room affair: wood stove, old-style icebox, no electricity, broken-down dinette, and a couple of beds shared by Ma, Pa, and the five kids.

Sue Ann told me her Daddy wasn't there, while Esther rummaged through a tallboy bureau probably handed down from Grandma. The home's only decoration was a picture of Christ's ascension tacked onto the wall. Their Christ had a nice tan and blue eyes.

"Figured that," I responded.

"You knew?"

I nodded. "I know most things. I know you're a good girl and help out your mom."

"Most times."

"Help her more."

When Esther finished her search, I asked her if her husband knew about his daughter's disappearance. She told me no, that he'd been working up at a line shack at the North Redmond Ranch, cleaning out springs and building fences. Almost as hot as tacking down asphalt singles, I thought.

"No phone up at the line shack, even so, it wouldn't be much good. We ain't got no telephone here either," she said.

I didn't relish the drive up to the North Redmond Ranch, sixty-plus miles over dusty washboard roads, twisted junipers, and overheated cottontails looking for shade. "I'll go up tomorrow and let him know. Man should know when his daughter is missing." I didn't tell her that it always paid to check out the family if one of the kids ends up dead or missing.

Esther nodded her thanks and handed me a black and white picture of her daughter. She seemed younger than I remembered her. Blond hair pulled back in a ponytail, she had worn her Sunday best, a print dress with what appeared to have been a doily fashioned as a collar. No hat, just a sad smile as if she realized what the future held.

"Confirmation picture?" Probably the only picture they had of her.

"June of last year," Esther said.

"Pretty girl."

Esther shrugged. We both knew she wouldn't hold her beauty long. Soon she'd be sucked down like her mother, premature wrinkles from too much sun, hands rough and chapped from washing with lye and chopping wood for the cook stove, tired and defeated from too many kids and not enough food. Down here, beauty for the Okies faded quickly.

"She was," Esther agreed.

"Is," I corrected. "I'll find her."

"There's always hope," she said. I tipped my Stetson and said my goodbyes. Virginia's sisters stood on the stoop and watched as I backed around and drove away.

Chapter 2

Three dozen young men, most of them towheaded, in football pads and cutoffs grunted as they pushed blocking sleds in the late afternoon sun. It must have been ninety-five degrees out, but thank God, not a hundred. It got so unbearable here 'bout when it cracked a hundred, the snakes and coyotes hid in their holes until the sun went down.

"Pick it up, Rob," Coach Conroy yelled in a high-pitched voice. "What are you? Some kind of pussy?"

I said my hellos to Conroy, an ugly man wearing a jarhead haircut, a permanent smile, and an Alabama sweatshirt—takes a special man to wear a sweatshirt in this heat. He asked me if I found Joey yet.

"We're still working on it," I said. "I understand that he disappeared after practice. Anything unusual happen yesterday? Anything that might relate to the boy's disappearance?"

"Like what?"

"Like anything." I felt a bit aggrieved. Smart folks playing dumb made my scalp itch. Good old boy drawl or not, Conroy was no dummy.

"Ordinary practice. Joey did break loose for a sixty-three yarder in scrimmage." Conroy tooted his whistle twice and, without further prompting, the kids broke into groups for specialized drills. How could a man smile so much?

"Joey especially close with anyone here?" I asked.

"Ronnie, over there." Conroy pointed at the quarterback, a lanky kid with fire-red hair.

"The Gearhart kid?"

"Good quarterback, nice kid," Conroy said.

I thought of his old man sitting in my lockup. "Maybe being a drunk asshole skips a generation."

Conroy looked at me quizzically for a moment. His masculine smell was overwhelming, like he was some great beast king. He opened his arms as if to embrace his team. "We're going to State this year, mark my words. We'll win State. Barnestown, State Triple A Champs, 1952." I didn't doubt him. He was a firecracker, but I found myself not caring. Ronnie Gearhart sprinted out on an option and tossed a clothesline pass down the field to a waiting receiver who muffed the catch. Linebackers and defensive tackles panted like Chihuahua's chasing a greyhound.

"We'll wrap up in half an hour." Conway was already moving toward his team and seeming to forget me. "Okay, ladies," he yelled. "Pick it up!"

*

Ronnie Gearhart joined me after practice. He was a straight-up kid with a fading case of acne. I remembered him from a few years back when I'd broken up a six-round prelim between his mom and dad. He had screamed in fury as I hustled his pa off to the bucket. He must have remembered me, but gave no sign, just yes-sir and no-sir'd me enough that if I was a married man I'd be looking over my shoulder wondering if he was sleeping with my wife.

"When was the last time you saw Joey?" I asked.

"At practice," Ronnie said. "We were supposed to get together for a burger, but he never showed up."

"Anything unusual going on with him?" I watched as a half-dozen elementary school kids emerged from the woods at the east side of the field and started a game of freeform football on the high school practice field.

"Like what?"

"If I knew, I wouldn't be asking."

"Nope." Ronnie looked at the kids playing football. They whooped as one team scored and then broke into an argument.

"He could be in trouble." I tried to shake his complacency.

"Joey can take care of himself."

"Like you?"

"Like me," Ronnie said, still watching the pickup game as if he was thinking about joining in.

"Looks fun," I said.

"Football should be fun."

"High school football isn't?" I asked.

"Kid's gripping the laces wrong." He motioned to one of the players.

"Tell me about Joey and Virginia Kelly," I said.

Coach Conroy honked and waved as he drove by in his Dodge pickup. Why did everyone have a nicer truck than me? There was a kid in the seat next to him. Ronnie waved a little tentatively, then returned his attention to me. "There's nothing to tell."

"Don't bullshit a bullshitter," I said. "She's missing, too. Disappeared about the same time as Joey. This past July, I found them making out in the back of Daddy McIntyre's Olds." I figured Joey had probably told Ronnie about getting caught. Boys share run-ins with the law with their best friends as if to verify a singular rite of passage. "I really need your help here, Ron. I'm looking after both Joey and Virginia, they come first. Did they pull a Romeo and Juliet and run off together?"

Ronnie shrugged. "Joey likes her. They're going steady, but no one is supposed to know. His old man will crap little green apples if he finds out."

"No one was supposed to know, but some kids did?"

"Small town," he said. "Hard to keep secrets."

I nodded, knowing all too well. "What about his old man? Was Joey frightened of him?" The pickup game changed from tackle to no rush, no run.

Ronnie laughed for the first time, showing even white teeth. Maybe Dr. McIntyre had worked on them. "Not scared in that way, Joey's tough. But he's worried about his old man getting pissed and taking away the Olds or not letting him play football. You need your parent's permission to play ball."

"Was Joey going to see Virginia after practice?"

"Don't know," Ronnie said. "Maybe."

"Anything out of the ordinary happen at practice yesterday?"

"Joey banged up his ankle. He was worried about it, but the Coach told him it wasn't that bad. He didn't think Joey would miss the opener. Still, Joey was nervous about it; said he'd stay late and have the student manager tape it up."

From faraway, a voice called, and the football players faded back into the woods. The field was empty except for the two of us standing in the five o'clock sunshine. "Where's the manager now?" I asked.

"Mike Barfield. That was him with the coach. He's probably back at his house by now." The big mill whistle hooted. Day shift done, next up was swing shift.

"Anything else I need to know?"

"You've got my old man in jail."

"Deserves to be there," I said. "He slapped your Mom around some last night. I haven't seen you there the last few times we've been to your house." "Let him out." His lips were compressed and pale.

"Why do you care?"

"He's my dad," he said, as if that explained everything.

My dad died when I was eight. I never cottoned much to my stepdad, and I took off on my own when I was all of thirteen. This kid was too good to do that. "Knuckleheads like that don't get better," I said. "He'll hurt your mom bad someday."

"I can take care of my mom," Ronnie said.

I made no bones about not liking Sam Gearhart, but our DA wasn't going to do anything about him. "Okay," I said. "I'll kick him loose this evening, but as of this moment you're responsible for your mother." Ronnie nodded, and I figured that unlike many folks in this county, he'd take me seriously.

*

A half-dozen little kids raced around the barren yard. Two black-and-white cow dogs herded them around with yips and nudges. When the dogs spotted me, they barked, half in warning and half in greeting.

"Duke. Duchess. Down!" Marybeth Oja called from the porch. A slight girl with black hair swept back into a bun, she wiped her hands on a dishtowel in a way that made her seem older.

"I'm Sheriff Harkness. Your parents home?"

Marybeth shook her head. "Coffee's on. Come in and set a spell," she said, as if she had been expecting me all along.

The Oja farmhouse was a step up from the Kelly household: living room, kitchen, two bedrooms, and running water. I settled onto a straight-backed wooden chair in the kitchen. Marybeth asked me if I took anything in my coffee and, when I said no, she handed me a steaming red and white metal mug. She poured a spot of coffee into another cup, filled the rest with milk, and sat opposite me.

"You know that Virginia Kelly is missing." When she nodded, I continued, "Her mom says she was here yesterday afternoon."

"She was," Marybeth said. "She left around five thirty. Her ma wanted her to get home for dinner."

"How'd she leave?"

One of the cow dogs followed a little girl into the house. "Potty," the girl said. Marybeth told her that she was old enough to go to the bathroom by herself.

Turning back to me, she said, "She walked."

"It must be a couple of miles back to town." The cow dog sat next to me and plopped his head on my leg. He had one blue eye and one brown.

"Maybe a mite more," she said. "Dad had our truck. He works

evenings at the mill."

"And your mom?"

The little girl came out from the bathroom, crawled up on my knee and asked me to tell her a story.

"Kathy, go out and play," Marybeth said. When we were alone again, she told me that her mom was out working in the fields.

"What about Joey and Virginia?" I asked.

"He's a buttface," she said.

"You don't like him?"

"He's just going out with her because he thinks that he can..." She shrugged. "You know."

"Yeah, I know." I wondered if she really did.

"I told her he'd break up with her when school started—Virginia and I aren't in the popular crowd—but she wouldn't listen."

"Think they're together somewhere?"

"Don't know."

I asked her if Joey was capable of hurting Virginia. For a moment, it was plain that she struggled to comprehend the question, then she took a deep breath. "No."

There was little else to learn from Marybeth. When I drove off, kids and dogs followed me down the dusty road 'til we reached the Oja mailbox.

*

The almost-new Ford police car spun down Grimes Flat Road, straight between two section lines, at a hundred and thirty miles per, siren wailing, coyotes and mama Herefords leaping away across pasture and field, and me and Tony smoking cigarettes and tipping back a bottle of Four Roses, laughing and whooping like high school boys out for their first drunk. The sense of danger set my stomach to quivering like I'd never gone fast before.

Telephone poles flipped by in a blur. The road was dark, dangerous, and with no white line to help guide the way. "There's a sharp corner up here," I warned. Tony told me he knew, but the yellow forty-five mph sign jumped up at us much too fast. The Ford squealed into the corner, the car's backend broke free, and I worried that Kate might not have believed me when I told her I loved her. Then Tony fought the wheel, and we were around the corner and off again, and I hoped that she hadn't believed me because I wasn't sure of what I wanted myself. Why hadn't she waited for me after the war? Hell, I was just hanging out in San Francisco for a while, only a year or two, then she up and married the fucking Judge.

"Hand me that bottle," Tony said, still laughing.

I realized the fucking siren was getting on my nerves, but when I turned it off, it wound down too slowly, wind pulling at the blades, until it growled to a stop. I turned up the radio, and Hank Williams yodeled some country blues song.

"I hear tell you're going to ride a horse in next year's rodeo parade." I could see his cocked smile in the dashboard lights.

"A nasty rumor," I said. "They don't pay me enough to ride no fucking horse."

"What will your posse say?" he asked. "A western sheriff that don't ride?" The Sheriff's Posse was a traditional organization, half-service, half-social, composed of local ranchers and want-to-be ranchers who do search and rescue when some hunter from Portland gets lost.

"As long as the county buys them some beer and a side of beef for their July barbecue, they're more than happy. It's not that I don't like horses. They have their place, and I have mine."

Maybe feeling he'd gotten enough mileage from that line of conversation, Tony asked me if I'd found out anything about Joey McIntyre.

"Both he and the Kelly girl are missing." I stuck my head out the window, and the wind brought tears to my eyes. I pulled my head back in the car. "Seems they're sweethearts."

"Nothing wrong with young love. They'll probably turn up in Reno, married," Tony said.

"I hope," I said, "but I'm not hopeful."

"Why don't you find yourself a honey?" he asked. "Rugged, handsome feller like you should do just right."

"You're better looking than most gals."

"And I ain't looking to get married," Tony said.

"You got me there." We both laughed, but my heart wasn't in it. When we passed the Grizzly Mountain turnoff, I spotted some headlights halfway up the mountain and speculated there might be poachers up there spotlighting mule deer. Tony wasn't too anxious to take his new Ford up the mountain, and I didn't blame him much. I figured tomorrow I could come up over the top of the mountain after seeing Virginia's dad at the North Redmond Ranch. It was a right nice drive, cooler on top of the mountain, and I had an urge to be away from Barnestown for the day.

Tony slid the Ford through a tight S-curve. I laughed with what felt like desperation and took a healthy knock from the fifth. I wondered if Barnes was fucking his wife. Kate told me she wasn't fucking him anymore, but I always had my doubts.

Chapter 3

The ride up the valley to the North Redmond Ranch was pretty enough in summer or winter, just too long on washboard roads for my taste. I kept the window down and hummed to myself as the countryside drifted by, sagebrush and juniper, up and over the hill out of town, then along wheat and alfalfa fields, faded to brown by August, and up the Paulina Valley. Maybe if I got a little ahead, I could buy a few acres up here. Good land, plenty of water, cheap, and undiscovered... so far.

I held my breath as I started up the long grade by Pilot Rock. Hoopie had a tendency to vapor lock, so I had brought along extra water and rags in case the heat caused air bubbles to block the fuel line. She hiccuped a couple of times, then stalled about halfway up the grade, but I expected that and didn't swear too much. Instead, I set about wetting down rags and tying them around the fuel lines. When I finished, I sat on the running board on the shady side of the truck, smoked a cigarette, and waited for the engine to cool off.

The engine was still ticking with heat when old Doc Silverman came by on his way down the grade. He stopped and explained he'd been out checking up on Elias Warner, who got bit on the cheek of his ass by a black widow spider. "Elias may waddle a bit for a couple of weeks, but he'll live." Doc was a likeable sort with skinny old man arms, a shock of senatorial hair, and a vague European accent. "You need anything here, Matthew?"

I told him no, I'd be fine, and he could head on out, but he stayed anyway, and we bullshitted for a bit. Being a history expert, he told me about how a band of Modoc Indians had wiped out a cavalry patrol up in the Ochoco mountains not far from here, and how the Modoc had gotten a raw deal by the white men. I allowed that I agreed with him, though I suspected neither of us would say that to many other folks in this county. Most just wouldn't understand, this being the white folks' land now.

It was along about noon when Hoopie cooled enough to start. Doc continued back toward town, and I drove over Sheep Mountain and down into the next valley. Kate had promised to come over in the evening, but I didn't feel hurried as I nursed Hoopie up the final grade through a basalt canyon to the North Redmond Ranch. The place seemed quiet enough, dust, sagebrush, and a curious cottontail peeking from beneath the crawlspace of the old homestead that served as the line shack, but I pushed my flapjack sap into my back pocket anyway and called out for Kelly. I hoped he might be somewhere close to the main building, it being almost suppertime and all. He was.

Ethan Kelly had his head stuck under the hood of a military deuce and a half converted into a hay truck. The flatbed had been cobbled on in some local garage, but the job looked good enough. If he was surprised to see me, he didn't show it, just wiped his hands on his overalls and offered me a drink of water. He was a smallish, slender man with bad teeth, sun-blackened arms, and the odor of three or four day's hard labor about him. I told him I was here about his daughter, and he got a long, sad look on his face. He invited me into the line shack to get out of the sun. "A man shouldn't hear bad news in the sun."

I told him it wasn't as bad as all that. I didn't add the 'yet' part. Maybe I didn't want to admit to that part myself.

The line shack consisted of a single room about as big as the Kelly home. Light came from kerosene lamps, and there was a hand pump next to the sink for water. As usual with those old places, the crapper was out back, and I got to thinking about how and where Elias Warner got bit by the black widow spider.

Kelly settled into warming up the morning coffee while I told him his daughter was missing. His shoulders sagged at the news. "I was just going to have beans for supper," he said. "Care to join me?"

I'd had more than my share of beans growing up and wasn't partial to them, but I wasn't one to let a man eat alone when he was in the sorrows, so I said yes. The line shack creaked in the afternoon wind while Kelly opened a can of pork and beans and dumped it into a battered saucepan. "Virginia's a good girl," he said. "A pretty gal, but smart, too."

"That's what folks tell me." My comment seemed to please Kelly a bit. "They also tell me she was seeing the McIntyre boy. What about that?"

"Her mama told her not to give it up too soon, not to get knocked-up and ruin her life. Us folks ain't got much in this life other than our reputation, she tells her." He handed me a plate of beans and a cup of Joe. "Esther seems to think that graduating from high school is important." He shook his head as if he wasn't sure he agreed. "Hope you don't mind cowboy coffee. Last line rider up here took off with the percolator. Now we have to boil the bejesus out of the grounds. Got some sugar if you want it."

"Black's fine." The stuff looked like something you'd swab onto a flat roof. "Joey McIntyre," I prompted. "Tell me about the boy and your daughter."

Kelly allowed that he didn't know much about his daughter's recent dealings with McIntyre, as he'd been over in Willamette Valley for most of the summer roofing and doing pickup labor. "The money's good enough, but too many people in the Valley." So he'd asked Dirk Redmond if he might have a job on one of his ranches, and Dirk said, "Hell, yes. Come on back." So he did. "Esther, she frets about Virginia, sneaking out all hours of the night with God knows who. Virginia was a hard girl to handle, being so smart and all, and Esther had her hands full taking care of all them kids and doing seamstress work on the side. Maybe we should take a switch to the child, but neither of us has the heart for it."

Kelly sighed and took a couple bites of beans. "Maybe we figured she'd grow out of her wildness. If only..." He sipped his coffee and spilled some on his t-shirt. "Shit," he said, brushing himself. He sat there in a straight-backed chair, mouth set in a tight line, and stared at the bare wall as if I wasn't there. Did he know or intuit something I didn't?

He roused himself and told me that Virginia wanted to attend beauty school. "She's got the gumption to do it. Fucking boys anyway. Sniffing around her like bird dogs."

I asked him if he knew the names of anyone else she might have seen other than Joey McIntyre. He told me he wouldn't be surprised if she had, but he didn't know who, and he didn't know where she might be.

He seemed pretty much talked out by then, so I asked him if he needed anything with the hay truck being broke and all, but he said "Nope." I left him sitting in his chair with a stained t-shirt and a plate of cold beans.

*

I decided to push my luck and go over Grizzly Mountain on the way back to town. Maybe I could find out who'd been behind the lights I had seen up there the night before. They were probably poachers; no one else would be dim enough to drive around on the mountain on a hot August night.

Grizzly wasn't a mountain in the true sense, only being six thousand feet high, but the snow would stick up there until early

June, and it was high enough to see most of central Oregon from the Cascades to the Ochocos. A gravel road ran up and over the ridge, and a dirt track led up to the top where the government had placed a radio repeater, or at least that's what they told folks. For sure, it was an electric thing, a tall tower and a squat bunker protected by a steel door and some serious locks. Rumor said it had something to do with the Commies, folks being frightened and always watching the skies for Russian bombers coming in from the West.

Hoopie huffed and chuffed over the ridge, but my luck held, and she didn't stall. Although it was getting along about four o'clock, and I didn't relish knocking around these roads in the dark, I thought I might check out a hunting camp close to where I'd seen the headlights the night before.

The side road to the camp had washed out with a flash flood, but it wasn't far in, maybe only a half a mile. My stomach grumbled from Kelly's beans and coffee, so I grabbed a roll of toilet paper from behind the seat before beginning the hike to the camp.

A rattlesnake lay coiled in the shade of a juniper just at the edge of the camp. Having no quarrel with him, I left him snoozing. Poachers must have been up here recently, because the smell of decay drifted down with the breeze from somewhere up above. After the war, I'd pretty much given up on hunting. Killing just wasn't as fun as it had been.

I heard the deer flies buzzing in a great swarm before I saw her. She hung by her heels like Mussolini in Milan from a great, grand juniper. Unable to stop myself, I turned and threw up what was left of the beans and coffee into an old fire ring. I felt ashamed for it. I'm stronger than this, I thought. I'd seen much worse in New Guinea. The Japs were bad, but I wasn't sure we were much better. Instead of killing our prisoners, we turned the Japs over to the natives. They did the murdering for us, but no one's hands were clean. I'd have to explain to the lab boys from Salem about the vomit. They wouldn't say anything. They'd been through the drill before with backcountry sheriffs and small town cops.

The murderer had slashed Virginia Kelly from breastbone to pubic bone. Dried blood, black and cracked, formed drip lines down her face and into her dark blond hair. Tan lines from a summer of swimming looped around her neck and at the top of her thighs—sparse pubic hair, a child, not yet a woman. With the flies and the gutting, she reminded me of a field-dressed deer waiting for someone to haul her home in a canvas bag, take her to the butcher, and carve her into chops and steaks. Her body twisted in the wind, and her breasts looked odd and misshapen hanging upside down.

No need to approach the body, Virginia had been dead for a while, but I sat there, not speaking. I'd never been good at talking with young folks. Kate was good at that. She should have been here with me. Instead, she waited at my place. When I got home, I'd explain, and she'd understand why I was late. She was good at understanding.

The sun began to dip behind Twelve Mile Table, and my bowels ached, so finally I told Virginia, "I'll be back soon, and I'll take you home." Then I hiked back to my truck and drove in a needless hurry down the mountain to the Flehardy ranch to call for reinforcements. I needed someone's help to get her down from that fucking tree.

*

Frank Flehardy helped me string rope around the crime scene. Once help started coming, the hunter's camp filled quickly. No one grumbled about having to hike to the camp, not even Doc Silverman with his gimpy leg. He doubled as the county coroner and pronounced Virginia dead at the scene. Jackson from the Crime Lab happened to be working a robbery case over in Bend and arrived sooner than anyone expected. He took pictures of the body, casts of footprints, and custody of the rope after we cut the body down and wrapped it in a canvas body bag.

The stars had come out by the time my job at the scene wrapped up. My deputy, George, volunteered to drive over to the North Redmond Ranch and tell Ethan about his daughter. We agreed that he'd drive Ethan back to town so he could be with his wife when we told her. "You've had enough to do," George said.

I didn't disagree. I hated delivering death notifications, watching the flicker of denial—'Are you joshing me, Sheriff?'—then the realization and the tears or the collapse. The hardest were the folks who didn't say or do anything, just held it all inside and let it simmer. George knew how I felt and bailed me out. Good, solid George. I could have kissed him.

As I was packing up, Dirk Redmond and the first wave of the Sheriff's Posse arrived with their pickups and horse trailers. They'd help secure the scene and search for evidence, and maybe Joey, if he was still in the neighborhood.

A hard-living cowpoke in his youth, Dirk had developed into a pot-bellied, skinny-legged, middle-aged man who owned most of the county. Most of the yahoos he ran with back then had ended up broke and lame, but not Dirk. His wife, Lucy, had something to do with that. She had more ambition than most men and better looks than most women, but America was a hard place for a woman to get ahead without a man. Though she was married, Lucy and I had had a short fling after I got home from the war. Neither of us seemed to take it seriously, and we parted with no regrets. Kate knew, but I assumed Dirk didn't.

Redmond settled his worn straw cowboy hat further down on his head. "I figure we can start a search for Joey McIntyre in the morning. Most of the boys will be here by then."

"Good plan," I said. "Just set up camp away from the crime scene."

He pointed. "Over there in the copse of trees will do just fine."

"Thanks for coming."

"Spiral or grid?" he asked.

"Pardon?"

"Search pattern," he clarified. "What kind do you suggest?"

"Rough country. Spiral would be best, too hard to set up grids in these gullies and buttes. Maybe go up to five miles from here. Keep an eye out for evidence or anything unusual." He already knew which search pattern to use, but deferred to me to be polite. I wanted to dislike him for all his money and power, but he was a deep-down decent sort of man, and I couldn't find the dislike within myself.

Redmond clapped me on the shoulder. "We have an extra horse in the trailer," he said. "Thought you might want to ride with us, help with the search, and get in shape for the parade." A horse whinnied and kicked the side of the trailer. "Handsome gelding by the name of Tornado, fine as they come."

I told him that it was right nice of him to think of me, but I had a passel of things to do.

Jackson and I loaded Virginia into the back of my pickup, and I started down the mountain. Grand vistas and open skies shortened into narrow bits of road lit by my headlights. Jackrabbits froze, blinded by the glare of the lights. I felt the thumps of their bodies against my undercarriage and regretted their deaths, but I didn't want to delay Virginia on her next-to-last ride.

*

My home was empty when I got in, the only sound the whine of the big saw at the mill. Dirk Redmond had added a graveyard shift in the spring. Business was good, and folks in America felt flush, except maybe for people like me who made fifty dollars a month and the Okies who lived on less than half that. Signs were that Kate had been here, then left. I crawled in bed, but didn't sleep until the false dawn.

Kate's reassuring warm body next to me when I awoke helped soothe my aching head. She smelled like fresh cedar.

"Hiya," she said.

"Hiya, yourself."

She wrinkled her nose. "You smell like a goat."

"Thanks for the endearments. We found Virginia last night."

"Dead. I heard." She got up and put coffee on the stove.

"You don't have to do that." I always made the coffee, one of those unspoken things between us.

"You don't like my coffee?"

Better move on to something else and enjoy the view. "News travels fast."

"I'm the judge's wife. I'm the first to hear things." She adjusted the burners.

"I never forget that you're married to him."

Kate clambered back into bed while the coffee perked. "How'd she die?"

"I'm not sure yet." The smell of percolating coffee reminded me that I'd live. "Doc Silverman'll do the autopsy later this afternoon. She was cut up some, but the cause of death is unknown."

"Cause of death unknown? That sounds like something Ed Dilkes would write for the paper."

"That's all I can say at the moment." I held up a finger. "Loose lips sink ships."

"Killjoy. Any suspects?"

"Logic says that Joey McIntyre is number one on the hit parade, but my gut tells me the murder was too mature for a sixteen-year-old kid. The crime scene was staged. No blood around the body. She'd been killed somewhere else and moved there. A kid killing in a moment of passion would have either left the body where it fell and run, or tried to hide it. This bastard left the body in an obscure place, but still out in the open. They knew someone would find it sooner or later."

"In short, no suspects." God, she looked good in the morning.

"Very aptly put."

Kate got out of bed and poured each of us a cup of black coffee.

"This is horrible. Is there any way I can help?"

My first instinct was to say, 'No, you're not getting involved', but I realized she might be helpful. "You have ears at the high school. Nose around; see if Virginia was seeing anyone else. Maybe snag a name of anyone else that might have been involved with either of them. Rumors are fine at this point; rumors are good. Did Joey have a rival? Did she? Ask around about the Gearhart boy, too."

"I thought you'd say no."

"Hell, honey..." I took her into my arms. "I'd never tell you no."

After we kissed, she said, "You really need a bath. Come on, I'll scrub your back."

Chapter 4

Doc and I laid Virginia on the embalming table in the basement of Doc's house, as there was no hospital in town. If a fellow got stove up, he'd either recover in an upstairs bedroom at Doc's or be taken to St. Charles Hospital over in Bend in a Cadillac ambulance driven by a volunteer firefighter who liked to drive too fast. I reminded myself every day not to get bad hurt; that ride to Bend was a killer.

"Someone already did a fair amount of my work for me when they cut her up," Doc said. When I asked if the killer might have known something about medicine, he said no, but he knew hunting. Doc started to work, and I leaned up against a bureau and chain-smoked. Smoke helped mask the blood-and-guts smell. I never got sick at autopsies, but I try to have only dry toast and coffee for breakfast on those mornings just in case.

Doc had me come over and hold a steel pan as he cracked ribs and pulled internal organs out of the body. They made squishy plop noises as he dumped them into the pan. He hummed while he worked. I wished I could be that content with my labor. Occasionally, he'd make a comment to no one in particular. "Someone took her liver," and "Gosh sakes, her heart, too." We'd been through this procedure before, and I knew enough to hold my questions until he finished. Murders not being too numerous in our county, the last time had been the previous summer when two drunk cowboys shot it out wild-west style behind the grammar school auditorium during the rodeo dance. One killed the other dead as dead can be. His prize for gunning down his buddy was twenty years of cracking rocks at the State Penitentiary in Salem. Being a good old boy, he'd probably get out in eleven.

After he dropped the girl's lungs into the pan, Doc pulled off his rubber gloves, sponged off his face with a towel, and directed me back upstairs into the kitchen. "I need a smoke."

I poured us some coffee from a pot warming on the stove while Doc fired up an evil, black cigar. I lit another Camel, and we both coughed for a while.

"What killed her, Doc?" I half-expected the method to have disappeared with Virginia's heart and liver.

"Strangulation." Doc took a bottle of bourbon from the kitchen cabinet and poured some into his cup. "Garroted, to be more precise.

Ligature marks suggest that he came at her from behind."

"He? A man?"

"Or a strong woman." Doc handed me the flask.

"Strangled, as with a rope?" Just a dash of bourbon to calm my nerves, I told myself. Can't waste good bourbon.

"Something thinner, like a clothesline. Thin, but strong, maybe a nylon clothesline." He sipped his coffee and grimaced. "Terrible thing, this." His accent slipped and thing came out as think. Rumor had it that Doc was German, though he claimed to be Dutch. Folks around here couldn't tell the difference, and I didn't care much.

"Clothesline, then?"

"I can't be precise, but I can rule things out if you have ideas."

I nodded. "Time of death?"

"Ten to fifteen hours before you discovered the body. As you theorized, she was murdered somewhere else."

"Was she raped?" Great motive for murder. Some bastard thinks she's easy, but she isn't, resists, he rapes her, then murders her to keep her quiet. A crime of violence, not passion. I'd solve the crime, find the bad guy, and he'd try to escape, run to the rodeo grounds. In my imagination, the murderer wore the face of Sam Gearhart. I'd tell him to stop, he'd pull a gun, I'd pull mine, then...

"Nope," Doc responded. "She wasn't a virgin, probably had sex within a few hours of her death, but no vaginal bruising that would indicate rape."

"Pregnant then?"

An older man could have gotten her pregnant, someone with a lot to lose for sleeping with a fourteen-year-old Okie girl. Barnes, that's it, Barnes. If he wasn't fucking his wife, then who? He'd have to fuck someone, not just for the sex, but for the power. He'd killed her, ripped out her internal organs, and discarded the fetus to cover up the crime.

"Nope." Doc knocked out another of my theories. "Not with child." "Goddamn, Doc. You're just a bundle of joy this morning, aren't you?"

"Sorry to disappoint you, Matthew." He poured me another shot of bourbon. I could have refused, but I felt I deserved a little pick-me-up. "You need to find yourself a nice girl," he said. "Settle down, have some kids."

"Bruises? Was she beaten?"

"A nice girl." He stared off into space. "I married a nice girl, but she died." Doc had come to town shortly after the war. A widower, he'd resisted the best efforts of our town's ladies to marry him off. He seemed to be one of those rare men who mated for life.

"Bruises?" I prompted.

"No bruises." The bottle of bourbon was almost empty, and we both sighed. Doc contemplated the bourbon bottle. "Find yourself a nice single girl."

I thought there seemed to be an emphasis on single and wondered how much he knew.

"Joey McIntyre is missing," I said to break the spell. "I think that his disappearance and Virginia's murder are connected. What do you know about him?"

"I saw him quite rarely. His parents usually took him to Prineville to see Doctor Richmond." Doc was also a Jew, which didn't please some folks. I suspected that included Jeff McIntyre. Being of the 'what the hell do I know' persuasion, a man's religion didn't make much difference to me. "Saw him last October when he broke his arm."

"His dad slap him around?" I asked.

He shook his head. "Not likely. Football. A barbaric sport that I will never understand, but I have no need to understand a sport to fix the injured."

"Think the boy is capable of murder?"

Doc sloshed what remained of the bourbon into our cups. We'd dispensed with the fiction of coffee. "Anything's possible," he said. "But in my opinion, Joey is a typical adolescent boy; arrogant with his peers but polite to his elders; he hadn't yet discovered his mortality, but could be very unpredictable when he was hurt."

"You're a philosopher."

"I was a communist in college." He slurred his words.

"And a Jew," I added. "Joe McCarthy is making a list and checking it twice; you'll move right to the top." Neither of us laughed. "What about Virginia McIntyre?"

"Some people don't think they can afford doctoring. I only saw her once. Double pneumonia when she was nine. Her father tuned up my Buick as repayment." He turned the bourbon bottle upside down. "Empty."

"Time for us to go back to work," I said. I stood to leave.

"You, perhaps. Time for my nap, an old man's prerogative."

*

The vagrant wiener dog had curled up in my office chair. "Well, make yourself at home." His wagging tail pounded the chair as if he were playing a drum solo.

Miriam emerged from the cellblock. "Judge Barnes is looking for you," she said. "He said he'd be at the barbershop."

"What the hell is this mutt doing here?"

"Addison needs to pee," she said. "Take him for a walk."

"I don't babysit dogs."

Miriam shrugged with apparent unconcern. "It's your chair."

"Fine, come on, dog."

"Name's Addison," Miriam said. Addison danced all the way to my pickup.

When we arrived at the barbershop, I paused to absorb the aromas—the hot lather and lilac water, the musk and the talc. Herbert, the barber, sharpened a straight razor with a deft practice, the rhythm like a primitive tune. "Judge is in the back," he said.

"Should I leave the dog in the truck?" Mighty hot in the truck, but I wasn't too thrilled to have him in here either.

Herbert looked out the shop window. Addison pushed his head out the passenger side window of the truck. "Sakes alive," Herbert said, looking out the window. "What a cute little feller. Bring him in."

The usual crowd played poker in the backroom. Barnes sat with his back to the wall, Harley, owner of the local haberdashery, on his right, Ed Dilkes, who owned and edited the local weekly newspaper on his left, and Coach Conroy in the final seat. During the school year, Conroy only appeared here on the weekends, but this was summer and there was time to kill before the second half of daily doubles.

"Pet store must have been all out of poodles," Barnes said. Harley and Dilkes laughed.

Conroy fed Addison a piece of venison jerky. "Ease off. A man and his dog is a personal thing."

"He's not my dog," I corrected. "I'm just looking after him for a spell."

"Sit in," Barnes said. "Draw poker, penny ante, nickel raises." Cheap, but on my salary still quite dear. I sat in anyway.

Harley dealt. I picked up a hand of nothin', eight high. "I'm out," I said, when the bet came around to me.

"Folks around here are concerned about finding Joey McIntyre," Barnes commented. Harley dropped out. Conroy bumped up to a nickel.

"Tell me something I don't know," I responded.

"We want to know what's being done." Harley was the only man in these parts that wore a double-breasted suit anywhere other than to church.

"Everything possible is being done," I said. "Dirk Redmond has the posse scouring Grizzly Mountain for any sign of the boy." Conroy won the hand with three sixes over Barnes's two pair. Barnes looked at the coach as if he had shit on his porch.

"So there's a connection between the Kelly murder and Joey McIntyre?" Dilkes was a narrow-faced man with a perpetual shadow of whiskers on his cheeks. His eyes glazed as if he were setting the type for the headlines. Conroy's turn to deal.

"Go fuck yourself, Ed." I picked up my hand—a pair of jacks. Against my better judgment, I raised a penny.

"I'll take that as 'no comment.'" Dilkes bumped me two cents.

Barnes dropped out and Harley followed his lead.

"We're pursuing all available leads." Horseshit and we both knew it, but this was a dance we danced. I drew three. A third jack showed his sweet little head. Dilkes drew one and frowned. I raised a nickel. Conroy scratched Addison behind the ears, considered his cards, then folded.

Dilkes bumped back. I checked.

"That your official comment?" I nodded and he called.

"Three jacks," I said.

"Sorry, heart flush." Dilkes spread his cards on the table.

"Son of a bitch." I tossed my cards on the table.

"Heard tell she was slashed from neck to navel," Conroy said.

"Like she was done in by some evil hunter," Dilkes said, as he dealt the next hand.

"I read a story like that once," Harley said.

"Evil hunter? Hey, that pretty much describes all of us." Conroy chuckled.

"Judge." I picked up my cards. "I can't discuss this case with Ed around. We can't have the details showing up in the local Bugle." Pair of aces, pair of eights. Against my better judgment, I opened for a nickel.

"Eddie will print what I tell him to print. Won't you, Eddie?" Barnes tossed his cards into the center of the table. Harley followed suit.

Dilkes bumped a nickel. "Yeah, sure."

Conroy bumped another nickel. "And a dime to you, Sheriff."

I dug into my pocket. Nickels and dimes added up. Fuck, I

knew better than this, but I tossed a dime into the pot and drew one. Another eight. Full house. I threw another nickel in.

Herbert came into the back. He opened a towel drawer and pulled out a bottle. "Anyone want a short snort?" Barnes and Conroy accepted.

Harley declined. "Got to get back to work."

My head still swam a wee bit from drinking with the Doc. I waved my hand and said that I'd pass, too.

Dilkes folded his hand. "I'm on the wagon."

"Har, har, har." Conroy bumped me a nickel. "How many times does this make?"

"It's not whether you succeed or fail, but the effort that counts," Harley said.

"Horse pucky. What are you, some fucking philosopher?" Conroy asked. Harley's face flushed, and he glanced at Barnes.

I searched my pockets for more money, but I was flat-busted. Dilkes peeked at my cards and staked me a nickel. He wasn't a bad sort, I decided, and flipped it into the pot before spreading my cards on the table. "Eights over aces." I felt rather proud of myself.

"Six high straight." Conroy smiled, then added, "All clubs."

"Fuck." I shook my head. "Who dealt this mess?"

"I did," Conroy said. I didn't voice what I was thinking.

"Coach, you know all the angles," Barnes said.

"I'd better get back to work." I stood. Betty McIntyre was the next name on the interview list. My stomach moaned, and I was broke. Maybe Miriam had brought sugar cookies to the office.

Addison followed me to the door, and Conroy laughed. That reminded me. "Oh, yeah," I said. "Mike Barfield, your manager."

"Student manager," Conroy corrected.

"I'd like to interview him. Will he be at practice today?"

"He'll be there, come hell or high water." Conroy laughed again, but I didn't see what was so funny.

*

Betty McIntyre almost skipped across her living room. "We just had this house built last year," she said almost gaily, but her face seemed tight and brittle as if it were ready to shatter into pieces. She pointed out their view of the courthouse, and the family's new couch. Good thing I left Addison in the truck. This woman wouldn't cotton to a wiener dog napping on her davenport. Mrs. McIntyre poured coffee in her second-best china, and we settled down at the dinette.

The coffee tasted like dirty water. "Tell me about Joey," I said.

Her hands fluttered as if they were birds, and she had the cross-eyed look of someone headed for a nervous breakdown. "He's a good boy." Is, her hope sprang eternal. Maybe that was the difference between this woman and the Okie—hope. "A good boy," she repeated. "He's never been in trouble. A 'B' student, but Jeff was hoping to get him into the University of Washington on a football scholarship." She sounded as if she wanted something else for her son.

"When did you see him last?"

"Afternoon before yesterday," she responded. "He left for football practice."

"How'd he get there?"

"His dad drove him," she said.

"What about Virginia Kelly?" I wasn't sure I could stomach her coffee.

"Who?"

"His girlfriend."

"Oh, no." Her hands swept and swooped. "Joey's going steady with Margie Weekly. Her father owns a mill. She's such a lovely girl." She leaned forward and whispered, "I think they've kissed."

"He's been seeing Virginia Kelly for at least a month," I said. "She lives over in Okie town."

"That, that..." she stopped, almost frozen. I decided to wait it out, see where she went when she thawed. The silence grew. Not proper for a woman like this to let a silence run. Her hands had stilled, but now her mouth flapped soundlessly. A knock at the door startled both of us. "The door," she said as if asking permission.

"Please." I waved her away.

While she went to the door, I dumped the coffee in a hydrangea. Mumbles drifted back from the entryway. Betty escorted Kate into the dining room.

"I brought you a tuna casserole," Kate said. "For you and Jeff."

"You know the sheriff, don't you, Kate?" Betty asked.

"We've bumped into each other now and again." Kate smiled.

I bit my lip. "We were discussing Joey's disappearance."

Kate protested that she should leave, but Betty asked her to stay. I agreed, saying that Betty shouldn't be alone right now. "We found Virginia Kelly's body up on Grizzly Mountain," I said. "It appears she and Joey disappeared about the same time."

"Joey's going steady with Margie Weekly," Betty insisted.

"Margie and Joey broke up last month. Now she's going out with Ronnie Gearhart." Kate had a good pipeline into the high school.

"Ronnie?" Betty asked. "They're best friends. What will people think?"

"It's kid stuff," I said. "They have a new steady every week."

"Virginia was a very nice girl," Kate said.

Betty went on as if she hadn't heard Kate's comment. "Jeff says that Joey's like any other boy, just a little more high-spirited. He wants to take him to Pendleton to a... a... one of those places men go." Great, a father taking his son to a whorehouse. I made a mental note to call the Pendleton Chief of Police, have him check out the cathouses there, and see if anyone had seen Dr. McIntyre or his son.

"Young men explore. You have to give them that." Kate glanced at me out of the corner of her eye.

"Anything unusual going on with Joey recently?" I asked.

"Just his letterman's sweater," Betty said. "It disappeared this past June. Joey didn't know where it had gotten to, but I gave him the money for a new one. Jeff would have kittens if he knew that he'd lost it."

"Was it that important?" I said.

"Maybe a clue," Kate offered.

I shrugged and asked Betty if she'd mind my taking a gander at Joey's room. "There might be something relevant in there." She didn't mind. Kate volunteered to come with me. I didn't mind.

Kate waited until we were in the kid's room before she folded into my arms and kissed me. She was a tall, lean woman, but in my arms she felt substantial.

"Nice work," I said, when we came up for air. "You should be a cop. You're a natural."

"You could hire me," she said.

"Yeah, a woman deputy in Ochoco County," I said. "That would go over like a lead balloon."

She disentangled herself. "Where should we start?"

The room seemed normal enough—a Southern Cal football pennant on one wall, Phillies pennant on another. I had Kate rummage through the kid's closet while I tossed the bureau. Joey's football playbook was in the top drawer. It smelled of mimeograph fluid and boundless teenaged dreams. Someone had annotated the pages in a looping, almost feminine, hand. Joey's handwriting, or someone else's?

"Aha!" Kate pulled her head from the closet. She held up two foil-wrapped condoms. "At least he was careful."

"Never buy a cow when milk's so cheap."

"Bastard." She tossed one of Joey's shoes at me.

I ducked, and said, "Let's not get started."

She grumbled and stuck her head back in the closet. I figured I hadn't heard the end of that. I returned to the bureau but didn't find much until the bottom drawer. Stuffed in the back were two bundles of letters, one held love poems written in red ink, hearts for dots on the I's, and signed, "Eternally yours, Virginia." Interesting that she had used her grown-up name. Grown up for just a moment, then she was gone.

The second bundle was in a different feminine hand, signed "M," for Margie, I assumed. These were simpler, less sophisticated, though no less passionate. Joey was a man with a gift, it seemed. In the back of the drawer was a crumpled 'Dear John' note, short, sharp, "I've fallen in love with Ronnie." The same looping hand as in the playbook had scrawled "Fuck her" across the page.

The last item in the drawer was a single sheet of white typing paper with two lines written in precise block letters with a fountain pen. "Don't cross me," it read. "You'll regret it." The nib had pressed against the paper hard enough to rip it.

"I found a gun. Twenty-two revolver." She held up a nine-shot Colt .22.

"Not unusual for a sixteen-year-old in this county," I said without looking up from the note. "Every boy here gets a gun when he turns twelve."

"He kept it under his pillow." She handed me the gun. I cracked the cylinder—loaded. I tried to touch Kate's fingers, but she pulled away.

"The plot thickens," I said.

Chapter 5

The large wringer washer sloshed and rattled as Mike Barfield, the student manager, lugged piles of dirty towels and gym shorts across the locker room. The afternoon session of daily doubles was in full swing. Feeling daunted by the prospect of the Kelly clan's Irish grieving and rending of garments, I had postponed a visit to the Kelly place until later in the day.

"Coach said you'd be by to talk with me," Barfield said when he saw me. A kid with more brains than muscles trying to survive at least marginally in the snake pit known as high school, he'd be darkly handsome if he dropped a few pounds. He would probably hit his stride later in life, maybe one of the few in this burg to go to college, but life as he knew it right now was bleak.

"I have a few questions for you." I perched on the training table. The room smelled of liniment and unwashed sweatshirts. Barfield stopped on his way across the room. "No," I said, "keep working." He started feeding wet clothes through the wringer.

"Coach Conroy says we're going to take State this year," I said.

"We have a scrimmage with Prineville a week from Friday," Barfield said. "We'll see how we measure up. Their coach, DeCoursey, has a crackerjack team."

"Might be tough without Joey," I said.

"The Coach is good at figuring stuff out." Barfield dropped the wrung-out clothes into a metal tub.

"Tell me about Virginia Kelly."

Barfield hesitated as if he hadn't expected the question. "Virginia's a sweet girl." "Was. Sad, her dying like that." He shook his head as if he couldn't understand what had happened

"How well did you know Virginia?" I asked.

"We were friends." He started to cry silently. When he calmed down, he glanced in my direction, then wiped his eyes with a dirty towel. "I'm sorry."

I wasn't sure if he was apologizing for his reaction or telling me how he felt about Virginia's death. "Did she talk to you about Joey or other people in her life?"

"We didn't talk about her love life. She wanted to be a poet. I wanted to be a writer. We talked about books and writing. We had things in common." He sniffed, and I waited for the waterworks to begin again, but they didn't.

"And Joey, what about him?"

Barfield unloaded the washer and put in more clothes. He started the washer and over the slosh, slosh of the machine, he said, "Joey was an asshole." He blinked as if he had said it louder than he intended.

"He beat you up?" I asked.

"More like he teased me, pushed me around, humiliated me."

"Joey was a bully, huh?" I nodded. "How bad was it?"

"Joey was the worst of the bunch," he said. "Some guys fuck with you because they think it's a requirement. Joey would slug me in the chest and laugh. He enjoyed hurting me." Barfield's face reddened with anger and shame.

"Enjoyed, as in the past tense?" I asked.

He shrugged as if to say he hoped so. He obviously had a couple of reasons to hate Joey. How much hate did this kid hold? "Tell me about Ronnie Gearhart. Did he tease you, too?"

"No, he's a straight arrow." Barfield sorted through some dirty towels as if he needed to keep his hands busy. "Sometimes he'd stop Joey. Ronnie's the only kid with the gumption to stand up to Joey."

"Rumor has it they're close."

"Not any more," Barfield said.

"Because of Margie Weekly?"

"That's part of it," he said. "After she dumped Joey, they were like two bull elk circling each other. Last week, they finally got into a fistfight after practice."

"Who won?"

"Joey got a split lip." Barfield smiled. "But the coach broke it up before any real damage was done. Made them both run thirty extra suicide sprints. Ronnie was fine with it, but Joey got PO'd. He feels like he's Coach's pet and should always get the breaks. I heard him yelling at the coach in his office. It sounded like Coach slapped him."

"Ever see the coach hit anyone else?"

"Just hacks," Barfield said. "He keeps a paddle in his desk and is always whacking a kid for something. Most of the male teachers give out hacks to the boys, but sometimes to the girls, too."

"And after the slap?"

"Joey slammed the door and ran out. The next day, everyone acted as if nothing was wrong."

Coach Conroy came in and asked how things were going. Barfield responded, "Fine, just fine." I figured I wouldn't get much more out of him with Conroy around so I said my goodbyes, but my gut told me Barfield knew more about this case.

*

A dozen people crowded the single room in the Kelly shanty. They had come bearing fried chicken and their best whiskey. Their voices sounded too loud for the circumstances, but no one tried to shush them.

Ethan Kelly seemed to take his daughter's death harder than Esther, or at least he showed it more. She probably had to be the strong one, holding things together for the kids if nothing else. Ethan just sat in a straight-backed chair as people flowed around him like water around a rock in the river. He chain-smoked alone, eyes red, sunken, and stared into nothing.

I'd already asked most of my questions of the family earlier, so I asked Esther if I could search through Virginia's things.

"Faith will show you," Esther said.

The eldest daughter took me to the two beds at the rear of the single room of the house, which contained one bed for the parents, one bed for the three girls, and a small closet shared by the entire family; three dresses belonged to Virginia, one of them her communion dress. "We hand things down, me to Virginia to Sue Ann," Faith said, as if she felt she had to explain.

I nodded toward a chest of drawers. "Anything in there belong to Virginia?" Faith opened the center drawer. It figured—middle kid, middle drawer. Inside were several threadbare white panties, one bra, two pairs of bobby socks—well-darned—two blouses, and a pair of cutoffs. To one side were two books, one a Bible with a bent-up cover and well-thumbed pages, the other a book of poems by Elizabeth Barrett Browning, beautiful book, almost new, bound in red leather. I found no inscription, but it was certainly a gift from someone. For certain, Virginia Kelly couldn't afford a book like that, and it wasn't a gift that Joey might give. Barfield, perhaps? I'd have to ask him. Other than what she was wearing when she disappeared, this was all that remained of Virginia's life.

Faith stood, arms crossed, with her back against the wall watching me if I might steal what little they had. "I understand Virginia was a poet," I said. "Are there any of her poems around?" Faith didn't answer, her faced closed with... what? Fear? Anger? "Maybe she wrote something that might help me find her murderer," I continued. "It could be important."

Faith didn't say anything for a long time, but she didn't tell me to git either. Finally, she reached under the mattress and handed me an English composition book with a black-and-white cover, like something I might have written in when I was in high school.

"Can we have it back when you're done?"

"Of course. I swear." I took the three books. Though I wanted to sneak out without saying anything to Esther and Ethan, I said my goodbyes. "Don't worry," I told them. "I'll find who did this."

Outside, the evening had turned cool, and the stars were bright. The farmers would worry about an early frost. Autumn couldn't come too soon for me—autumn, when the old died away and made way for the new.

*

I lit a fire in the oven for heat and made myself an onion sandwich with lots of salt and pepper. The silence of the night got on my nerves and made me feel lonesome. I turned on the Philco and listened to Fibber McGee and Molly. The sound of other voices reassured me.

I had half-figured that Kate might have come by, but it was past nine, too late for that. Sometimes women didn't talk when they were pissed. Sometimes women wouldn't talk when they weren't pissed. Women were a mystery, and I'd never figured out how to tell when I was in the doghouse and when I wasn't. When Kate didn't come by my little house that evening, I didn't know if it was something I said or did, didn't do or say, or if she had just gotten entangled with Barnes. Things were never simple with women and certainly never simple with Kate in particular. Surely she wasn't serious about me hiring her as a deputy? Fifty dollars a month and hemorrhoids from jostling on washboard roads, who'd want that?

I dozed off on the couch and awoke to someone scratching at my front door. "Kate, you minx," I said, but it turned out to be Addison, all jumpy and excited. Miriam must have dropped off the dog on her way home.

I offered Addison the rest of my onion sandwich, but the ingrate ignored it and scooted his ass across my one and only hook rug. Worms, I thought. A dog adopted me, and the son of a bitch had worms. I thought about all the things I would do to Miriam, but the county offices would fall apart without her. Our local vet was good about carrying people on account. I'd take Addison there in the morning.

My cupboards held a single can of beef hash, so I offered it to Addison. While he wolfed it down, I screwed up my courage and called Kate. If Barnes answered, I'd unload some bullshit about the investigation. Kate answered the phone.

"Hey, sweetheart," I said.

"Good evening, Sheriff Harkness." Her voice felt like a dull knife.

"I missed you tonight," I said.

"Yes, Porter's here," she said. "I'll get him." Pissed for certain, I thought.

When Barnes came on the line, I tap-danced for fifteen minutes, filling him in on the case. He'd always loved being on the inside. After I hung up, I cracked a can of Olympia beer and lay on my couch drinking and wondering how I got in the doghouse.

"Addison, you son of a bitch," I yelled. "Don't you scoot on my rug."

*

The next morning, I puttered around the office for a while, but the Kelly grief had drained me, and I decided I had earned a break. I loaded Addison into my pickup and headed up Grizzly Mountain to see how Dirk Redmond and the posse were coming along. It was well past eleven, and thunderheads, white and pillowy, almost luminescent on top, rose up in the south. The wind pushed them north toward our county. Big storm coming for sure, I thought. *Lightning bust*, the Bureau of Land Management crew would call it. I'd have a fine view from this side of the mountain. The problem would be getting down if it rained too hard. Hoopie was a fine truck, but she didn't do well in the mud. I should have turned around, but I didn't.

I passed by the Flehardy ranch and made a mental note to talk with Frank. He might have heard or seen something up there that evening. I needed to make a list. I needed to do a lot of things.

A caravan of horse trailers surrounded the hunter's camp where I had discovered Virginia's body. Most of the posse was still out searching for evidence. Jackson, the state crime lab guy, was still there tending the campfire. He had the rumpled, unwashed look about him that told me he'd slept in the back of his panel van—Army surplus sleeping bag, Spam for dinner, Spam for breakfast, almost like being in the service. How had Jackson escaped being shipped off to Korea?

He was young enough, and with the Red Chinese aching to get in the mix, we'd need all the able bodies we could get.

He offered me a cup of coffee too black for a normal man to drink. I took him up on his offer, but declined a slice of Spam. Jackson tossed the slice to Addison who wolfed it down raw and had the guts to beg for more.

He mentioned that Redmond would be back in camp soon, and I asked him what he'd found.

"Not much," he said. "Hard to differentiate between the leavings of hunters and evidence left by the murderer. Whoever did this was smart enough to erase his footprints with a piece of brush. Maybe they were Injuns." He chuckled.

"Do you really believe that?" I asked with a sober face.

He rubbed his jaw. "No. The posse did find a tire track that might be related. I've taken a plaster of Paris casting and will try to match it up with the exemplars we have back at the office."

"Brand of tire and size sure would help."

Jackson told me he'd work on it. There really wasn't much out here that would hold a fingerprint. Someone had taken a crap a little ways east of the body. The shit was fresh enough to belong to the murderer. He walked me over to the spot—a fat, smelly, brown log with lots of deer flies looping around it. "Big pile of droppings," he said. "The guy must have been saving up."

"Marking his kill," I said. "Any blood?" Addison, probably looking for more Spam, sniffed around the camp's food bag that hung high in a tree. I carried him back to Hoopie and had him curl up on the seat.

"Not much to speak of in the camp," Jackson said when I returned. "As we thought, she was murdered elsewhere and hauled here. As of yet, the posse hasn't found much in the way of blood traces."

"One killer?" I asked.

"Can't tell for certain," he said. "Hard for one man to haul her up into the tree, but not impossible." He thought for a moment. "You think it may have been a local?"

"Maybe," I said. "Someone would have noticed a stranger. They don't get far in this county without someone noticing them. Some folks are pointing the finger at Joey McIntyre, but I'm not so sure."

"Two perpetrators would simplify things for you," he said. "Hard to keep something like this secret for long when two people know about it." The crime lab hired smart kids.

The south wind accelerated, blowing straight into our faces, and the thunderheads boiled up across the rimrock on the distant side of the valley. The undersides edged from dark gray into black. Jackson asked me if I was going to wait for Dirk Redmond, but I told him it was time to go. I hadn't been paying close enough attention. "I don't want to get caught in the storm," I explained. He told me he'd file a complete report in a couple of days.

I left Addison in the front seat rather than having him tossed back and forth in the bed of the truck. He stuck his nose out of the window and sniffed the clean ozone smell of the air, seeming almost happier than was possible for man or beast.

As I negotiated my way down the grade, I reviewed what I'd learned about the murder of Virginia Kelly. Based on what I'd seen earlier, she'd been sleeping with Joey McIntyre. Maybe her notebook would tell me more about her love life. Just before Joey went missing, he'd had a fight with Ronnie Gearhart and a set-to with the coach. More questions to ask. Kate was pissed at me; maybe I could buy her a gift, a lamp or a can opener or something.

Thunder roared far away at first, but moved closer. Addison yelped and hopped down off the seat. He tried to scramble underneath it, but failing that, curled up on the floorboards. Rain plopped down in huge splattering drops, and the fierce wind blew from hot to cold. Lightning marched up the side of the mountain. Multiple strikes, sounding like mortar shells thumping through the jungle, shredded tall junipers. I had visions of Japs charging the perimeter of our landing strip. *Tat-tat-tat.* The .30 caliber machine gun bucked in my hands. Addison whimpered down below.

I stopped the truck for a moment to roll up both windows. By the time we moved again, hail had begun to mix with the rain. In what seemed no more than seconds, the hail became so heavy that my wipers couldn't clear the windshield. Confused by the bang of thunder and blinded by the deluge, I crunched over a large rock and hung up on it. I rocked the truck back and forth until she freed herself. No need to get Hoopie's undercarriage high-centered on a rock, so I stopped in the middle of the road to wait out the storm.

I'd brought Virginia's notebook with me and scanned through it to the sound of hail hammering on the roof of the truck. Diary entries were interspersed with poems, sad examinations of her family's poverty. Some depressing stuff, vignettes of the cruelty of her classmates—Margie Weekly seemed especially cruel.

She teases me because my clothes are mended. Kids know that I wear the same thing day after day. I have nothing else. We can't afford nylons. My legs go bare.

The descriptions were vivid. She would have grown into a good writer. A little later:

Dr. M is going to check and clean my teeth. O Golly, they're so dirty. What will he think of me?

The exam was Joey's doing, I assumed. A big deal for a poor girl. The next several pages had been torn out. Was the exam that embarrassing?

Barfield seemed to be her one true friend.

Mike is such a sweetie pie. I tell him everything.

The back half of the notebook contained love poems. No names, just poems. They started as kid's stuff, things that Kate might have written me in high school, but became more passionate later. In the end, I found an allusion to jealousy. Someone intruded in the relationship:

He hides in the shadows, watching us. J is frightened, but won't tell me his name. In my dreams, I see his face. It is the beast.

I flipped through the book of Browning poems looking for underlined passages or annotations, but there was nothing. I hit pay dirt in the Bible with a scrap of a notebook page folded into the flyleaf.

Forbidden fruit,
his touch a sin
the book a sign of our love
my fault
I hate myself
God hear my prayer

The thunder rolled further up the mountain, and the wind shifted from south to north as the leading edge of the storm passed. The rain kept on, perhaps even harder than before, and the gravel road had become a creek. A croad, I called it in my mind, half creek, half road. Hoopie shivered, then slid sideways beneath me, carried by the rush of the flash flood. My stomach slid with her, and Addison mewed like a cat, eyes tight shut, his muzzle pressed between his paws.

Hoopie slithered right, then slid ass-end into a ditch. A coyote jumped yellow-eyed from her hiding place. I wasn't sure if she was scared of me or the storm. Mud splattered up on the windshield, and the truck yawed like a fighter plane banking for an attack. It crunched into something hard and unyielding. I slid across the seat, smashing my head onto the doorpost. Fog descended for a moment. When it cleared, Addison had jumped onto my lap and stuck his cold nose against my cheek as if he realized I was injured.

As quickly as it started, the rain faltered and petered out. For a moment, I thought I smelled gunpowder, but realized it was wet sagebrush and juniper. A thin rivulet of blood trickled down my cheek, and I mopped it with my handkerchief. The engine caught quickly enough, but Hoopie's tires spun fruitlessly in the mud, burrowing deeper and deeper. Would Kate cry for me if I died up here? Rocking the truck back and forth only liquefied the mud, and the truck sank up to the axles.

"Okay, mutt. We're going on a little hike to the Flehardy Ranch."

My cowboy boots slid in the mud, and I plopped on my ass. My ma didn't raise no fucking cowboy. Combat boots, I needed combat boots for this job. Addison skipped and capered down the mountain as if happy to be free of the pickup. I stumbled down after him.

*

Addison barked at a chicken when we hit the Flehardy's yard, and Frank came charging out his front door packing a double-barreled shotgun.

"Jesus Christ, Frank," I said. "The war's over."

"Some lowlife stole a couple of horses." He lowered the shotgun. "We haven't even had time to call your office."

"My truck is stuck up on Grizzly Mountain."

"Come on in," he said.

Agnes Flehardy made me a cup of coffee while Frank got on his rubber boots and overalls. Their ranch house was simple but efficient, a wood range for cooking, a fireplace for heat, filled with plants, porcelain knick-knacks and paperback books. Raymond Chandler for her, Zane Grey for him, Agnes explained. The coffee was good and hot and, from somewhere, Agnes found a soup bone for Addison. She fretted about the horses, and I told her I'd find them for her.

"Let's go," Frank said. "Will your dog be alright here?" Addison gnawed contentedly on his bone by the woodstove. He looked as if he was in no mood to move. I told Frank that he'd be just fine.

Frank cranked over an ancient Ford tractor, and I perched precariously behind the seat. Frank drove with slow resolve back up the mountain, and I took the opportunity to ask him if anyone unusual had passed by his place in the past few days. "No one person in particular, though I did hear a rig go by the night before last."

"Car or pickup?" I asked.

"I wouldn't venture to say for sure," he said. "Pipes weren't loud enough for it to be a haying truck or such. Figured it might be some kids out for a joy ride, or one of Dirk Redmond's crew heading back to the North Ranch."

Frank wasn't too keen about lying in the mud to attach the towrope to Hoopie's frame, so I laid down a canvas tarp I kept for emergencies and wiggled underneath the truck. The oil pan had a fair-sized dent in it. I hoped Frank could fix it at the county maintenance shop. With the aid of the tractor, Hoopie popped out of the mud as sweet as you please, and I headed back down to pick up Addison.

Chapter 6

While on my way home, a stranger's car, a rattletrap Desoto with California plates, passed going northbound on the highway. Chasing taillights had never been one of my passions, but I couldn't let this one pass, not now.

I spun a U-turn and came up on the Desoto with my red lights flashing. I never did convince the county to spring for a siren, so when the driver didn't stop, I pulled up alongside of him and motioned for him to stop. The driver was a negro, something one rarely saw in these parts. I checked for my sap before climbing out of the truck.

"Was I doing something wrong, Officer?" He added an extra syllable in 'officer' as if he was used to being stopped by white coppers. I shined my flashlight in his face forcing him to shade his eyes with his hand. He was a little younger than me, though not by much, neatly dressed, with a porkpie hat on the seat next to him. A cardboard suitcase lay in the backseat.

"Sheriff," I said. "Sheriff. License and registration please."

"I wasn't doing anything wrong," he said, as he handed me his paperwork. I had him step out of the car and move to the front of my pickup.

I scanned his license. Thomas Jefferson Stewart from San Francisco. "Little far away from home, aren't you, Mr. Stewart?"

"Free country," he said. He stood at parade rest. A vet, I figured.

"Where you headed?"

"Portland," he said. "I got me a job at the shipyard up there. I start next Monday. What's the problem?" He shifted his weight from one foot to the other. Even though the night had cooled, sweat beaded on his forehead. White cop, negro out here in the middle of nowhere, I could imagine what he was thinking.

"Tell me where you've been the last couple of days," I said.

"I wasn't speeding."

"That's not what worries me," I said. "Where were you day before yesterday?"

"I started out from San Francisco on Tuesday. I spent that night in Red Bluff and last night in Weed. Thought I'd try to drive all the way through to Portland tonight."

"Got any motel receipts?" I asked.

"I have one for Red Bluff."

"And in Weed?"

"Why?" he asked.

"A young girl got herself murdered day before yesterday," I said. "A white girl."

Stewart's eyes widened. They looked yellow in the headlights. "A white girl?" His composure broke, and he skittered back one step. That spooked Addison, who stuck his head out the open pickup window and barked. "A dog?" Stewart squinted into my headlights.

"A killer."

"I stayed with my uncle in Weed," Stewart explained. "He works on the railroad. You can check."

"Let me see the receipt for Tuesday night." I held the flashlight while he fished through the jockey box for the receipt. It verified his story.

"I didn't kill anyone." He started to put his hands in his pockets, then seemed to think better of it.

"Were you in the service, Thomas?"

"I drove a truck in Italy."

"Dangerous duty," I said. "As one vet to another, I'm going to give you a break. Turn around, head back to Bend, make a hard right and follow Ninety-Seven up through Madras into Portland."

"That's a hundred miles out of my way." Stewart's voice got louder, and he shifted nervously. Addison took up barking again.

"I'm a practical man," I said. "Negro man driving through Barnestown right after the murder of a white girl is a sure recipe for a disaster. Town marshal isn't good for much other than writing parking tickets and chasing loose dogs, but he'd love to get his hands on you. Be smart, take the long way around. I don't need the complication."

"I'm not a complication," he said, waving his arms. "I'm more than a complication."

"Turn around," I repeated.

"No." He raised his hands as if to push me back. Addison buzzed by me, latched onto Stewart's pant leg, and shook it with vigor. "Son of a bitch." Stewart kicked at Addison with his foot. I didn't think about it; I just sapped him behind the ear. That would have been enough to stun a normal man, but this negro had a hard head. He struggled to his feet, and I slapped him alongside the head again, harder this time. He folded down onto the pavement. Then regret hit me. He was a man like me, just trying to get along. He didn't deserve this treatment, but I had to do my job. I lifted his head to make sure I hadn't killed him. I hadn't, but he did have a bloody nose. I rolled him over and propped him up in a seated position against the tire of his car. Addison licked his face. Crazy dog.

I took the opportunity to search his car. I found two things of note. In his cardboard suitcase was a picture of his family, mama and two smiling little girls. Under the front seat, I found a loaded .32 semi-auto handgun, something he may have carried in Italy. I stuffed it behind the seat of my pickup.

I smoked and petted Addison while waiting for Stewart to come around. A magpie worked on a dead rabbit in the pool of light near the side of the road. My thoughts turned to Kate. How could I make things up to her for whatever I had done wrong? Flowers were out; Barnes would catch on. Quo Vadis was playing at the Tower in Bend. She'd like that. Wait, a picnic. A picnic would be perfect.

Stewart groaned and touched his nose. The blood on his hand looked almost black. "You aren't going to hit me again, are you?" he asked.

"You are one hard-headed S.O.B."

Addison sniffed at Stewart, then crawled onto the man's lap and nuzzled his hand. "A real killer," Stewart commented.

"Here's the deal," I said. "You can turn around and head to Bend, or I can whack you up alongside the head again."

"Ain't much of a choice."

"Thirty-two under the seat. That's worth five years breaking rocks with Billy Ray in the hot sun over at the state pen. Mama Stewart and those two pretty little girls sure would miss their papa, wouldn't they?" Stewart's chest swelled, and he started to get his dander up. "Before you say something you'll regret..." I slapped my hand with the sap. "Think about your options."

He sighed. "Fine, you've got me, Boss. I'll turn around."

"Smart man." I nodded. "Just looking out for your interests."

Stewart clambered back into the Desoto and turned back toward Bend. He didn't say goodbye, but I silently wished him luck and hoped I'd never see him in this county again.

*

The next morning, I decided to visit Margie Weekly. Her parents had a new ranch-style house up on Crest Drive, not too far from the McIntyre home. I envisioned Margie climbing out of her window and paying a midnight visit to Joey now and again before they had broken up.

Margie herself, all blond curls and rouge, answered the door. After I introduced myself, she batted her eyes, and said, "Come on in and sit a spell, Sheriff." She wore shorts and was quite a sight from behind as she led me into the parlor. Seeing as how I was stuck on Kate, the sight didn't do as much for me as once it might have.

I pulled up an ashtray and lit a cigarette. "Sorry about Joey disappearing."

She shrugged. "We broke up a few weeks ago. Ronnie Gearhart and I are going steady now." She showed me a class ring on a chain around her neck. "See?"

"Who broke up with who?"

"I broke up with him."

"Because?"

"I liked Ronnie more," she said.

"What about Virginia Kelly?" I asked.

She screwed up her face. "That tramp," she said.

"I hear tell someone was spreading rumors around the high school that she was pregnant."

"Do tell." All her prettiness had deserted her.

"You're not sorry she's dead?"

"I'm a girl," she said. "You don't think I had anything to do with it, do you?"

"I'm a man with an open mind." I could have used a cup of coffee, but decided not to ask.

"My daddy owns Unified Pine," she announced with prim certainty.

"Do tell." Unified was the second largest mill in the county. "Would Ronnie know where Joey's gotten off to?"

"They aren't friends anymore." She seemed proud of the fact.

"I heard they had a set-to at football practice on Monday."

"What?" Her face told me that she didn't know about the fight. I was about to follow up when the phone rang. Margie answered it, then held it out to me. "It's for you."

"I left this number with my office," I explained. On the phone, Miriam told me that a neighbor had called to report a fistfight at the Gearhart place. Sam Gearhart whipping up on Ronnie, I figured. The town marshal was tied up, so the state patrol would have to roll to back me up, but they were twenty minutes out. No worries, I told Miriam. I could handle Sam Gearhart by myself. "Got a domestic disturbance down the road," I said as I left.

*

Ruby Gearhart ran screaming into the street wearing only a short blue housecoat and a couple of fresh bruises. “Murder! Murder!” she cried.

I unlimbered an axe handle from behind the seat and locked Addison in the cab of the truck.

Inside, Ronnie Gearhart held down his old man and punched him merrily about the head and shoulders with both fists. As he worked, he chanted, “Fuck you! Fuck you! Fuck you!” I had half a mind to let him continue, but old Sam was pretty much done. Blood covered his face and his ripped work shirt, and he had stopped defending himself. The kid’s fists sounded like they were hitting a side of beef.

I dropped the axe handle and tugged at Ronnie’s chin while telling him that Sam had had enough, but the kid paid no attention. I could have been talking to a potato. I wrapped my forearm around his neck and squeezed on his carotid until he passed out from lack of oxygen. The condition would be temporary, so while he was out, I rolled him over and snapped my handcuffs on him.

Sam blew bubbles of blood and wheezed and gasped in a way that made me afraid he was going to die. I rolled him onto his left side and whacked him hard between the shoulder blades a couple of times. He coughed up a fair amount of blood, goo, and beer, then settled down to breathing with a stuttering regularity that was better than nothing.

He woke up for a moment, mumbled, “Damned kid kicked my ass,” almost as if he were proud of it, then slipped back into unconsciousness.

Ruby Gearhart ran back into the house with her housecoat flopping open, nothing underneath, screaming all the while.

I took her by the shoulders, and yelled, “Hot water! I need hot water.”

She spun into the kitchen while I phoned for Doc and the local ambulance.

I lit a cigarette and perched on the edge of the davenport. After a while, Ronnie Gearhart came around. I sat him up and told him that he had sure thumped his old man. He looked over at the bloody lump that was his father, and said, “I did. He was whupping up on my mom.”

“You need to learn when to stop, or your temper will get you in a bind that you won’t get out of.”

"How would you know?" he asked.

"I know." He reminded me of myself when I was a kid. I wanted to tell him more, but this wasn't the time or place.

"Coach'll be pissed," Ronnie said. "First Joey's gone, now I'm in trouble. The team will be sunk."

"There's more important things than football going on right now." He told me he knew that, but he didn't seem convinced.

Doc Silverman and the volunteer fireman that drove the ambulance arrived about the same time. Ruby calmed down enough to tell me she didn't want me to take Ronnie to jail. Sam had beaten her, and Ronnie stopped him. "He saved my life," she said. "Sam can't control himself when he gets his temper up."

"The ambulance is going to take him to St. Charles in Bend," Doc said. "Sam's in a bad way, and I think he may need surgery."

"Bad enough," I said to Ruby, "that I'm going to have to take Ronnie into custody. Don't worry. I'll make sure no harm comes to him."

She was okay until I started to walk Ronnie out in the cuffs. He cried like some boys do when they're headed to the pokey, and Ruby went off again. She called me a beast, a bastard, and a shit, which were probably all the bad words she knew.

Doc Silverman wrapped his arms around her shoulders and pulled her back into the kitchen.

I maneuvered Ronnie out to the truck and made Addison ride in the bed. The kid cried and the dog barked all the way back to the office.

*

The town marshal, Peter, met Addison and me as we were coming down the stairs into my office with Ronnie Gearhart in tow. "I caught your murderer," he said with his satisfied smile that always got on my nerves.

"Bullshit." I half-hoped it was true, half-hoped it wasn't. I wanted to catch the son of a bitch myself. The arrest would make me look good to the voters, and I'd have the satisfaction of smacking the bastard in the gut a couple of times.

"Sure enough," Peter said. "Wait and see." Though the town was nominally the marshal's jurisdiction, he was lazy and a coward, so I usually ended up taking all his criminal calls along with my own. I'd complained to Barnes, but he said we needed someone to do the job.

"He can't and you're been elected by the people."

We walked Ronnie Gearhart back to the small cellblock. Thomas Stewart, black as you please and holding his head in the palms of both hands, sat in cell number two, swaying back and forth. Addison slipped into the cell, jumped up onto the cot, and licked Stewart's face.

"Get that dog away from me," Stewart said.

"You stupid nigger," I said before I could control myself. "You had to be righteous."

"You can't talk to me that way."

"My jail, I'll talk to the prisoners any damned way I please."

"You two know each other?" Peter asked.

"Never you mind," I said. "He'd didn't do it. Let him go."

"City is my jurisdiction," Peter said. "You may run the jail, but you can't release one of my prisoners without a judge's permission."

"You need to do a report before I can book him in."

"I was just getting to it," Peter said.

"Get to it," I said, and he scampered back into the front office.

"There's no evidence against me," Stewart said. "I want a lawyer."

"Hold your water." I guided Ronnie into cell number one. Now he was a scared kid, not someone who had just beat up his old man. Before he could start crying, I told him not to worry, but he'd have to stay in jail until we heard how his father was doing. "You'll be fine," I added.

He sniffed, and asked, "What about the coach?"

"I'll talk to him," I said.

"I'm an innocent man," Stewart said. Addison had curled up next to him for a nap.

"I should have escorted you to the county line," I replied.

"A lawyer?"

I offered to let him use the phone, but he said he didn't know any lawyers in this county.

"Then the circuit judge will appoint one. He'll be in town next Tuesday."

"The Constitution says I have a right to a speedy trial." Stewart grabbed the bars and tried to shake them.

I laughed. "Why in the hell do you think I wanted you to take the long way around? You just don't get it. Speedy trial for colored folks in these parts means a mob escort to the railroad bridge and a long drop with a short rope."

Stewart turned to Ron. "He's shitting me, right?"

"It was a long time ago, 1898," Ronnie said. "They have a picture of it upstairs in one of the courtrooms. Man's body swinging from the bridge. You can't miss it, steel bridge, just south of town along the highway. My great-grandfather was there."

"Problem was," I said, "they hanged the wrong guy. Thought they caught a horse thief, but the horse had wandered off on its own." I ran my fingers through my hair. "Now it's my job to keep you alive." George and my reserve deputy, "Happy" Jack Sparks, would have to trade off babysitting our prisoners until the circuit judge hit town.

"He was shitting you," Ronnie said. Stewart laughed nervously. "White. The guy they hanged was white."

"Oh, fuck me," Stewart said.

"You damned mutt, get out of that cell," I said to Addison. "We've got work to do."

Chapter 7

Coach Conroy had purchased the old Jackson homestead up on the backside of Horseshoe Mountain, just a jump and holler east of Twelve Mile Table. The second half of daily doubles, football practice, was at least a couple of hours away. I didn't call ahead for any other reason than I hadn't been to his place before, and I was a nosy jackass.

Roberta Conroy swung a two-handed sledgehammer with authority, dead on the wedge, splitting pine logs with well-intentioned blows. I'd seen the Coach's wife in town now and again but never had the occasion to talk with her. She seemed a reclusive sort, and I hadn't really formed an opinion of her.

Roberta had to have seen my pickup coming up the way, but she kept right on working. She'd finished at least half a cord of firewood already and had a couple of cords of cut-rounds waiting for the sledge and wedge.

When Addison and I hopped out of my pickup, Roberta leaned the sledge against her chopping block and wiped the sweat out of her eyes. She was a large, stocky woman, not fat, but what my mama might call big-boned. If she were a man, they might call her a bruiser. Her eyes were veiled and held no greeting for me.

"Afternoon, I'm Sheriff Harkness."

She nodded. "I know who you are."

"Going to town on that woodpile," I said.

"Not necessarily a man's job." Addison sniffed around her shoes, and she rubbed the scruff of his neck.

"Some men can't handle an axe." I showed her a deep slice in one of my cowboy boots. "Came damned close to whacking my own toe off last fall."

"No toe Joe. A poem." She laughed at her own joke, and I laughed with her. The laughter changed her face, and she seemed prettier, in a stark sort of way. She whistled and a black and tan Australian Shepherd bitch bounded from the wood shed. She and Addison nosed around each other's nether parts as a way of getting acquainted. I'd have to watch that fool; he was too irresponsible to become a father.

"Coach around?" I asked.

"Conroy's working on his game plan for the scrimmage with Prineville. He's out back." I snapped my fingers for Addison to follow me, but he would have none of it. "Looks like he's found true love," Roberta said. "He'll be fine. Tippy and I will watch over him."

Twelve Mile Creek formed the border of the backyard that had a small green lawn and a birdbath. The Table loomed above the yard to the east. The sun would rise late here. I found the Coach sitting at a card table set up in the shade of the back porch. The table was piled with notebooks.

"Pull up a chair and rest a while." He put aside his pen, leaned back, and offered me some water from a screw-top Mason jar.

I declined and told him that I had Ronnie Gearhart locked up in the clink. "He kicked his old man's ass," I said. "Put him in the hospital."

A covey of quail cooed from the brush at the edge of the creek. Conroy sighed and rubbed the short hairs on the top of his head. "Shame. Any chance of him getting out of this?"

"Depends on what happens with his old man. He's hurt pretty bad."

"I'm sure he was provoked. Ron's a good kid."

"Like Joey McIntyre's a good kid?"

Tippy raced pell-mell around the corner of the house with Addison in hot pursuit. They tumbled together and woofed happily; neither of them showed any interest in the quail.

"Joey McIntyre is a good football player."

"Not the same thing," I noted.

Conroy took a long pull from the Mason jar, then screwed the lid back on and shook it. "True enough." Something spooked the quail and they disappeared down the bank of the creek.

"Sorry that your two star players may miss the season," I said.

Conroy shrugged. "Being a champion is learning to overcome adversity."

"Tell your kids that?" I asked.

"Got a poster to that effect hanging in my locker room." I lit a Camel.

"Those things will kill your wind."

"They keep me skinny," I said.

"Skinny and dead."

"I hear that Joey and Ronnie had a little fracas in practice the day Joey disappeared," I said. Addison and Tippy stopped playing and looked toward the creek. A gray tabby cat skulked at the edge of the bank.

"Kid stuff," Conroy said. "Gave 'em both wind sprints for show, but I like emotion in my players. Shows they got moxie."

"I heard Joey didn't take it too well, and that the two of you had an argument in your office after practice."

"The walls have big ears," he said.

"Hear tell that you slapped him when he protested about the punishment," I said.

"Not a slap." The cat pounced on something in the bushes and reappeared with a small quail in her jaws. "Fucking cat." He tossed the half-full Mason jar fifty yards on the fly, and it exploded less than a foot from the cat. The cat dropped the quail and skittered away upstream as the two dogs took up the chase.

"Wouldn't slap the boy," Conroy said after a bit. "Wouldn't do that, but I'm not above giving the kid a hack with my paddle if he needs it. Common practice at the school. Ask anyone."

Common practice when I was growing up, too. Didn't make it right. "That might make you the last person to see Joey before he disappeared."

"That so?" Conroy asked.

"That's so," I said.

"I seem to recall that Joey was headed down to the haberdashery after practice to get fitted for a letterman's sweater."

"I'll check that." I remembered that Betty McIntyre had mentioned the sweater had gone missing.

"Sounds like you doubt me," he said. Addison and Tippy returned from chasing the cat. I scratched Addison behind the ears. Tippy curled up at my feet.

"Just being thorough." When the coach didn't reply, I asked him if Mike Barfield would be at practice today.

"Hell to pay if he ain't."

*

I peeked around the corner into the high school locker room. Barfield jumped when I said, "Hey."

He'd been reading a Life magazine. "I didn't expect anyone to be around."

"I need to ask some more questions about Virginia," I said.

"Coach Conroy isn't here." He got up and tossed a bag of footballs onto a top shelf.

"I need to ask you," I said.

He told me fine, and we moved out of the locker room into the gym and sat on the bleachers. Sweat lined the kid's upper lip.

"Tell me about Virginia and the older man," I said, working on my hunch based on Virginia's poetry.

"I don't know anything about that." He clasped his hands as if to keep them from trembling.

"She talked about forbidden fruit in her journal."

Barfield just shrugged.

I scooted closer to him, and said, "Let's cut the bullshit. You had a crush on her. You gave her a leather-bound book of poetry by Browning."

He shook his head. "Not true."

"You loved her. What happened when you told her and she rejected you? Did you slip into a rage and kill her?"

"It wasn't that way."

"What way was it?" I asked. He looked away for a moment, thinking, and when he looked back I shoved my face up close to his. "Help me find her killer. I know she confided in you. That you may have been her only true friend. She was seeing someone else on the sly. Who was it? A teacher? Coach Conroy?"

"Ha!" he said. "No, not the coach."

"Who, then?" I put my hand on his shoulder, easy, just to establish a presence.

He didn't look at me as he spoke. "Joey's dad."

"Dr. McIntyre?" I didn't know whether to whoop or feel sick.

Barfield nodded. I asked him if Joey knew about the affair.

The kid shrugged as if it say he didn't know. "Virginia told me it just happened. Joey talked his father into filling one of Virginia's cavities, and Dr. McIntyre seduced her. She wasn't sure what really happened, but afterward he gave her a book of poems. It tore her up. Virginia said she felt dirty."

"She didn't feel like she could tell anyone," I said.

"Just me."

I chewed on the revelation for a bit—son of a bitch McIntyre fucking a fourteen-year-old girl. I relished putting the screws to the bastard. And Virginia had mentioned that J. was frightened of someone. Was that Joey or Jeff?

"So you don't know if Joey knew about it?" I asked again.

"Virginia didn't say. Maybe."

*

McIntyre's office was closed for lunch, so I decided to visit Harley's Haberdashery and see if Joey had gone there to get fitted for a letterman's jacket on that last day. If you were a man in Barnestown, your first option for clothing was the haberdashery. Your second option was the long drive to Prineville to the Men's Wear or Erickson's Department Store. Harley stocked just about anything you might want in his cluttered shop: work boots, cowboy boots, loafers, oxfords, saddle shoes, shoe polish, work pants, dress pants, belts, buckaroo belt buckles, cowboy hats, fedoras, porkpie hats, suits for funerals and weddings, leather gloves, pocketknives, pocket watches, money clips, and boy scout shirts, bandanas, handbooks, and merit badges.

Harley's daughter Ruth—twelve and already an accomplished shopkeeper—greeted me at the door. Harley had three good kids, two younger boys and the girl. When Harley heard me say "Hello" to his daughter, he came out from the backroom.

"Matthew." He shook my hand. "What can I do you for?" Harley was a medium man, medium height, medium build, neither fat nor skinny, unremarkable except for a thick thatch of rusty brown hair that he swept back from his forehead. Today, rather than a suit, he wore a white western shirt with pearl buttons and snakeskin boots, less a fashion statement, I suspected, than to comfort his customers.

I grabbed Harley by the elbow and guided him to the front door. "Let's take a little walk." He stiffened as if to resist, but then came along.

The day had shaped up to be an idyllic fading summer day. Warm, yet cool in the shade, mosquitoes almost all gone because of an early frost. The old-timers, men who by custom had carried sidearms when they were young, lounged against the granite wall of the First National Bank sunning themselves and talking perhaps about how sweet this country had been before motor cars had been invented and when the ryegrass still grew six feet tall on the spot where they now stood. When I had a moment, I'd stop and listen to their stories and wonder what it would have been like to live in a simpler time.

Harley's Adam's apple twitched as he asked me what this was all about.

"Did Joey come in the day he disappeared?" I asked.

"No, sir," Harley said. "He had made an appointment to get fitted for a letterman's sweater, but he never showed up." We paused in front of the drugstore.

"Didn't he already own a sweater?" I asked.

"Yes, indeed," he said. "But I'll be darned if I know what happened to it."

"So he didn't say?"

"No."

"Was Ruth working in the store that day?"

Harley frowned at the mention of his daughter. "As a matter of fact, she was," he said with some reluctance. "Do you need to talk with her?" The frown stayed. I figured he didn't want her involved in this.

"Do you stock Army surplus combat boots?" I asked. "Damned cowboy boots make my arches ache."

"We stock arch supports."

"Not the same thing," I said. "High-heeled shit-kickers just don't suit me."

"Not much call for them," Harley said. "Take a few weeks if we ordered them. You could try the Army-Navy Surplus store in Redmond."

"You could ask your supplier to rush the order," I suggested. "Ruth will measure me, and I'll ask her some questions about Joey real gentle-like. I won't upset her." Barnes and Kate walked out of the drugstore, content but not touching. They seemed more like brother and sister.

"Harley." Barnes nodded in our direction. "I need you to alter my gray pinstripe suit. I'm giving a speech at the legislature."

"Too many strawberry sodas." Kate glared at me as if that was my fault.

"Judge, don't worry, you haven't gained an ounce," Harley said.

"The boots?" I asked. "Gentle-like."

Harley glanced from Barnes to me. "Fine. Ruth will take care of you. Come along, Judge, let's get that suit, and I'll whip it out in no time."

After Barnes and Harley moved out of earshot, I asked Kate, "Are you mad at me, Sweetpea?"

"Why would I be mad?" She turned and walked back up Main Street. I trailed along, and the old geezers by the bank buzzed. I wanted to tell them to shut up.

"I don't know what this is about," I said.

"Ask Lucy Redmond," she replied. "She can explain it to you."

Kate would toss Lucy up at me whenever she was on the warpath. It was an old rub between us, and I knew that something else had to be bothering her. "We need to talk. Seriously."

"Seriously?" She paused to check a yellow print dress in Penny's store window.

"It's about the case."

She sighed. "Fine. Your place tomorrow. We'll talk."

"Wonderful." I rubbed my hands together.

"Hold your water. We're just gonna talk."

*

Kate and I were high school sweethearts, engaged to be engaged was what we called the state of our relationship. After graduation, she headed off to college to study English. I was a poor kid living with my uncle, so I went to work in the mill, pulling green chain. We pined for each other when school was in session, made up for it during the breaks. She graduated, and I'd just gotten a job selling Buicks, so we set the date to set the date, then the Japs decided to attack Pearl Harbor. My draft board said, "We want you." The Army taught me how to hurt people, handed me an M-1, and shipped me off to the Pacific Theater. Kate said she'd wait for me.

I wish I could say that war ennobled me, but it didn't. I killed more than one man. I found myself a hero on one day, and a coward on another. I tended to say it didn't bother me, but my actions would hang with me the rest of my days. Some men liked to brag about what they did in the war. I didn't.

The Army wanted me to stick around, attend Officer Candidate School, be a gentleman, but I said, "Nuts." They discharged me at Treasure Island, San Francisco. Ironic name, that. I should have headed home, but reason left me, and I stuck in Frisco, earning enough for booze and a room working with a hammer and saw. I took up with a little Chinese gal by the name of Ming Li. She eventually left me for a Chinese insurance broker. She said she wanted to make her family happy. I reckoned I should have been more disappointed.

I could have headed home right after the war, started selling Buicks, settled down and gotten married, but I didn't. My childhood had been agony, and I ran away from my mom and stepdad when I was thirteen, rode the rails for a while, and finally ended up living with my uncle. Maybe because of how brutal my mom was, I couldn't face settling down or having kids or being responsible for anyone other than myself. Or maybe I needed to work the war out of my system—killing people before they killed me, living in the mud and grime, rats as big as dogs, jungle fever eating away at my guts, wondering when I was going to die. I told myself I'd never kill again, yet here I was carrying a gun. Maybe as much as I hated that life, I discovered it was what I was good at.

By the time I drifted back home, Kate had gotten married to Barnes. She told me later that she figured I was gone for good. Maybe I could have broken things up, but I took up with Lucy Redmond instead, she being a woman of fire and lust, and her husband Dirk being a man who appreciated an Arabian mare as much as he did his wife.

Lucy was a fine woman, as smart and practical as her husband. She knew exactly what she was getting into and, unlike me, knew exactly when to get out. "You still love Kate, and she loves you," Lucy said when we broke up. "You two belong together."

So Kate and I were back together again, after a fashion, but she hadn't been able to make a firm decision to leave Barnes. She kept saying she couldn't be sure I was serious. Looking back at how I had fiddle-farted around, she probably had good cause.

Chapter 8

"So I hear tell you were fucking Virginia," I said to Jeff McIntyre, my mind still tumbling after my conversation with Kate.

"That's a lie," McIntyre said. "Repeat it and I'll sue." When I had first mentioned Virginia, the good doctor had hustled me into his office, a small side room that he apparently used more for storing records than for doing paperwork.

"I have her notebook. She was very graphic about what happened." Bullshit, but he couldn't be sure. Guys like this were used to lying to their wives, not to the cops.

"A schoolgirl fantasy." He fiddled with some papers on his desk, not looking me in the eye.

"Someone gave her a book of poems. Elizabeth Barrett Browning, not your usual teenager fare. The stationary store would probably have a record of who ordered it. When your son turns up, maybe he could shed some light for us."

McIntyre's hands trembled, and he wiped tears from his eyes. That didn't surprise me. Older men who are predators often rationalize their crimes by believing they have deep feelings for their victims, easier to live with love than guilt.

"Such a sweet girl," I said. "So beautiful. She was almost angelic."

"She had so much possibility." He pulled a handkerchief from his pants pocket and blew his nose. "I wouldn't do anything to hurt her. You have to believe that."

"Tell me about it."

"Maybe I need to talk to a lawyer," he said.

"Nah, if we call a lawyer, everyone will find out about you and Virginia. Let's keep this just between us and the fencepost." I scooted my chair closer to his and put my hand on his shoulder. "You want to help me find her killer, don't you? You help me, and I'll help you get out of this mess." If he had killed her, I would make sure he fried. If not, he'd still do ten to fifteen cracking rocks at the State Pen with a cellmate named Butch.

"She and Joey started going steady," McIntyre said. "Betty didn't approve. She wasn't the right kind of girl."

"Mothers never think their son's girlfriends are good enough."

"She was a good enough gal," he said, "pretty, polite, smart. You have to believe me, I didn't intend for anything to happen."

"It just happened," I said.

"Her teeth were in dreadful shape," McIntyre said. "Her family couldn't afford proper care, and Joey asked if I couldn't do something."

"You did it for your son," I said.

McIntyre almost smiled. "Sure. I gave them a good cleaning, found a couple a cavities during the examination, and told her I'd fill them for her." I bet, I thought, but bit my tongue and nodded for him to continue.

"It was in the spring, May, pretty May. A Saturday morning. I had gone for a walk and seen a golden eagle. She came to my office wearing a white blouse, threadbare and missing a button. My assistant had the day off." His eyes glazed as if he was reliving the moment. "When she lay back in the chair, I realized that she wasn't wearing a bra. So sad, yet erotic."

"That was when it began?"

McIntyre nodded. "She said no, but she was a woman. She really meant yes."

"You made love to her in the examination chair?"

"You think I'm a monster," he said.

"I'm just trying to understand what happened. Did Joey know?"

"Not in the beginning. He found out later. It was our secret, Virginia's and mine," he said. "You have to understand how she felt."

"But she wanted more," I said.

"She wanted to marry me, but she didn't understand my position. I couldn't just haul off and do something rash like that."

She was fourteen, I thought. How could she understand? "She hadn't had any experience in love, not like you."

"She had potential," he said.

"And Joey, how did he find out?"

"Virginia told him," McIntyre said. "He was furious. Threatened to hit me. Imagine that, hit his father. I told him to leave the house. He stomped out."

"When was that?" I asked.

"The day before he disappeared," he said. "He didn't come home that night. Betty was frantic, but I told her everything would be okay."

"He attended daily doubles the next day," I said. "Do you have any idea where he spent the night?"

McIntyre shrugged. "Maybe with Ronnie Gearhart. They were best friends. You have to believe me; I didn't kill her."

"Joey," I said. "Could he kill her?"

"Of course not," he said. "Joey's a good boy, a solid citizen. When he turns up, you'll see."

"Sure I will." But I had to wonder. If he knew about the affair between his father and his girlfriend, would he be enraged enough to kill her? If so, he was probably on the run, either that or holed up somewhere. "What now?" McIntyre sniffed as if he'd begin to cry again.

"We'll keep looking for your boy. Don't worry, we'll find him." Rather than toss McIntyre in the pokey right then, I decided to play him out on a line and see if he'd lead me to his son.

*

When I got back to my office, my two prisoners, accompanied by Miriam and Ed Dilkes from the local paper, sat around my desk in straight-backed chairs eating a late afternoon supper of fried trout and potatoes. The Motorola record player played some round-toned crooner.

"Who in the hell is that?" I asked. Crooners made me feel all mushy inside.

"Nat King Cole," Miriam said. "Isn't he dreamy?"

"Dreamy isn't a word I'd expect from you," I said. "What's Dilkes doing here?"

"Smile." Dilkes raised a camera.

"I'll break that Kodak over your head," I threatened.

"Speed Graphic," he said, as he lowered the camera. "Reporter's best friend, a Speed Graphic."

"They're all the same to me."

"Ed's waiting to interview you about the murder," Miriam said. "I told him he could have lunch with us." Addison hopped into Stewart's lap and begged to be petted.

"Does the term sedition mean anything to you?" I asked.

"Did you know that Thomas here played in the Negro leagues before the war?" Ronnie Gearhart asked. "Pee Wee Stewart, shortstop for the Atlanta Black Crackers."

"This is a joke, right?" I asked.

"Nope, I'm writing a profile on him," Dilkes said.

"Eddie, do that," I said, "and I'll shoot you where you sit."

"Grumpy fart, isn't he?" Dilkes asked.

"I think he's got love problems," Miriam said.

"You don't know what you're talking about," I said.

"Some in the community have expressed a concern for Mr. Stewart's safety here in the jail," Dilkes said. "Would you care to comment for the record?"

"Miriam, hand me my shotgun."

"How 'bout a nice plate of scrambled eggs with your trout?" she asked. "I made my jalapeño sauce extra hot, just the way you like it."

"What's a jalapeño?" the Gearhart kid asked.

"You'll feel much better," Miriam said.

My mouth watered. "Fuck me."

"Love problems?" Dilkes asked. "Must be, right, Miriam?"

"I don't know what you're talking about," I said.

Miriam served me a plate of eggs and trout smothered in green sauce. Before I forgot, I asked Ronnie if Joey had spent the night at his house before he'd disappeared. He told me no. I turned to Stewart. "Don't worry about your safety. Eddie works real hard to get a rise out of folks. People around here are levelheaded, but most of them have never ever seen a negro before."

"Do you know Roy Campanella?" Ronnie asked Stewart. "Could you get me an autograph?"

While I worked on my eggs, Miriam told me that Ron's dad was still in the hospital in Bend. Seemed like they were still trying to decide how long to hang onto him. I figured I'd keep the kid for another night. When I finished talking with Miriam, I shooed Dilkes out of the office, and told Stewart, "Stand up, we're going to take a ride." I wasn't exactly sure why. Maybe I felt guilty about having him locked up, or maybe I wanted the company. Maybe I was worried about his safety.

"If I turn up killed, tell my family what happened," Stewart said to Miriam. "You're my witness."

"If I was gonna do something to you, witnesses wouldn't be a problem," I said. "But don't worry; I gave up murdering people for Lent,"

"Lent is over."

"So it is."

*

We ran back roads looking for signs of Joey McIntyre. Addison nestled in between us with his ugly muzzle propped in Stewart's crotch. After a couple of hours of eating dust and enduring doggy farts, we headed back into town. At the city limits, I pulled up and stopped. The sign read: "No Colored Folk within the City Limits After Sunset."

"I don't believe it," Stewart said. "You folks up here are crazy."

"Not my sign, not my law." I tried not to feel guilty. "City ordinance, so I don't have to enforce it, but I figured you should know what you've fallen into here. You should have listened to me when I told you to turn around."

"This ain't right," Stewart said.

"I agree, but lots of cities and towns in the West have sunset laws. The laws were enacted right after the first war when black folk started to move up north looking for work. Lots of white folk got nervous. Funny part is, most folk in these parts have never seen a negro before."

"Nothing funny about it," Stewart replied.

Already some townspeople were pushing to repeal the law, but this fact wouldn't ease Stewart's pain, so I kept my mouth shut and drove us over to the McIntyre house. We'd set up there and wait to see if Doctor McIntyre would go out into the advancing night to see his boy or futz with the evidence.

The McIntyre place was a grand house, brand new, built on the Heights overlooking Barnestown. So new that McIntyre hadn't put in a lawn yet. The Heights held just a scattering of houses served by dirt roads, but the subdivision held promise. The city had put in water lines, and there was power. If I had had extra cash, I'd have bought a lot up there, maybe two. A feller could work the angles—build on one, hold the other, and sell it down the road for a profit. Kate had told me she wanted a place up there, something with room for her animals. I didn't want to reflect on what could have been.

I must have been too silent because Stewart cleared his throat and asked me where I'd served during the War.

"New Guinea. Nothing glamorous, just a lot of grunt work. How'd you like Italy?"

"They told us it was beautiful," he said.

"But it wasn't?"

"Never seen so much mud in my life," he said.

"You should have tried New Guinea," I said.

"Were you kidding about killing an unarmed man?" he asked after a while. "Was it a Jap?"

"I was just joshing you." But I hadn't been. I did kill an unarmed man, a white man, not a Jap. New Guinea did something to all of us; somehow it made us less than human. Snakes as big as fire hoses, strange sounds in the night so you couldn't sleep and it rained every fucking day. The natives were good to us, God knows why, black fellers with hair like bushy thickets. Good folks, but I learned not to get on the wrong side of them. We didn't have the wherewithal to take care of Jap prisoners, so we'd hand them over to the natives. We found one poor Jap's head on a pike out in the jungle a couple of days after we had handed him over to the tribe. We didn't ask what happened to the poor fucker.

There was a girl in the tribe about the same age as Virginia. Sweet kid. We called her Sal; she hung around the camp a lot, helped the army nurses with the sick and wounded. The local girls went bare-chested; we never could convince them to cover up. After a while, we stopped noticing, except for one private named Roger. Roger always sniffed around for pussy, laughed funny-like at the jokes, like a teenager who'd never gotten laid. He took a shine to Sal, tried giving her smokes and chocolate, but she was a kid. She didn't get it.

Just before the Japs made their big push, I was stuck in camp recovering from jungle fever, fighting off the sweats and night terrors. I had just come out of a bad patch and awoke to what sounded like a scream through the white noise of the rain. The camp was empty; everyone was out on patrol. At first I thought it was a dream or a delusion, but it wasn't. Figuring the Japs had snuck into camp, I grabbed a .45 and went to investigate. I found Roger in his tent raping Sal from behind. When I pulled him off her, he stood there, dick at half-mast and laughed half-crazy like. "We'll have to kill her," he said, "or the natives will kill us." I thought about the Jap head on a pike.

"Sure," I said. "Let's take her out in the jungle, do it there."

Even though I was still weak with fever, I carried her, half-conscious, to a small clearing a few hundred yards from camp. The racket of the birds drowned out the sound of the rain. A coven of monkeys watched from the trees.

He asked me for the gun. "I'll shoot her."

"No, it's my job," I said. She was awake then and knew enough English to know what was going on. She didn't beg, just looked at us.

"Sorry." I put a round right between his eyes, blew the back half of his head off. The report spooked the birds, but not the monkeys. Sal didn't say a word, just picked herself up and trudged into the jungle. I buried the body as deep as I was able in the wet loamy earth. I expected the natives to come at us with hammers and tongs, but they didn't. Either she didn't tell anyone, or they figured we were square. Everybody in the camp figured Roger got captured by the Japs or wandered off into the jungle. Guys disappeared from time to time. I kept my mouth shut.

I must have been lost in my thoughts, because Addison yipped and brought me back. The sounds of the high-desert night enfolded us. Bullfrogs croaked down by the creek, and the ten o'clock whistle hooted at the mill. Lots of work at the mill, Americans on the move, we were optimistic, except maybe for the Commies kicking our asses in Korea and Joe McCarthy telling us that they were already here. Some folks danced to McCarthy's melody, not me. I had more important things to worry about, like Virginia hanging from a juniper tree and Kate brushing me off.

McIntyre came out and hopped in his car. I figured I had him, but he drove straight to the Spur Roadhouse, out on Highway 26. After he parked and went inside, we cruised the parking lot and used my spotlight looking for cars I recognized. The place was jumping, new singing in town. Barnes's Cadillac was there, as was Doc Silverman's Ford and the coach's pickup. Sam Gearhart's Chevy would have been there except he was laid up in the Bend hospital.

I backed into a spot that gave me a view of the front door, killed the engine, and settled down to wait. I thought about getting the bottle from behind the seat and taking a short snort, but looked at Stewart and thought better of it. "See that tree over there?"

"Let me guess," he said. "Your dog wants to pee."

"Hell if I know what he wants," I said. "At the very top of the tree, there's a flag. The Wops put one up there every time a baby is born, supposed to be good luck. Over one hundred feet up. You know how they do it?"

"Wops?" he asked. "You hate Italians, too?" He scratched Addison behind the ears, and the dog moaned.

"Wops," I repeated. "I love them dagos. Some of my best friends are I-talians."

"Fuck," he said, almost under his breath. "I don't want to talk to you anymore."

"What's the matter with you?"

He didn't answer, just kept staring out of the window. No accounting for city folk, I thought and scrunched down in the seat. Moths flitted around the yellow light over the front door of the roadhouse. With Barnes here, maybe I could drop by and say howdy to Kate. What could I do with Stewart? I could handcuff him to the bumper of the truck. I laughed, and he glanced in my direction.

Coach Conroy came out with Judy Smalley on his arm, and they adjourned to his pickup. Judy was known to have round heels and wasn't above turning a trick now and again, a necessary service, even in backwater country like this. The pickup's windows clouded up quickly, but I didn't have the inclination to break up the clinch. Hell, it was only midnight. Kate would be awake if I called, wouldn't she?

Without ado, the front door of the roadhouse exploded, and a crowd poured out with Barnes and some tall cowpoke riding the crest. Barnes and cowpoke proceeded to whang on each other without the usual 'fuck you's'. The cowpoke smacked Barnes on the chin with a decent one-two combination, but Barnes dropped his head and charged his opponent.

"Aren't you going to do something?" Stewart asked.

"Better to let 'em wind down a bit." When you're a cop in the middle of nowhere and your backup is forty miles away, you learned not to rush these things. It was best to hang back, wait for the fighters to bang on each other until they're too pooped to pop, then step in and pick up the pieces.

The cowpoke had Barnes in a headlock, but his blows struck without noticeable effect on top of the older man's bald skull. He wasn't going to get anywhere that way. Barnes threw a fist to the cowboy's testicles which loosened his hold considerably.

Then, Barnes caught the cowpoke with a Joe Louis uppercut that dropped him like a palooka at the Olympic Forum. Barnes immediately jumped on top of the half-conscious cowboy and tried to kill him by pounding his face with meaty fists.

"Time to saddle up." I cuffed Stewart to the steering wheel.

"What the hell are you doing?"

"Stay here," I said. "Watch my dog."

Barnes was still working over the cowboy when I pushed my way through the shouting crowd. I dug my fingers into the nerves at the base of his neck and hauled him off the unconscious man. I wrapped a forearm around his neck and held him still. "Come on, Judge. Enough. You're the high-desert champ."

"Harkness," he said between gasps. "You're fired."

"Can't," I said. "I'm duly elected by the people."

"Judge." Harley appeared out of nowhere. "Are you all right?"

"Harley? Your car isn't in the lot." I dusted Barnes off as well as I could. His shirt had been ripped down the front, and blood streaked his hands and face as if he was some ancient tribesman.

"No crime in having a quick jolt," Harley said.

The cowboy was semiconscious and mumbling something about

riding bareback. Doc Silverman appeared from the crowd and started to attend to the cowboy.

"What happened here?" I asked.

Harley pointed at the dazed man. "He was badmouthing Judge Barnes's wife."

"Yeah," Barnes said. "Let me at 'em. I'll kick his ass again. Nobody can talk about my Kate like that."

The cowboy came around enough to say, "That ain't necessarily so."

"Are you calling me a liar?" Barnes asked.

I pushed Barnes back a few feet. "Simmer down, Judge. We don't want an incident, do we?" I told Harley to hang onto Barnes and make sure he didn't do something stupid.

I took a moment to look around. Neither Coach Conroy nor Jeff McIntyre were in the crowd, but Judy Smalley stood front and center. I asked Doc Silverman how the cowpoke was doing.

"Other than a couple of stitches, he'll be fine."

The cowboy staggered to his feet and leaned against one of his friends.

My life was tough enough without worrying about hauling Barnes into court. "Mutual combat," I said. "No one goes to jail." The crowd cheered.

"You're hired again," Barnes said.

Harley promised me he'd drive Barnes home. The cowpoke and his friends wanted to have a snort to celebrate the battle, but I told them the bar was closed. After the crowd dispersed, I checked the parking lot. McIntyre's car was gone, as was Coach Conroy's pickup. I waved at Doc as he headed back toward town.

The crowd had cleared the parking lot by the time I walked back to my truck. I'd done a good job of not stepping into a political snake pit. Neither Barnes nor the cowpoke would gripe about the outcome, and I figured Barnes owed me one. He'd never admit it, but he wouldn't forget either.

Addison should have barked when I approached the truck, but all I heard was the croaking of frogs down in the cattails. Both doors to my pickup stood open, and the truck was empty. Stewart had made off with my steering wheel and, for Christ's sake, taken my dog with him. There hadn't been a wrench in my truck, and I was unsure how in the hell Stewart had unscrewed the large hex nut that secured the wheel to the steering column. After I finished jumping up and down in the dust and swearing, I trudged back to the roadhouse to call

Frank Flehardy. Jeanie offered to fix me a plate of ham and eggs for breaking up the fight, but I told her, "Not now."

When Frank Flehardy arrived with his tractor, I stewed about not being able to drive my truck. "Don't worry," he said. "I've got an old tractor steering wheel back at the garage that might work as a replacement. You can ride back with me."

"Good," I said.

"Slim, the way you're going, the county should invest in a tow truck."

"Go fuck yourself, Frank."

"Hee hee." He giggled like a girl all the way to the county garage.

Chapter 9

I was still sleeping when Kate tapped on my door the next morning. She wore my favorite yellow cotton dress that showed the ripe curves of her figure. Something inside of me leaped, but I knew I had slim to no chance of getting her out of it this morning. Then again, my mood was so foul that the realization came almost as a relief. She put some coffee on the stove while I got dressed, then she perched on the edge of a kitchen chair as if she were ready to bolt out the door.

"How shall we begin?" I asked. Even in the bright morning sunshine, the world seemed foggy as if I were coming off a three-day bender.

"Porter came home all beat up and bloody last night," she said. "He wouldn't tell me what happened."

"He tangled with one of the Redmond cowboys at the roadhouse," I said. "He told me that the cowboy bad-mouthed you, and he was defending your honor."

"Why would he do that?" The way she said it, I wasn't sure if she meant her husband or the cowboy. I shrugged. "Was Porter with another woman?"

"Hell if I know. I had other things on my mind, but I do know that Harley drove him home. I could look into it further, if you'd like."

"Please." She lit a cigarette.

"Sure." I poured coffee into blue porcelain cups that I had rescued from the local secondhand store. "My prisoner escaped."

"The negro?"

"Yeah, and he took Addison with him. It's not common knowledge, so keep it to yourself."

"People will know soon enough," she said.

The bitterness of the coffee cleared the fog away. "Yeah, you're right."

She tasted her coffee, made a face, and rummaged through the fridge looking for cream. She found some, smelled it, and frowned for a moment, thinking about something, I supposed. Then her face relaxed, and the tiny lines around her eyes and mouth smoothed. She had a fine down on her cheeks that some women of a certain age develop. She put back the cream and stood by the fridge. "Your fridge is disgusting."

"You're mad at me," I observed.

"No... yes, I'm mad as hell at you."

"I'm smart enough to have figured that out," I said, "but dense enough not to know why."

She sat kitty-corner from me at the table with her legs crossed. Her skirt rode up to just below her knee. "I want to be more than your mistress."

"Barnes will shit little green BBs when you leave him," I said, "but we can work it out."

"Matt, you don't get it. Life should be more than just being a good hostess or lover."

"More like what?" I asked.

"I want to be a police officer."

"And carry a gun?" Kate knew how to shoot. She and Barnes hunted chuckers and doves in the fall, but I couldn't picture her carrying a sidearm on her hip.

"Coppers do a lot more than just carry big guns and break heads," she said.

"A big gun. Sounds a little Freudian to me," I said, repressing a laugh,

"Fuck you, Harkness."

I raised my hands in supplication. "Honey, what can I do?"

"During the war, I buckarooed on my uncle's spread. Broke horses, bucked hay, built fence line, shoveled shit out of the barn; I'm as good as any man. Maybe better." Her face had set like baked clay.

"Of course you are," I said.

"And another thing," she said. "Tell me again what took you so long coming back from San Francisco after the War? I still don't understand."

An old argument, revisited. "You know what I was doing there. I told you about that." My coffee was cold, so I added more to warm my cup.

"I know how you passed the time, but I don't know why. You keep telling me you don't know." She turned to look out the window. A sage grouse waddled across my tumbleweed yard. My faucet dripped, and the fridge hummed. She was pissed enough to leave me?

"Okay," I said. "I'll see what I can do. Maybe I can create a special deputy position, someone to help the Valley folks at the new reservoir in the summer. We could call it a marine deputy, maybe not a full commission at first, but we could ease into something more permanent. People like you, they'd get used to it." How could I tell her that there weren't any women deputies in this state? I wasn't sure there were any in the United States. "Pay wouldn't be much to begin with," I added.

"Money's not important," she said.

"But," I said, warming to the idea, "the position might even pay for itself in fine income. Hell, we can't have them city folk bulldogging our lake."

"Then you'll hire me?"

"Hold your horses, honey." Sometimes I spew so much bullshit that I work myself into a corner. "We've just moved into the new budget year this past July. I can't spring this one on Barnes and the County Commission until the spring when I submit my next budget proposal. We don't want to move too soon with this."

"So this is just horseshit." Her eyes became diamond hard.

"No, seriously." I laid my palms flat on the table. "We need a plan of attack. Show our hand too early, and someone will oppose us. You know some folks like to fuck with the county for sport." I composed my face with care. "We'll move carefully with this. Continue helping me with this investigation. Joey's a complicated kid, not a real good kid, more like a stinker in some respects, but I don't think he's got it in him to be a killer. His family's like a yellow onion, layers upon layers, and you can help me peel them back. It seems our esteemed Dr. McIntyre was sleeping with Virginia."

Kate's face turned white. "You didn't tell me."

"I just found out. Maybe you could cozy up to Betty. She's hiding something."

"Bastard." I wasn't sure she meant me or McIntyre.

"When we catch the killer, I'll make sure you get a large dose of the credit. Do a good job, and we can slip you into the job without a lot of fuss."

"People wouldn't mind?" she said.

"Not as much as you might think." I could already envision the angry letters to the editor. Dilkes would have a heyday with this.

"I'll drop by Betty's house this afternoon with a casserole," she said. "Maybe you're wrong. Maybe she doesn't know anything."

"Some women make it a point not to know."

"And some women know, but hide it for the good of the relationship."

Apparently we were dancing, but I didn't know the tune. "Find out for me."

She got up and headed toward the door. "I can do that."

The sun silhouetted her in the open doorway, and her hair shone red in the backlight. I asked her to stay a little longer, but she said "I've got to run," and left me sitting alone, drinking lukewarm coffee. After a bit, I whistled for Addison, but he wasn't there.

*

The Spur Roadhouse was my kind of place—cool, dark and quiet during the day, hot and noisy at night, good whiskey, cheap women, and Jeanie, the owner, let me carry a tab until payday. When I was on duty, the coffee was free, but I didn't dare drink whiskey at the bar when in uniform.

Jingling came from the backroom when I walked in; some fool was playing the slot machines. The state said they were illegal, but Judge Barnes had given the Spur a special dispensation. Jeanie left off her sweeping and fried me up some ham and eggs while I worked on my fourth cup of coffee that afternoon. "How's that new singer working out?" I asked.

"She belts out one hell of a Kitty Wells" Jeanie said. "Have you seen her yet?"

I shook my head. "One doosie of a fight between Barnes and one of Redmond's cowpokes here last night."

"Not much of a fight," she said. "Mostly name calling—'I'm a better man than you' horseshit—a few wild swings, one or two good punches on each side, then we pushed them out into the parking lot. You know."

"I know," I agreed. Jeanie was just a whisker shy of fifty, thin and wiry, and tough enough to do a fair share of her own bouncing. "What started it?"

"Hard to say, I was working the bar at the time." She flipped my eggs. The ham sizzled on the grill. "Heard tell you lost that negro last night."

"Hear tell the Liquor Control Commission is looking to shut down rowdy roadhouses. Might be some surprise inspections coming to a town near you."

"A little touchy, are we?" Jeanie slipped the ham and eggs onto a plate and plunked it down in front of me. "That's fifty cents for the special. Put it on your tab?"

"I thought it was on the house?"

"Just the coffee, Matt. Were you kidding about the Liquor Control Commission?"

"Tell me about Judge Barnes." What was another four bits

between friends?

Jeanie shrugged. "Barnes, Harley, and a couple of others were playing shuffleboard. Cowboy from the Redmond Ranch, not sure of his name, wanted to play. Harley told him no. Cowboy called him out, and Judge Barnes jumped into the middle of it. Cowboy said something to Barnes I didn't catch. Barnes shoved the cowboy, he pushed back, a 'cocksucker' there, a 'motherfucker' here, and the fight was on. A couple of the boys helped me push them out the door, and most of my crowd followed."

"Someone said the cowboy bad-mouthed Judge Barnes's wife."

Jeanie smiled as if she knew a secret. "Not that I heard."

"Dr. McIntyre with Barnes's group?"

She stopped to think for a moment, then shook her head. "He came in late, chatted with Coach Conroy, then they scooted out the back door. Conroy came back in fifteen minutes later, but not Dr. McIntyre. He picked up Judy a while later, and they headed out to the parking lot."

"Seen Conroy and McIntyre together before?"

"Conroy is here now and again, trolling for a little strange," she said. "But Doctor McIntyre sightings are pretty scarce. He hangs his high hat at the Cinnabar Lounge. We're a little too pucker-brush for him, if you know what I mean."

I told her to call me when either Conroy or McIntyre made an encore appearance. I heard a cough from the back of the club, but couldn't see who it was in the darkness.

"What about the Liquor Control Commission?" she asked.

I waved my hand and told her I'd let her know. Someone coughed again, so I left my eggs and hustled to the back, where I found Sam Gearhart huddled with Ed Dilkes.

"Sam, I thought you were on death's door at St. Charles."

"They wanted to keep me, but I said,'Hell, no.' Don't trust no fucking doctors." Gearhart sipped his coffee. His left arm was in a cast and his left eye was swollen shut.

I settled into a chair and told Dilkes to take a walk.

"I'm interviewing Sam for a story," Dilkes protested.

"This is official business," I said.

"Don't do anything stupid." Dilkes knew how I felt about Gearhart.

"What are you, my guardian angel?" I asked.

"Somebody's got to look out after you," Dilkes said.

"I'm fine," Gearhart said. "I'm not afraid of the big bad sheriff."

After Dilkes left, I said, “Now that you’re healthy, I’m going to release your son. I don’t expect you’ll be pressing charges.”

“Boy kicked my ass,” Gearhart said, as if he were still trying to comprehend it. “My boy kicked my ass.”

“And you’re not going to do anything about it,” I stated.

“Don’t worry, my boy don’t belong in jail.”

“This is the end of it,” I said.

“Who says?” Gearhart chugged his coffee like it was a beer.

“Me.” I popped up, planted the heel of my boot on his instep, and hauled him to his feet. “Listen, you piece of shit,” I said in a steely whisper, “if anything happens to your son or your wife, I’ll fuck you up so bad that you’ll walk like a duck for the rest of your life.”

“Help!” Gearhart cried.

“Harkness!” Jeanie said. “Outside.”

“No problem here.” I pushed Gearhart back into his chair. Cowboy boots were good for something after all.

“You broke my foot,” he said, massaging his instep.

“I’ve been a good boy for a long time,” I said, standing over him. “But you could have a little accident. Maybe break the other arm or maybe worse. Who do you think people would believe? Me or some trash drunk? I’ve earned a free pass, and I’ve been saving it for you.”

“Why do you hate me so much?” he asked. “What have I done to you?”

“You fuck with your kid, you fuck with me,” I said.

“Hell, I was proud of my boy. He’d been acting like some candy-ass.” He smiled almost shyly. “I didn’t think he had it in him.”

“You’re a piece of work, Gearhart.” I went back to finish my eggs. On my way out the door, Jeanie asked if I was nuts. “Could be,” I said, but she didn’t laugh at my joke.

*

Ed Dilkes, Ronnie Gearhart, and Miriam were playing cards when I returned to the office. “No gambling in here,” I said.

“It’s gin rummy,” Miriam said.

“She’s a whiz at rummy.” Ronnie picked up another card.

“What are you doing here, Eddie?” I asked. “I can’t shake you.”

“Just nosing for news,” he said.

I told Ronnie to collect his belongings and hit the road. “What about my dad?” he asked, almost as if he’d found a better home in the pokey.

"Your old man is home from the hospital and is somewhat healthy. I know where to find you, so go home. He shouldn't cause you or your mom any problems," I said, "but if he does, you're to call me right away. Let me help you. Don't be a chump and push your luck or someone could get killed."

"Yeah, sure," he told me, but he didn't seem to be buying what I was selling. Miriam handed me a roast beef sandwich and told me to eat while she processed his release and called his mother to pick him up. When I asked if he wanted me to drive him home, he looked at me like I was nuts.

After he left, I took a bite of my sandwich. "Eddie, what's going on with you and Sam Gearhart?"

"As I said, I'm interviewing him for a story," Dilkes said.

"You're a better liar than this, Ed."

"Sam's going on the wagon. He asked me for some advice."

My laugh popped out louder than expected. "You don't believe that crap?"

"What have you got against the man?" Dilkes asked.

"He's a drunk, a brutal drunk," I said.

"And...?"

"And nothing," I said.

Ed frowned and shook his head as if he were disappointed.

"And," I continued, "my old man was a drunk. He died when I was six, left me with my mom."

"And he was brutal?" he asked.

"I think you have him confused with my mom."

Dilkes was licking his lips as if deciding where to take the conversation next, when a clatter and hoots of laughter sounded from the head of the stairs.

State Trooper Tony Giovanni blew into the office. "So, you lost your nigger."

"This is where I leave," Dilkes said. "I hate to see blood shed." He grabbed his hat and headed up the stairs.

"If you don't have any business," I said to Tony, "you can go with him."

"Touchy, aren't we?" He dropped his flat-brimmed trooper hat on my desk and sat in the chair opposite. He sniffed my sandwich. "What flavor?"

I handed him the uneaten half. "Roast beef."

"Any mustard?"

"Go fuck yourself," I said.

"Don't worry, we'll find your missing prisoner," Tony said. "It's not as if he can blend in with the local folks around here."

"That's what's bothering me. Someone should have spotted him by now. Colored city boy shouldn't fare too well out on the high desert, especially when the sun's down."

"Maybe he's holed up in someone's barn," Tony said.

"Or maybe somebody's hiding him," I said. "But why? He's got no family or friends around these parts."

"Before I forget." Tony passed me a piece of paper. "The Major wanted me to hand this to you." It was the forensics report. Tony rustled himself up a cup of coffee and finished his sandwich while I scanned the report. Not much there. Someone had taken great care to erase their footprints. They did find one tire track good enough for casting.

The killer had hung the body from the tree using a doubled-up nylon clothesline, probably the same clothesline that had been used to strangle her. The ends of the line had been burned with a match to prevent fraying. Whoever had done this had put some thought and planning into it. Some murderers fantasize about their kills beforehand. Would Joey have been this premeditated? And why hadn't she been raped? Pretty young thing like that would have been a pervert's wet dream. But then, maybe the guy couldn't get it up.

The evidence indicated that the killer had tossed the doubled-up clothesline over the juniper branch and hauled her up. One man could do that, one strong man. Field dressed, Virginia didn't weigh much more than a medium-sized buck.

The crime scene people had discovered a few cigarette butts in the fire ring—Philip Morris, common enough brand. Too bad they weren't something more exotic. The butts looked fresh, but cigarettes didn't deteriorate quickly in this dry climate. They could have belonged to the killer or someone else. No spent matches, so I figured the smoker used a lighter. Why erase footprints and tire tracks and not police your butts?

No fingerprints anywhere, but I didn't expect any. There weren't any smooth surfaces at the scene that would take a good print. The killer had been precise, a man that planned ahead, maybe Dr. McIntyre. Dentists were precise, careful. I couldn't recall if McIntyre smoked. That seemed silly, a dentist smoking, ruining his teeth, but then Doc Silverman smoked, and he was a man that knew better.

What about the missing heart and liver? The rumor in New Guinea was that a few of the tribes ate the hearts of their enemies, not the tribes that we held as friends, but some further back in the bush. It was a warrior ritual to take the courage and strength of your enemy, and become stronger and braver. But if so, why Virginia's guts? Her innards wouldn't be of use to a warrior, but I had forgotten. I wasn't dealing with a warrior, but with a perverted son of a bitch.

Tony asked if I'd run the roads with him that afternoon to look for speeders; Californians flocked to the area in the summer for vacation. The end of the month approached, and Tony needed a few more citations to keep the Major happy. "Got to finish up some work here," I said, "but I'm up for a jab this evening."

"Let's hit Prineville," he suggested.

"I was thinking of the Spur." The place held currents and eddies that my gut told me were important. "Keep an eye out for my missing prisoner."

"Always," Tony said.

After he left, the office was silent. Miriam had already retreated back upstairs to the Assessor's office, and George was out on patrol. My eyes kept drifting shut, and I decided to head back to my place for a nap. Blackout curtains covered my windows and, when I awoke, confused and alone in the darkness, I didn't know if it was day or night. Seeing the setting sun when I opened the curtains seemed to reassure me somehow.

Chapter 10

Couples whooped and whirled across the dance floor to a breakdown tune. The Haystack Trio—slide guitar, accordion and bass fiddle—played with unrestrained joy among swirls of gray-white cigarette smoke. Preserved in this moment of time, the place smelled of beer, sawdust, and hard labor forgotten.

Two men from the Redmond spread, Ethan Kelly and the cowpoke that had tangled with Barnes, leaned against the bar pounding back neat shots of whiskey. Ethan looked just about as mournful as a man could look. Tony and I watched for a moment, then we joined them.

"My condolences again, Ethan," I said to Kelly.

"A shame," Tony said.

"Do I know you?" Kelly asked Tony.

"He's with me," I said.

Kelly nodded to the cowpoke. "This is Frankie. We're having a wake for my girl."

"Next round is on me," I said.

Jeanie lined up double jiggers of rye for the four of us and told me not to break up the furniture. "Oh no, not me," I assured her.

"I know you, you be the Sheriff," Frankie said.

"Sure 'nuff." I patted my pockets. "Got a spare smoke? I'm out." The cowpoke handed me his pouch of tobacco and rolling papers. Any port in a storm. "What were you and Judge Barnes tussling about?" I asked while I rolled a butt.

"Frankie can be an asshole when he's got a load on," Kelly said.

Frankie laughed. "Yeah, I can. Harley said no, I said yes. That baldheaded fireplug jumped me. All there was to it."

I asked him if he'd badmouthed Barnes' wife.

"Never met the lady." He tossed back his drink and motioned for another. I told Jeanie to put it on my tab. On stage, a blond built like Olive Oyl gnawed on Goodnight, Irene. The crowd shouted to cover the wail.

"Usually there's a word or two that starts things off," I said.

"Not me," Frankie said.

"Probably 'motherfucker,'" Tony said.

The cowboy laughed again. I could tell he was feeling fine. "Cocksucker," he said. "That's the one. Wouldn't 'motherfuck' a man unless I had cause. The fancy guy said I couldn't play shuffleboard; I called him a cocksucker and came out swinging. You friends with Barnes? I assumed the fancy guy was Harley."

"We get along to go along," I said.

"Just because a man's important doesn't mean he can step all over common folk," Frankie said.

"Boy howdy." Kelly looked into his drink as if he'd find something there. "It wasn't Virginia's fault," I said, trying to guess his thoughts. "It wasn't your fault either. She happened to be in the wrong place at the wrong time." The platitude didn't cheer him up, but it did seem to draw a bit of the sorrow out of him.

"Look at that." Tony pointed to the door with his voice full of anticipation.

Frankie turned and looked. "Boss lady. Time for us to leave."

"She won't mind," Kelly said. "She's a decent sort."

Coach Conroy squired two ladies into the club. One of them was Lucy Redmond. Tony, not being a local, didn't know who they were. I told him the redhead was Lucy. It had been a few months since I had seen her. Though pushing forty, she looked to be in her late twenties dressed in calico and buckskin with her red hair pulled back into a cowgirl ponytail. I felt a warmth in my chest that I wasn't altogether sure was pleasant.

"How 'bout the brunette?" Tony asked.

"Catherine Steelhammer," I said. "Lives up by Sheep Rock." The two women took a table in the back as the coach headed to the far end of the bar. Up on stage, the Olive Oyl blonde had been deposed, and the trio played a snappy waltz in country four/four time.

"Let's go say 'Howdy.'" Tony stood. "Night's young."

"They're married. Catherine's got two kids," I said.

"Never stopped you," Tony said. That stung a bit.

We picked up our drinks and threaded our way through the swirling crowd. When she saw me, Lucy smiled showing her gums, pink and clean. "Oh, Slim." She touched my hand. "Sit down, join us."

I said it would be a pleasure and introduced Tony to Catherine. "State bull stationed out of Bend." He liked that. He and Catherine huddled immediately, seemed they both liked golf.

"Been a long time," Lucy said to me.

"Nice to see you," I said.

"Nice to be seen," she said.

I asked if Dirk had come down from Grizzly Mountain yet. She told me he was due back in the morning. There was an invitation in her voice that neither of us took seriously. "I miss you," she said. That sentiment was genuine.

By reflex, I almost replied in kind, but Catherine saved me by asking if I was going to join the golf club. Dirk Redmond and Barnes were developing a parcel of scrub pastureland down by the creek, working it into a nine-hole private country club.

"Fuck golf." I considered switching to gin. I hadn't had gin in a while, but couldn't remember why.

Three gin gimlets later—light on the lime—Lucy talked me into taking a whirl on the dance floor. The skinny blonde on stage did a passable job on a Kitty Wells ballad. Lucy snuggled in my arms, and I made believe Kate and I were doing the two-step again for the first time. Lucy wore Chanel, Kate wore gardenia perfume, but for that moment, I didn't make a distinction.

Somewhere along the line, I cracked an eyelid and spied Dr. McIntyre whisking through the front door as if he was trying to stay invisible. He needn't have bothered, the crowd reeled and hollered, and no one seemed to notice him but me. He squeezed in at the bar a couple of places down from the Kelly wake. For a moment, I considered if the two fathers knew each other, but decided from the neglected state of Ethan's teeth that he probably hadn't visited McIntyre's office.

Jeanie poured McIntyre a whiskey neat, the good stuff judging from the bottle, and he threw back the shot like he knew what he was doing. The blond singer dedicated the next song to the 'good-lookin'' sheriff, and then proceeded to make a mess of "Are You Lonesome Tonight.'

McIntyre ordered another bourbon and hammered it back. The coach walked by and tapped the dentist on the shoulder. McIntyre frowned, but followed the bigger man into the back hall which led to the heads and the back door. I disentangled myself from Lucy and pushed through the crowd. The only person in the bathroom was a drunken logger on his knees singing "Jingle Bells" into the toilet.

I banged through the backdoor and stumbled into the back parking lot. The light over the door had burned out, but the three-quarter crescent moon lit the lot enough for me to see only two cars were parked back there. One belonged to Jeanie, the other—a Model A—sat silent and empty up on blocks.

"Slim," Lucy said from the doorway. "Did you get lost?"

"I'm detecting," I said.

"Catherine and I are leaving," she said. "Be a gentleman and say goodbye."

"I'll meet you out front." I quickstepped around the side of the roadhouse. The lot was fairly full. A solitary drunk had passed out across the fender of a Ford coupe. McIntyre's empty car was still parked in front, but the Coach's pickup was gone. Somewhere on the highway, tires hummed on the warm summer pavement.

Outside the front door, Lucy touched my hand and said goodbye. We had gotten past the time when we would have kissed. Tony tossed a quick pass at Catherine who deflected it with the skill of someone who had been very popular in high school.

"Catherine's keen," Tony said.

"Catherine's very married," I said.

"We could play golf," he said.

"Trust me," I said. "She's not on the market. You'll have to work your magic on the new bank clerk."

He saw my point. I talked him into lead-footing it back to town to see if we could overtake the Coach. We zipped past a couple of cars, but not the pickup. He and McIntyre must have headed up the valley, but what for? Nothing up there but scrub brush and rattlesnakes.

*

The next morning, I drove up through the canyon lands checking out a report of a colored man running through the gullies. All I found were barren dry gulches and jackrabbits humping each other. When I returned to the office, I had a message to check in with Dirk Redmond. He'd given up on the search and returned to his ranch, but there was something he wanted me to see.

The new Redmond ranch house was a one-story rambler. Their old place, a two-story clapboard affair, still stood up on the hill and now housed the ranch foreman and his family. Dirk and Lucy had built their new place further down the valley a couple of years ago. My shack could fit into their living room.

"You know the old cinnabar mine up on Barnes Butte?" Dirk asked, as we took a seat in the shade of the porch.

"Know where it is, but I've never been inside." I wondered if Lucy was home this morning. Up early, I supposed. She had always been an early riser.

"I had one of my range riders, Prometheus, check to make sure kids weren't fooling around up there, and he found something in the mine," Dirk said. Prometheus was an ageless desert rat who set traps for beaver and muskrat on the Redmond spread. "The road washed out in the flash flood. You can ride one of our horses up there."

"I don't ride horses."

"Not even for a body?" Dirk asked.

"Whose?"

Dirk shrugged. "Theus didn't pull it out. The body's wedged headfirst into a ventilation tube at the back of the main shaft. He thought he should leave it 'til you had a chance to examine it."

"White body or black body?"

"Didn't say," Dirk said. "You can ride Tornado. I'll help you get him saddled up."

"Tornado? Hold on there, cowboy," I said. "Jackson from the crime lab is still over in Bend. I'll call over there, and we'll take him along with us. Do things by the book. Two or three hours won't make a difference to a dead person." Dirk agreed, and we sat on his porch drinking percolated coffee and swatting mosquitoes.

When Jackson arrived, we chatted a bit about how we'd get the body down the Butte while I puffed down three cigarettes, lighting each one on the butt of the last. Finally, no one seemed to have much to add, so I said, "Let's hit the trail. Daylight's wasting."

"John Wayne, right?" Jackson asked.

"Never heard of him," I responded.

Gelding gentled the savage stallion. Horseshit. Tornado, dapple-gray and long-ago gelded, was still pissed off about missing his nether parts and wanted to blame me for it. Theus held the bridle while I clambered aboard. Tornado swayed and pranced, and I screamed, "Whoa, Nelly!" This inspired the smelly beast to sidestep to the left, hop to the right, and buck straight up in the air. I tumbled ass over teakettle and bounced on the hard-packed barn floor.

Theus chuckled. "He gets a wee frisky now and again." Years of exposure to sun and swirling dust had permanently darkened Theus's face and hands to a grimy brown.

"I'll cure that." I drew back my fist.

Theus stepped between us and held the horse's muzzle in both hands with some degree of affection. "He's just a dumb animal."

"Okay, fine," I said. Theus helped me scramble back on board while I tried to figure out who was dumber, me or the horse. Jackson got a sleepy mare named Elizabeth who probably had never bucked in her life. This had to be a commie plot.

My ass started aching during the first mile on the trail. Theus sang a song about some poor hunter that got his leg caught in a bear trap and died of starvation. When he wound down, Jackson chattered about taking his sweetie to the amusement park at Janzen Beach over in Portland.

Theus stuffed a large plug of Red Man chewing tobacco into his mouth and offered me a pinch of the brownish-black fibrous stuff. My stomach rolled as if we were on stormy seas, and I thought about shooting myself. Instead, I reached for a cigarette. Dirk stopped me, saying that even with the last deluge, the high desert was still bone dry and could go up in a flash. Earlier this month, a hundred-thousand-acre fire had obliterated a large chunk of the Wagontire Range. Theus launched into some tall tale about how back in '27 a range fire had surrounded him, and he'd escaped by running through the flames to safety. "Flames are hot, but if you don't slow down you can get through them."

I wanted to call bullshit on that, but Tornado turned and gave me the evil eye. "Knock if off," I said to him, "or you'll end up as dog food."

"Ain't this a grand adventure," Jackson said.

"My ass hurts," I replied.

"Got some green chili and juniper berry liniment I could rub on it," Theus offered.

"Just you fucking try," I said.

"Mine shaft's just around the corner," Dirk said.

"That's what you told us an hour ago," I said.

But he was right, it was. Barnes Butte was an extinct lava dome overlooking the valley. Back in the nineteenth century, miners pulled cinnabar out of there by hand and transported it to town, where the red ore was refined into mercury. Once a rutted wagon road had served the mine, but it had washed out over the years, so we'd have to haul the body out on the pack mule that we'd brought along.

The mineshaft had been blasted from a solid rock outcropping about halfway up the Butte. We hobbled the horses, and I walked around to work the stiffness out of my butt and legs. I thought about black widow spiders and tight dark places.

Dirk said, "Let's go," and we stepped into the entrance of the mine.

The mine itself ran straight back for a hundred feet or so, then doglegged to the left. Light faded quickly as we proceeded, and we lit our hand lanterns. Theus walked point, Dirk and Jackson next, and I took the rear. Soot from long-dead miners' torches covered the walls and ceiling of the tunnel. The floor was roughhewn and uneven, hacked by hand after the lava rock had been loosened by dynamite. Near where the tunnel turned, the roof had collapsed, and we stepped lightly over a pile of rubble.

"When did this happen?" Jackson asked.

"A while back," Theus said. "Cave-in back in ought-six, killed three miners up here."

"Thanks for the cheery thought," I said.

"Place is safe enough now," Theus said.

"That's what they said about the Hindenburg," I replied.

The tunnel angled down from there, and a shaft branched off to the right. "Not that way," Theus said. "Dead end, the vein played out." Past the branch, the walls wept from nearby groundwater.

"Feels hot down here," I said.

"Something touched my face," Jackson said.

"Probably spiders," I said.

"It's all in your head," Theus said.

The shaft ended in a round gallery chiseled out of the rock. Theus shone his lamp on a small ventilation shaft six feet high on the left side. Something stuck out of the shaft. If a fellow wasn't looking closely enough, he might think they were timbers left by long-gone miners, but they were two feet, bare and dirty and white.

Jackson photographed the scene, took measurements, and sketched a hasty diagram, then he supervised while the rest of us tugged on the body, pulled it out, and laid it on a waiting tarp.

My lantern's light played across the half-nude body and onto Joey's face, his eyes half-open and clouded as if he had cataracts. I couldn't read his expression. Anger, fear, sorrow? The smell hit, and my stomach twisted. Goddamn, the town would explode over this.

We carried Joey outside and laid him on the rocky trail at the mouth of the mine. His grayish tongue stuck halfway out of his mouth. Clad only in ripped cutoffs, Joey had abrasions on the pasty skin of his shoulders and forearms. Even with his muscled chest and thick forearms, a man could see he was only a kid.

Jackson bent to fuss over the body. Theus volunteered to help the tech while Dirk and I sat in the shade of a grandpa juniper. A nicotine fit overwhelmed me, and I asked Dirk for a chew. The chewing tobacco tasted sharp and salty, and I had to hold the urge to spit it out.

"How do you think someone got Joey's body up here?" Dirk asked.

"They could have used a pack mule," I said. "Why haul a body up here, but then put it somewhere that someone would find it?

Everyone knows kids explore up here all the time. I think Joey either walked or rode up here on his own for some unknown reason, and the killer murdered him close by, then carried the body into the mine and stuffed it in the shaft." Hard purple juniper berries and bits of cinder rock dug into my ass. I swept off a patch of ground with the side of my hand and resettled.

"Then why did Joey come up here?" Dirk asked.

"When I know the answer to that question, I'll be one step closer to finding out who murdered him and Virginia." I spit out a glob of blackish tobacco juice and hiccuped. "Is the only way up here the way we came?"

"If a feller had a good pony," Dirk said, "he could ride up through the saddle there from Twelve Mile Table." The trail wound up to a small saddle between Barnes Butte and an unnamed sister butte.

"Walkable?" I asked.

"Take a fair bit of time," he said. "You think they came that way?"

"I don't know," I said.

"You're a smart man," Dirk said. "You'll figure it out." Images of Kate and Barnes flashed through my mind. "Not smart enough that a man would notice. Let's look around the area." When I stood, the nicotine from the chew rushed to my head, and I felt like I was ten and had just finished my first smoke.

Nearby, we found several empty bean cans hidden in a copse of sagebrush. One of the cans was half-empty, and the remaining beans were still moist. I reckoned the can had been opened no more than a couple of days ago. A little further on, we found some semi-fresh human shit, but no toilet paper. Maybe a rushed trip? Our last find was a dinged-up army canteen in the rocks with a slosh of tepid water still in it. It could have belonged to some kid adventurer or the killer. I'd show it to the McIntyres to see if it had belonged to their son. Someone had been camped up here for a while. I figured it was Joey, but I didn't know if it was before or after Virginia's murder.

"Look at this." Jackson turned Joey's head to one side. A small amount of black-cracked blood had pooled in the boy's ear and dribbled down his neck. "I'm no coroner," Jackson said. "But I'd bet my boots this kid was killed by a twenty-two round close up. One shot to the ear."

"How'd you figure?" I asked as I spit. My head wobbled as if it was on a spring. I dug the tobacco out of my mouth with my index finger and flicked it onto the ground. That was enough of that.

"We had a murder like this up in Portland just after the war.

Organized crime killing. Victim had cooked the books for a crooked car dealership. Seems he got a little too greedy. We found him stuffed in the trunk of a car at the airport. This is pretty much the same M.O. This guy knew what he was doing."

"Any chance it was the same guy?" I asked, though I couldn't imagine the mob being interested in a high school fullback from our little burg.

Jackson shook his head. "They gassed the guy last year. Couldn't be him unless the ghost of Twinkle Toes Dick haunts this mine."

"Any idea about the gooey stuff smeared on his body?" The nicotine high still bothered me, and I squatted down on my haunches to clear my head.

"My best guess is petroleum jelly," Jackson said.

"No shit," I said.

"All the better to squeeze the body into that little hole," Jackson said.

We rolled the body up in the tarp, loaded it on the pack mule, and headed down the Butte. The bottom edge of the sun nudged the far horizon. It would be dark by the time we reached the ranch house, but I figured, what the hell? I couldn't ride very well in the daylight. How much worse could it be in the dark?

I fell off Tornado three times, lost my cigarettes and lighter, and opened up a half-inch gash over my right eye, but I'd pretty much mastered the son of a bitch by the time we rode over the last hill and down toward the ranch. Unfortunately, just as we entered Dirk's barnyard and I was feeling like I might become a passable horseman, the world exploded with an unnatural white light. Tornado snorted, hopped, and bucked so hard, we both flipped over backward. My back and head thudded on the ground alongside the damned horse. I lay wheezing in the dust for a spell trying to recover what little sense I had.

"Think he'll be alright?" Dirk asked.

"Don't rightly know," Theus said. "He might be bad hurt. We may have to shoot him where he lies. Shame. He wasn't really the bad sort."

"Hey, I'm a good sort." I worked on opening my eyes. "Don't shoot me yet! Give me another chance." My eyes opened, but my head wouldn't move.

"They aren't talking about you, Matt," Ed Dilkes, that bastard, said. "They're talking about the horse."

"Tornado?" I asked. "Dilkes, what the hell did you do?"

"Sorry, a misstep." Dilkes aimed his Speed Graphic camera at my face and snapped a picture. For a moment, I was blind again. "The image of Joey's body on a pack mule will be a great lead for Wednesday's issue."

I popped to my feet. The world reeled, and I plopped back down on my fanny. "If they shoot that horse, I'll shoot you."

"Thought you didn't care for horses," Dirk said.

"I feel for all dumb animals," I said. "Dirk, help me up so I can wring Eddie's pea-picking neck."

Dilkes put down the camera and grabbed me under the shoulders. As he lifted, something caught in the middle of my spine. "Wait!" I said, but he hoisted me onto my feet.

"You're stronger than you look," I said.

"Looks can be deceiving," Dilkes said.

"Let me look at your camera," I said. "I might want to buy one for our office."

He scooped up his camera and hid it behind his back. "Maybe you should see a chiropractor."

I considered cold-cocking the son of a bitch just to alleviate my aches, but my better sense prevailed. "Keep the camera," I said, "but hold off publishing the picture until I give you the word."

"Fine," he said. "As long as it's by Wednesday."

Tornado snorted and lifted his head. Dirk and Theus pushed and hauled until the gray horse regained his feet. He skittered my way with bad intent in his eyes.

"Not me." I danced out of the way. "I wasn't the one." I scooped up a flat-bladed shovel and held it at port arms in an attempt to defend myself. The horse wheeled, and we faced off.

Theus took Tornado by the reins and pulled him away. "Come on, big fella. A curry comb, a bucket of oats, and you'll feel better." I swear the son of a biscuit-eater looked back at me with murder in his eye.

Jackson and I loaded Joey's body into the back of my pickup, and we rumbled off the ranch and headed back toward town. My next task was to transport the body to Doc Silverman's for an autopsy, then tell Jeff and Betty McIntyre that their boy had been killed. I pictured Betty McIntyre wailing with grief. Maybe Kate could help me break the news. I'd give her a call.

Chapter 11

Dr. McIntyre took only an instant to figure out the score when he opened the door, but his wife's eyes held hope until I said, "I'm sorry to say...," then she swooned and hit the hardwood. No one caught her, and she bounced once and seemed to fold in upon herself, making a tidy pile on the floor. Kate and I hefted her up onto the couch while her husband ran his hands through his hair. Someone had clocked McIntyre in the left eye, and it shone bright and black. By the morning, it would begin to fade to purple and brown. What had passed between Coach Conroy and him last night?

Kate dabbed Betty's forehead with a wet dishtowel while I herded McIntyre into the dining room. "How did he die?" he asked, when we had gotten settled. He rocked his chair back and leaned it against the china cabinet.

"We're not sure," I said. "Doc Silverman will do the autopsy in the morning. We found his body up on Barnes Butte."

"Murdered?"

"Presumably," I said.

"Jesus." McIntyre held his head in his hands, hiding his face. I kept my silence and let him gather himself. A single sobbing gasp came from the living room. Betty had hung a Degas reproduction on the far wall. Ballet dancers, little girls... no, on second thought, maybe it was her husband's idea.

Kate came in and used the telephone to call Doc Silverman and the family's preacher. We should have thought of that earlier. Kate told me that Betty McIntyre had regained consciousness, but not her wits. "Maybe Doc can give her something," she said.

After she returned to the living room, I pulled the battered canteen from a paper bag and asked McIntyre if he recognized it.

"It's my son's." I figured he might start crying soon.

I scooted my chair close enough to see the sweat on his upper lip and asked him what else Joey might have taken with him.

"Sleeping bag," he said, "an army surplus mess kit, boots, warm clothes."

"And a knife?" I prompted.

"Pocketknife," he said. "His grandfather gave it to him for his eighth birthday. It's a whittling knife; a man couldn't gut someone with it."

"You didn't tell me any of this before," I said.

"Joey's a good kid." McIntyre put his head in his hands again. "I was trying to keep my son out of trouble. He said he needed to get away for a while, but he didn't tell me why. You're not a father; you just wouldn't understand."

I asked McIntyre why Joey needed to get away, but he said he didn't know. I didn't believe him, but moved on. "We found him up on Barnes Butte. Has he ever been up there before?"

"I haven't had the time to camp much, but Joey and Ronnie Gearhart camped out a lot during the summer. Ask him."

"Quite a shiner," I observed. "Tell me what happened to your eye."

He touched underneath his eye with his fingertips. "Stepped on a rake. Darned handle flew up and hit me in the face."

"I saw you and Coach Conroy at the Spur last night," I said. "Wanted to have a word with you, but you disappeared. Where to?"

"My car wouldn't start," McIntyre said. "Mr. Conroy was gracious enough to give me a ride home."

"Sure he didn't sock you?"

"Why would he do that?"

"Why indeed?" Something was fishy between Conroy and McIntyre; I could feel it in my bones. Had Conroy had something going with Virginia, too? I thought about slapping McIntyre upside the head to get him talking, but just then Betty started screaming. We hustled back into the living room, where Kate was trying to control Betty. I helped Kate hold Betty down on the couch until Doc Silverman arrived. He stuck a hypodermic needle in her arm, and she yelped, struggled for seven seconds, then hit the highway to dreamland.

"Doc," I said. "I need some of what you gave Betty. I can't sleep at night."

"Doc, don't you dare," Kate said.

Doc checked Betty's pulse and nodded, apparently satisfied. He put his equipment back into his bag. "I'll do the autopsy tomorrow morning, eight o'clock sharp."

"Can't it wait until nine?" I asked.

"Find that errant dog of yours yet?" he asked.

"You're an evil man," I said.

"Not evil, just bad," he said. "There's a difference. Never fear, Addison will come back in due course. I'm sure he misses his master."

Before I could belt the old fart, the parson, Reverend Hasty, arrived.

"Evening, Parson," I said.

Hasty ignored me and took Jeff McIntyre's hand in both of his. "I am deeply sorry for your loss." The parson wore the same bad toupee he'd worn when I caught him and Judy Smalley in a private prayer meeting in the church pump house last year. Not being a religious man, I didn't judge him too harshly, but he'd avoided me ever since.

Things had wound down, so I took Kate by the arm and steered her to the door. "Come over to my place," I said on the stoop.

"I can't tonight," she said. "My husband's home."

"I thought he'd be hanging out with Harley," I said.

"Why, whatever do you mean?" she asked.

"I'm not sure," I said. "They always seem to be together lately."

"They're friends," she said. "They play poker, bowl on Thursday nights, and like to fish." I tried to picture Barnes bowling, but failed.

"Tomorrow?" I asked.

"Maybe I could spring free for an hour or two in the afternoon," she said. "We can talk about the case." She stood on tiptoe and kissed me on the cheek. I whistled on the drive home. It wasn't a firm promise, but I held out hope.

*

Barnes called early the next morning and demanded an audience. I found him in his office almost obscured by smoke and puffing on a fat cigar. "Tell me about Joey's body," he said.

I fired up a butt and plopped my fanny in a side chair. "Someone stuck the departed in the cinnabar mine up on Barnes Butte. He was half-nude when we found him." I kept my affairs with Tornado to myself, but I did forewarn him about the photographs Dilkes had taken for the local paper.

"We're losing control of this thing," he said.

"Hard to keep tabs on a murderer when you don't know who he, or they, are," I said.

"I'm talking about the investigation, you nitwit," he said.

I sat up straight in my chair, shifted my weight, and gathered my feet underneath it. "Watch the name calling, Porter." I picked up a gavel from his desk and rolled it around in my palms.

He caught my drift. "Sorry, Harkness." He held up one hand. "It's the pressure."

“Eddie will tread easily for the time being,” I said. “He knows from whom all blessings flow.”

Barnes nodded. “How’d the kid die?”

“We’re not sure yet.” I wanted to keep the .22 round to the ear to myself for the time being. “Doc Silverman is starting the autopsy as we speak.”

“Aren’t you supposed to be there?”

“That was my original plan,” I said.

“Don’t let me keep you.” He nodded toward the door.

I groaned as I pushed myself to my feet. My ass hurt worse than when my old lady had lit into me with the strap. Fucking horse. “Harley okay after the fight at the roadhouse?” I worked a hunch.

Barnes looked at me with weasel eyes. “He’s my friend.”

“Never said any different.”

*

I pounded on Doc’s front door and waited on the porch while he unsnapped the locks. “Worried about protecting the evidence,” he said, as he let me inside. I grabbed a cup of coffee and went down into the basement. Doc cracked the kid’s ribs, dug out the heart, and weighed it. “Everything seems to be normal,” he said. “Heart, large intestine, small intestine...”

“Still got his testicles?” I asked.

“Think your guy is some kind of warrior throwback?” Doc snipped off the kid’s shorts with a pair of scissors.

“Covering my bases,” I said.

“Nope, they’re still here,” he said. “There’s a flask in my desk drawer if you have a mind for it.”

“I’m on the wagon ‘til at least noon.” Kate didn’t like me drinking early in the morning. “Jackson said that he thought Joey might have died from a gunshot through the ear. Whatcha think?”

Doc turned the kid’s head. “Obvious something entered through the ear, probably a bullet, but you’ll have to wait until I remove the skull cap and examine the brain.” He started sawing on the kid’s head with what looked like a hacksaw, and I decided to meander up to the kitchen to make myself some toast. Doc said he had the Sawyer kid quarantined with three-day measles up in the third floor dormer. I told him not to worry; I couldn’t climb that far with my aching ass.

With his wife long gone, Doc’s kitchen had become a one-man operation, not much different than mine, albeit more organized—

one good knife, a potato masher, mismatched spoons and forks, and maybe a couple more plates than I owned. I snitched some orange juice from the fridge and buttered my toast. Someone thumped and bumped upstairs, and I yelled, "You should be in bed. Don't make me come up there." The Sawyer kid quieted down after that.

Doc had the skullcap removed and was futzing around with Joey's brains when I went back down to the basement. My stomach still growled. Maybe the Doc would stake me a couple of eggs, too.

"He wasn't shot," Doc said. "The killer stuck something in his ear and jimmied it around. See?"

"Any idea on the instrument?" The kid's brain looked like slug pudding whipped by an eggbeater.

"Perhaps." He had me help roll the body onto the stomach. "My best guess would be an ice pick. Time of death would be forty to forty-eight hours ago."

"After Virginia?"

"With a certainty, yes."

"Ice pick. He'd have to get up close for that."

Doc examined Joey's lower back and buttocks. Something seemed to attract his attention, and he looked closer with a magnifying glass. "There are signs of a struggle."

The basement felt chilly. Other than the smell of ether and formaldehyde, this place would be a nice refuge from the summer heat.

"Joey was a tough kid, he must have trusted his killer to let him get close enough to do this."

"Perhaps." Doc peered closer at the body, his nose no more than a couple of inches from the kid's butt. My stomach rumbled. Didn't I see some bacon in the fridge? "Aha," he said. "That's why."

"Why what?" I asked.

"Joey McIntyre was sexually assaulted before his death."

"Sexually assaulted?" I wasn't sure I wanted to know what he meant.

"Buggered. The boy was buggered. There are several small tears in the delicate tissues in the boy's anus, made shortly before his death, but not enough time had passed for them to heal."

"Rape?" The word tasted funny in my mouth.

"Either that or very violent consensual sex." Doc pulled off his gloves. He went to the sink and washed his hands. I noticed a small string of numbers tattooed in gray-blue ink onto his inner forearm. "My best guess is that he may have struggled against the buggery, but that the death blow probably was a surprise."

I chewed on that for a moment. "Know any faggots in town?"

"Homosexuals aren't necessarily prone to murder," Doc said.

"That wasn't my question," I said.

"But that's my answer," he said.

I dropped it and waited while Doc finished stitching up the body. We wrapped Joey in a canvas shroud. Doc would make sure the body made it to the funeral home.

*

Harley called to tell me my combat boots had arrived, so I stopped by the Haberdashery to pick them up. Ruth greeted me and said her father was out to lunch, so she'd help me try on the boots.

"How do they feel?" Ruth was a smallish girl with close-set eyes and a ponytail.

I flexed the stiff black leather, pushing my toes back toward the heels. They'd shine up real nice. "Did Joey McIntyre come in here to get fitted for his letterman's sweater? Maybe the same day he disappeared?"

"He was supposed to," Ruth said, "but he didn't keep his appointment."

"He already had one sweater, right?" I fumbled with the laces on the boots trying to maneuver them through the hooks and eyes.

"Dad ordered one for him last year." Ruth opened a ledger book. "Joey picked it up in January." When I asked her if she knew what had happened to that one, she merely shrugged.

"Joey come in here often?"

"Not much," she said. "The McIntyres did most of their shopping in Prineville or Bend." She bit her lip as it to say maybe they weren't good enough for their family. "Walk in the boots," she said. "See how they feel."

I walked to the far end of the store, turned at the rack of Boy Scout uniforms, and returned to her. They were tight in the arches, but I told her they'd do. "What did you think of Joey?"

"He thought he was cute," she said.

"Was he friendly with you?"

"I'm twelve years old," she said. "He didn't know I existed." I couldn't tell if she was wistful or relieved. "What about the boots?"

"I'll take them." I tried on suit coats I couldn't afford until Harley returned. He came in alone. "Let's talk," I said.

He took me into the office, a small windowless room in the back of the larger stock room. The place smelled of new leather and wool blankets. The only adornment was a picture of his family on the desk. "We found Joey." I shut the door behind me.

"I heard," Harley said. "Dead. A shame."

"Where'd you hear that?" I asked.

"A birdie told me," he said.

"Had to be Barnes," I said. "You two are close as thieves." Harley merely shrugged. "What the birdie didn't tell you, what he doesn't know yet, is that someone fucked Joey in the ass shortly before he died."

Harley sat down, his face pale except for two bright red spots on his cheeks. "Why share that information with me?"

"Why indeed?" I said. "I keep thinking about that time a couple of years back when you got roughed up on a buying trip in Portland. I'd always assumed it was probably a trick roll by some pimp. Local yokel goes to the big city and gets in over his head. Not all that unusual."

"A baseless speculation," he said.

"Perhaps, and not something I'd speculate about in public, but now I wonder if it might have been something else. Something a little," I searched for a word, "a little more extreme."

"Be careful," he said. "Judge Barnes—"

"Ah, Judge Barnes," I said. "A buddy of mine works for the Portland Police Bureau. I could give him a jingle, get a copy of your report, and find out what really happened. I might be interested in the exact circumstances of the assault."

"What do you want?" he asked.

"Let's talk about Joey." I lit a fag and instantly regretted it. Smoke choked the tiny office.

"I barely knew the boy," he said.

"I can accept that," I said. "But do any of your friends like the younger trade?"

"Friends?" he asked.

"Men who waltz to a different tune," I said.

"You're a complete asshole, Sheriff."

"Guilty as charged, your honor," I said. "But I'll do what I must to protect the people in this county." I stubbed out my cigarette.

"That includes persecuting honest citizens?" Harley asked.

"Harley, make no mistake, I can be a real asshole if need be. Don't try me. You're a good family man, pillar of the community, all that falderal. Hell, I've always liked you, thought you're one of the saner people in this little burg. I don't care who you fuck or what sex they are, but you need to tell me anything that might help me with my investigation. Help me, and I won't tell your secret."

"You don't know anything to tell," he said.

"Harley, don't piss me off. Otherwise, I may have a talk with your best buddy Barnes and tell him how you let your hair down."

Harley became as still as I've ever seen a man become. I could hear the ticking of my watch and Ruth's voice drifting back from the front of the store. He had frozen like a fawn waiting for the hunter to pass.

"He knows," I said. "He knows, doesn't he?"

"You'd better leave." Harley pointed to the door. "I've said all I'm going to say."

"We'll talk again."

Chapter 12

As I drove back to my place to meet Kate, I mulled over what I had learned. Barnes knew about Harley. I figured Harley had a crush on Barnes. Were they lovers? That might help my case with Kate, but if I made the accusation and was wrong, Kate would lose any respect she had for me. If Harley and Barnes were a couple, could they have committed the murders together? I struggled to picture either of them gutting Virginia or raping Joey. I wasn't certain Harley had it in him, but Barnes was more complex. He'd served with distinction in the war, survived the Battle of the Bulge. I respected the way he ran the county, but found him to be a rough and abrasive man. We'd been aching to tangle for a long time, like two tomcats claiming the same territory.

Barnes knew how to kill a man, but I wasn't sure what Harley had done during the war. Did either of them possess the urge, the spark, to do it? What would have been their motive? Barnes ran the county his way, and people usually crossed him only once, but what would have been the connection between the kids and Barnes? Exposure? Perhaps. But if Joey had discovered their secret, why kill Virginia? And why display her body like that? I decided not to tell Kate what I suspected about Barnes, at least not yet.

Kate sat on my steps waiting for me.

"You could have gone in," I said. "I made my bed this morning."

"I have someplace to be," she said.

"You're not coming in?"

"It's important," she said. "Betty McIntyre and Esther Kelly are planning a double funeral for their children, and they want me to help them with the arrangements."

"Jeff McIntyre isn't going to be too pleased with that ceremony. In fact, he'll probably be downright pissed off about the whole thing."

"He doesn't have much choice," Kate said. "Betty's a stronger woman than you think. She's paid for Virginia's funeral plot, next to her son's."

"When's the funeral?" I asked, trying to nudge Kate through the front door. No dice.

"Tomorrow," she said. "You'll have to be there. The murderer will show up."

"Pardon?"

"Ellery Queen. The murderer always appears at the funeral. It's in the killer's code of ethics."

"I hate to break it to you, Pumpkin," I said, "but killers don't have codes of ethics. That's why they're killers."

"Shows what you know." She turned and walked toward her car.

"Besides," I said following her, "just about everyone in town will be there; people from both sides of the tracks, the entire high school, just about anyone who's everyone."

"You mean everyone who's anyone?"

"Yeah, that too."

"Have you been drinking again?" she asked.

"Not yet," I said. "But if you're not going inside with me, I might start."

"Blackmail doesn't suit you." She took my hand. "Tell you what, let's have a picnic after the funeral. Just the two of us."

"Nice spot up by Wasserman's Pillar," I said. "Secluded." She laughed and told me goodbye. I'd forgotten to show her my new boots.

*

I checked with my office around five o'clock when the heat was the fiercest in this country. No sign of my missing prisoner or my dog, but there was a message from George to let me know that he'd found Frank Flehardy's horses down in Bolton's Hollow at the base of Twelve Mile Table.

I parked my truck up on the county road and hiked the last three hundred yards down into the Hollow. Frank was waiting when I arrived. "Goldarn son of a biscuit-eater shot 'em," Frank said. He looked as if someone had painted dark circles under his eyes.

The dead horses lay in a shadowed, rocky dry wash. The pinto mare was swollen and bloated as if she had eaten too much sweet grass. The roan gelding's stomach had burst from the internal pressure. Insects crawled in and out of the split in his side. Between the six o'clock heat and the smell, I thought I might pass out. I took Frank by the arm and moved him upwind to escape the stink,

"Mighty sorry, Frank."

"Agnes will be just sick at heart," Frank said. "She loved that little Appaloosa mare."

I could have said something about getting another horse, but I'd lived in this country long enough to know how folks felt about their horses. A rope had been looped around the little pinto's nose. "That bridle yours?"

"Halter," he said. "That's a halter, but it ain't ours."

"Think someone might have used the gelding for a pack horse?"

"Maybe." He squatted on his haunches and stirred the dust with a stick.

"When did you say the horses disappeared?" I asked.

"Afternoon of the big rain," Frank said. "Somewheres between two and four in the p.m., I was driving the county grader and Agnes was in town shopping. Our stock was gone when she got home."

"Before we discovered Joey's body. Maybe before he was murdered," I mused. "I checked up here the next day, and the gully was empty then. He didn't kill your horses right away."

Frank stood up and rubbed his back. "While I was waiting, I found something else over in the sagebrush, half-buried in the rocks."

"What?"

"Bloody clothes, sleeping bag, and a mess kit."

"Knife, rope, anything like that?" Finding a murder weapon would be helpful.

"Once I saw the bloody clothes, I stopped looking," Frank said. "Figured you'd be the one wanting to dig through the pile." I told him that was good thinking.

"No tracks, he must have hiked out of here," Frank added.

"He erased them with brush like someone from a Western picture," I said.

"Smart cuss."

"Maybe not smart enough." Though I shouldn't have, I poked around in the pile of clothing. No knives or guns, but there was a length of clothesline, one end burned, the other frayed. I'd check with the hardware store, see if anyone had bought this particular kind recently. Maybe our murderer had made a mistake. I told Frank that the discovery was between us. "Let's play out a little line, see if our murderer bites."

"What sort of man does something like this?" Frank held up his hands as if in supplication. The nails were split and black from missing the head of a nail once too often.

Twelve Mile Table's shadow had finally enveloped us. The hollow was on a direct line between the Flehardy Place and the cinnabar mine. I wanted to tell him the same kind of man that murders kids and does terrible things to their bodies, but instead I said, "I'll get him. Don't you worry, I'll get him."

"Heck, Slim, I ain't worried about that. Just don't you kill him when you find him." He asked if we should bury the bodies.

I told him that we'd have to wait for the crime scene folks to photograph the remains. "I'll help you bury them when they're done." Bedrock in this country was six inches below the surface. It'd take dynamite to blast a hole deep enough for the horses.

"I'd take it kindly if you did," he replied.

*

A man needed to spruce up for funerals and for courting. Today, I would deal with both, so I decided to get a haircut. Herbert greeted me with a smile and asked if I wanted the usual. I told him sure. I wasn't much of a talker when I was in the chair—I did some of my best sleeping there, but Herbert rattled on about fishing and baseball. I nodded appropriately and let my mind roam. Herbert had a couple of outdoor prints on the wall that I coveted: wild bears invading a hunting camp and chasing the hunters up trees. Where did he get them?

Harley didn't acknowledge me as he drifted through and went into the back. Barnes came through five minutes later. He waved his cigar in my general direction and grunted.

"Anybody else back there?" I asked Herbert.

"A couple of the boys," Herbert said. "Coach Conway for one, but I'm not sure who else." Some men came to the poker game through the back door. They may have wanted a little anonymity, but the whole town knew what went on in there.

Herbert stropped his straight razor and shaved the back of my neck. I always felt little chills when he did that. Hot towel next, then the lilac water. I hoped the aroma would hold up through the funeral and into the picnic. Herbert asked if I wanted my boots polished. I said, "What the hell, it's a special day." The buffing cloth snapped and slid on my combat boots. When he finished, I headed into the back to check out the poker game.

The participants were the usual bunch: Barnes, Harley, Coach Conway and Ed Dilkes. "Don't you guys have real jobs?" I asked with a smile.

"Look what the cat dragged in." Sam Gearhart stepped out of the head, wiping his hands on a towel.

"What the hell you doing here?" I asked.

"Shooing the ducks off the porch," he said.

"Oh, a wise guy," I said.

"This is neutral ground," Dilkes said. "No affrays in the barbershop."

"No what?" Conway asked.

"Affrays," Harley said. "Fights."

"Harley," Conway said, "I just heard a rumor you were a spy in the War."

"A canard," Harley said.

"I can vouch for him," Barnes said. "He drove a desk in Maryland."

"Rest a spell, Harkness." Ed Dilkes pushed back a chair for me. "I'll deal you in."

"I've got to dress for the funeral," I said. "Side's, I'm stone broke."

"I'll give you an advance on your paycheck," Barnes said.

Conway offered me a beer. I passed, but did munch on a fresh glazed doughnut from the bakery. In my first hand, I picked up a pair of nines, pushed my way through with them and won the pot. Maybe this would be a good day.

"Everyone going to the funeral?" I asked.

They all nodded except for Harley. He explained that his daughter was going to attend, so he'd have to stay and run the store. "Didn't know him that well," he added, without looking in my direction. Barnes nodded. Harley might have told him about our conversation, but Barnes wouldn't say shit with a mouthful. He was a cool customer.

"Coach," Dilkes said. "What're you going to do now that Joey is gone?"

"Pass," he said. "Pass, pass, and pass some more. Ronnie Gearhart is the next coming of Y.A. Tittle."

"Except he's still got his hair," Sam Gearhart said.

"You're the best coach in the state," Barnes said. "You'll work it out."

"I've got a plan." Conway put a finger alongside his nose.

The next hand I picked up three treys. I bumped the pot a quarter before the draw; only Gearhart and Conway stayed with me. A pair of nines came my way in the draw. I bet the limit again. My full house beat his flush.

"How's the investigation coming?" Dilkes asked.

"Making headway," I said. "Slow but sure. Don't worry, I'll nail this son of a bitch's hide to the barn door."

"I'll put your photo on the front page," Dilkes said.

"We'll give you a medal," Barnes said.

"Better go home and change. Funeral's in an hour." I grabbed a maple bar and my winnings and made for the door.

"I'm out," Harley said. "Gotta relieve Ruthie."

"Come back after the funeral, Sheriff," Conway said. "Give us a chance to get our money back."

"Can't today," I said. "After we put the kids in the ground, I'm headed up to Wasserman's Pillar to look for some lost horses. Got a report they were up there." A convenient mistruth, no one needed to know yet about the discovery of the slaughtered horses.

I stepped outside. The morning looked like it had the makings of a glorious day. I was picnicking with my sweetheart this afternoon, and I'd won over a buck in the game. I felt flush.

*

The funeral service had been set for noon, and the sun shone down on the juniper-spotted cemetery with late summer intensity. Most of the town made an appearance that day—boys in sports coats and high-water pants, girls in their summer finest, the cheerleaders in their uniforms, and the football players in letterman's sweaters.

I felt absurd, like a faker, standing with the other mourners. After watching my mother leak crocodile tears at my dad's funeral, I'd come to hate funerals and had skipped most during the years, but I felt compelled to attend this one.

Teachers filed in front of the students, and the townspeople flanked them on either side, middle class and rich folks on the right, Okies and mill hands on the left. Mike Barfield stood in the student section doing a good job of fading into the woodwork. Coach Conroy stood with the teachers. He wore a short-sleeved white shirt and narrow black tie. Eddie Dilkes took photos with his Speed Graphix. Doc Silverman had joined Barnes next to the casket. Kate hugged Betty and Esther, then took her place next to her husband. She looked fine as ice in a simple navy skirt and jacket.

As for me, I had only one suit, a black wool number barely fit for weddings, funerals, and court appearances. Sweat trickled down my cheeks, and I had compounded my discomfort by wearing a fedora rather than my straw cowboy hat. Miriam and George completed the Sheriff's Office delegation. Miriam mouthed, "Handsome." I took it she meant me and said thanks.

Someone sobbed behind me and I turned, expecting it to be a woman. Instead, Jeff McIntyre cried as if this day was to be his last. Were the tears for his son or his lover? Betty and Esther stood between their husbands holding hands and bridging the gap between their communities.

Both the preacher and the priest would take a turn at orating, Joey being Scotch Protestant and Virginia being Irish Catholic. This arrangement couldn't have made Jeff McIntyre happy, but at this point I figured that Betty was driving the truck and he was along for the ride.

The priest read the 23rd Psalm and tossed around some Latin, lulling the crowd into a listless fog. It slipped past me without sticking, but if this mumbo-jumbo consoled the Kelly's, then it was fine by me. Kate glanced my way just once during the service. Was that a wink or just my imagination?

The preacher took the stage and worked at waking up the crowd. Apparently, the McIntyres held with the fire and brimstone point of view like my ma. I worked at ignoring the words and studied the crowd. Dirk and Lucy Redmond stood in the back. She wore a black swirling number that probably doubled as a cocktail dress. He wore a huge white Stetson and string tie. I wondered why they were here until I remembered that Ethan worked on the Redmond spread. Barfield stared at the ground; Conroy looked lost in thought, probably scheming about his next game. Barnes chewed his cigar, and Sam Gearhart stood next to his son with his head down. All I could see was the shine from Sam's bald spot. Someone had clocked his kid and had given him a black eye. I growled when I saw them, and Miriam patted my hand.

Besides Barnes or Harley, who could have killed those kids? Virginia had been sleeping with both the McIntyres. Joey had been raped before his death, but Virginia had not. A mysterious reversal in what I'd normally expect. The lack of defensive wounds led me to believe that the kids had known and trusted their attacker or attackers. One man or two? Suspects? Jeff McIntyre, for sure. Motive, opportunity, and trust of the victims. Coach Conroy? Barfield said that he'd slapped Joey. Slapping the kid put him on my list. Sam Gearhart? Logic told me no, but I didn't like the man and left him on the list just for spite. How about one of their classmates? Barfield probably obsessed about Virginia sleeping with both the McIntyres. He went on the list. Ronnie Gearhart? This time my gut told me no, but logic told me to add him.

Coach Conway had decided to lead the students in a cheer. "Joey, Joey, he's our man, if he can't do it, no one can. Hurray, Joey!" Margie Weekly appeared at the front, her cheerleader's skirt swirling up when she kicked showing her slim, tanned legs. She didn't seem too broken up at the death of her ex-boyfriend. After the cheer, Conway spun the student section off into a rousing rendition of Onward, Christian Soldiers. Jeff McIntyre wailed louder. The more respectable folks in the assembly looked shocked at the goings on. I muttered, "This is where I came in," and tried to skedaddle, but Miriam grabbed my arm and told me I wasn't going nowhere, nohow.

The priest had a quick word with Conroy, who then turned and quieted the students. The service wound down to a predictable end; Esther and Betty held out until four strong men lowered each of the children into the ground, then they cried.

The crowd began to dissolve and drift away. I started toward Sam Gearhart and his family. Miriam stopped me. "Matthew, be nice."

"I'm always nice," I replied.

"This is a funeral," she said.

I told her I was just fine and caught up with the Gearharts. "Nice shiner," I said to Ron.

"Ran into a door," he said.

"A door named Sam." I moved toward his father.

Ronnie stepped between us. "Pa didn't do it."

"I didn't wear my hip boots," I said.

"I've reformed," Sam said.

"Eddie said you're on the wagon," I said. "But you're full of shit."

"Don't talk to my dad that way," Ronnie said.

My head felt as if it would explode. I wasn't sure why, but I realized I'd better not continue the conversation, so I walked away. Knots of people remained here and there. Barnes and Kate chatted with the Redmonds. I tried to sneak off to Hoopie, but Lucy waved me over. "Matt, join us for a sec." Kate's look could have peeled wallpaper.

"We were saying what a grand service this was," Dirk said.

"Grand service," I said.

"Too much speechifying for me," Barnes said. I suspected he was upset because he hadn't been asked to speak.

"There's a reception at the Methodist Church." Lucy swirled her dress. Kate's throat turned crimson.

"Can't make it," I said.

"The Sheriff is heading up to Wasserman's Pillar," Barnes said.

"Looking for thieved livestock." I didn't look at Kate.

"Someone should shoot them rustlers," Dirk said.

"We could lynch them like in the old days," Kate said, looking at me.

"Not in an election year," Barnes said. "Trial first, then hang them."

"Mind your manners, Judge," Lucy said. "Here comes Ed Dilkes."

"Gotta run." I'd had enough of probing questions for the moment.

"Seen you soon," Barnes said.

"Soon." Kate smiled at me. My heart soared.

Chapter 13

Near where Mill Creek meandered down from the foothills and emptied into the Crooked River, the junipers gave way to pine woods, and the creek cut around a basalt pillar that jutted three hundred feet over the creek bed. Early pioneers had named it after Frank Wasserman, but it looked like a giant prehistoric penis, and locals had given it a more colorful nickname: The Chief's Cock. A gravel road led to the Pillar and, except for the occasional gyppo logging truck, the area was only visited during hunting season.

I picked up Kate behind the Spur Roadhouse. The sky was blue enough to hurt my eyes and, though it was day, a pale crescent moon hung in the afternoon sky. Kate rested her head on my shoulder once we left the main road. The sun warmed the landscape--hot, but not too hot. Just right for a picnic, I thought. I'd fried up some chicken and opened a can of pork and beans. Couldn't have a picnic without pork and beans. Kate had baked a pound cake and iced it with lemon frosting. I hadn't been on a picnic since my real dad died and, even with the murders and my dog running off, I felt grand.

A lone poplar tree marked our picnic spot, a sure sign that homesteaders had set up shop here back when sheep still roamed this range. The old-timers talked about how rye grass grew as tall as a man when the first pioneers entered this valley, but overgrazing by sheep at the turn of the century had changed all that. Now only cheatgrass grew on the range, and most of the sheep were gone. Farming without water was next to impossible in this hardscrabble, lava rock soil, and most homesteaders had lost their parcels to the bank and moved into town to work in the mills. Though deserted and lonely, it was still a lovely spot, secluded, with a creek bubbling nearby.

I parked Hoopie at a wide spot in the road, and we scrambled down the bank. Kate wore bib overalls and a white blouse, something a woman might wear on a farm, but she looked just fine to me. I longed to have my hands roam inside of the overalls, but when I touched her hips, she slapped my hand and said, "Not yet."

Kate spread the blanket by the poplar while I unloaded the basket--beans, cake, chicken and beer. I crossed my legs Indian style and chugged a beer. When I reached for another, Kate placed her hand over mine. "Just one."

"Why?" I asked.

"Because you're a nicer man when you're sober," she said.

"You know what I like about you?" I asked.

"What?"

"You don't drink hard liquor straight from the bottle."

"Sometimes your humor isn't funny," she said. "Eat."

We nibbled on chicken and beans. The ants discovered us straight away, as did a couple of chipmunks who chattered at us from the rocks. Cheese, I should have brought cheese for the chipmunks.

"What's with Harley and Barnes?" I asked.

"You asked that before," she said.

"They're thick as thieves," I said. "I'm just curious."

"Porter has his faults," she replied, "but at heart he's not a bad man."

I tossed a piece of cake at one of the chipmunks. She stuffed it into her mouth and lit out with a couple of the other 'munks chasing her. "I know," I said. "Otherwise you wouldn't have married him."

Kate didn't laugh. "I've been nosing around at the high school. There's a secret there that the kids won't talk about."

"I'll reinterview the Weekly girl and Mike Barfield. Put a little pressure on them, see if they fold."

"Not too hard," she said.

"I've got a touch like velvet."

That got her to laugh. "Betty McIntyre knows more that she's telling," Kate said, "or maybe she doesn't realize what she knows. I'm going to chat her up more. Apparently, something happened to Joey a few weeks ago. He'd been moody and remote."

"Sounds like a typical kid," I said. "Remember, I was like that when I moved to town."

Kate was quiet for a long time, then she looked up at the rimrock and said, "After all these years, I still don't feel as if I know you, Matthew." When I asked her what she meant, she told me that she'd been thinking about us and about me a lot over the past few days, figuring out what to do. "You moved to town and lived with your uncle while you went to high school. You never have told me much about your childhood, your mom, your dad. You have a brother, don't you?"

"Two, two half-brothers. One lives in Texas. One lies in a Flanders' field."

"I'm sorry," she said.

"We weren't close," I said. "I left home at thirteen."

"Ran away?"

"Left." I decided to tell her the cleaned-up version of my story:

Dad died when I was six, a drunken Mick with tuberculosis and no money for doctoring. I hated him for leaving me with my mother, but I didn't tell Kate that part. Mother remarried to a stone mason. He and I didn't get along that well. I had been a rotten kid, maybe I still was rotten. The Depression crushed our family and, being the oldest, I worked three jobs. "Got tired of it," I said. "Got tired of working fourteen hours a day on weekends, my mom taking all the money I made, got tired of my stepfather sitting around, not working, being a failure. I left home. Lied about my age and worked for the CCC building roads for a couple of years. My uncle said I could stay with him. I figured that was better than sleeping on a cot and swinging a pick all day long."

Kate asked me if I missed my mother and I shook my head. "No?" she asked.

Sadness engulfed me like a wave. I felt like a kid again, and the shame and the hurt and the pain overwhelmed me. I tried to contain it but couldn't, and the truth escaped. "My mother beat me," I said. "Not the normal kid stuff with a hairbrush, but nasty. The last time she whipped me, I'd used some of the money I'd made to buy myself a hat. In the mornings before school, I'd deliver newspapers on my bike, then sweep up the butcher shop before heading to school. It was January, and the east wind howled down the gorge. My ears were frostbit and stung all the time. I couldn't stand the pain anymore so I bought a hat, a fucking hat. She tied me to the bed and worked me over with a strap. My half-brother heard my screams and ran out to the shed to get my stepdad.

"Stepdad was an asshole, but when he saw what my Mom had done, saw my blood on the bedspread, he smacked her around the room with his fists like only a half-drunk Mick can do. Closed up both her eyes, knocked out a couple of teeth. Told her he'd kill her if she did it again. I'm not sure why he did that, but my old lady never did hit me again. When the weather warmed, I hitchhiked south, bummed around the country for a while until Uncle John told me I could come here and live with him."

"Life must have been terrible for you." Kate put her hand on mine. I had almost forgotten she was here. "When was the last time you saw your mother?"

"Christmas," I said. "I was sixteen."

"That's the last time?"

"We didn't talk," I said. "She wanted to, but I told her we didn't have anything to discuss. She lives over in the valley, but we don't communicate."

"I'm sorry," Kate said.

"My brother calls once in a while and lets me know how things are going. My stepdad died a couple of years ago, and Mom's not well," I said. "Diabetes."

"So sad," Kate said.

"I'm over it," I said.

Kate handed me a piece of cake. "No, you're not."

A covey of quail kicked up from the brush and startled both of us. "Must be a coyote about," I said. The mama herded the little ones across the clearing and into the pine woods on the other side.

"Matt," Kate said, "you're one of the smartest men I know. There's so much good you could do with your life. If I were to leave Porter, we can't live here. He would make life impossible for us."

I chewed on telling her about Porter and Harley, but didn't want to pop that one unless I knew it was true.

"I'm not sure where we would go."

"Let's move to the city. You could get a job as a big city cop."

"Being a sheriff is what I'm good at. I like what I do. I like it here"

I'd lived in San Francisco and in Portland, too many people there, rushing about being busy about nothing.

"We could get a house, start a family. I might start a career. I have dreams, too."

I sighed. "Having kids scares me. Like mother, like son. I won't let myself hurt a child." Mama quail peeked out from behind her pine tree, then disappeared. A chipmunk chattered.

"Things have a way of working themselves out," she said. "If we work as a team, we can find a solution. Just like with these murders."

I warmed to the idea. "Why not? If we dream big, anything's possible." Kate was a strong woman. Maybe her strength could sustain me. I imagined that it could. Maybe we could make a plan before we left. My head felt like it was buzzing.

She touched my face. "I love you. Don't let me down again."

"I won't. I promise." I kissed her. "Maybe, we could..."

She caught my drift and laughed. "You'll never change. Dessert first." She uncovered her pound cake, lemon icing and pink stars. "Then we'll see."

"My favorite," I said.

The bullet whirred, and I flinched. Bullets had whirred past me before in the jungle. There, they usually pinged against the rocks, thunked into a tree, or splat into a man's flesh. This one thwacked into the side of Kate's head. The pop of the long gun came a half-second later, the sniper at least a couple of hundred yards away, probably more. Kate's skull, blood, and brains splattered against the trees and sandy dirt. Conscious thought fled, and I knelt in the dust trying to scoop the pink froth and white slivers of bone back into her head, but everything seemed to slip through my fingers.

My teeth chattered, and I sat there with Kate's body cradled in my lap. I screamed and waited for the next shot to come. Part of me wanted to crawl on the ground, slither behind a tree, find cover, but I didn't want to be a coward in front of Kate. "Shoot me, too!" I waited for the next shot to finish me, but my only answer was the bubbling of the stream and the rustling of the wind in the pines.

After a bit, the mama quail moved from here to there, and the chipmunk chattered again. The bastard must have decided to let me live. I closed Kate's half-open eyes and tried to gather what remained of my wits.

I needed a gun. There was a snub-nosed .38 Chief's Special stuffed behind the seat of my truck. I scrambled up the bank on my hands and knees. A log truck roared and rumbled down the valley toward where I parked my truck. Hauling ass, full load of timber, I reckoned, going too fast for this road, but log truck drivers knew these roads better than most and trusted their skill more than fate. I reached the road, rummaged through my truck, and found the gun. The log truck rounded the far bend, and I stood in the middle of the road, revolver at the ready. The truck's brakes hissed, and it slewed left, then right. The driver's eyes widened as if he couldn't believe what he'd seen. Maybe God would let the truck hit me, but at the last moment, instinct overcame despair and I dived out of the way. The truck slid past me and crunched into the upside bank of the road; the trailer jack-knifed and tipped up. Chains snapped, and logs bounced onto the road and rolled off into the creek.

I ran to the truck, opened the door, and jumped up on the running board. The driver yelled, "Hey!"

I stuck the barrel of my .38 in his ear, and yelled, "Get out! Get out! Get out!" The dust caught up to us and swirled around like a dirty brown mist.

The driver slid out of the truck and put his hands on his head. "Oh, Jesus, don't shoot, Sheriff. I have papers for the logs. Honest. Don't shoot."

"She's dead." I twisted the gun deeper into his ear.

"Dirk Redmond hired me to haul a load," he said. "Honest

Injun."

"Killed dead," I said.

"Dead?" he asked. I'd seen him around town before, a young logging man, all youthful bluster and angles and elbows. Ray? Was his name Ray? He worked for some gyppo logging outfit upcountry, sometimes hauling honest loads, sometimes hauling off the books. "You hit a deer?"

"Kate," I said. "Kate's been shot dead."

"Kate?" he said. "Blood. You're covered with blood."

"Blew her brains out from a couple of hundred yards at least."

"Kate who?" he asked. "Please lower the gun. You're scaring me."

"Kate Barnes. Watch your head, the sniper's still up there." I pushed him down, and we crouched in the dirt next to his truck.

"Judge Barnes's wife?" he asked, as he peered up at the rimrock.

"She wants to leave him." I realized I didn't want to kill this man and lowered the pistol. "She loves me; she told me so." My hands shook, and I couldn't stop them. "Loved me. I'm a dead man."

"Were you in a fight?" Ray asked. "Are you hurt?"

"Anyone else up the road?" The dust seemed to have settled a bit.

"Falling crew," Ray answered, "setting chokers." Chokers were chains to pull the logs up the grade to waiting log trucks.

"Murderers. A killer up there." The mist closed in again, and I felt cold.

"Sheriff, you're not making sense. Do you need a doctor?"

"Get help," I said. "I'll stay here with Kate."

"My truck won't move. We'll need a tow truck to get her back on the road again." Most of the logs had bounced off the road and down the bank. Hoopie could just squeeze by on the downhill side.

"Take mine." I pulled him back to my truck and tossed him my keys. I dug around behind the seat and took up the dusty bottle of gin I kept there for emergencies. "Not right for a woman to be down there all by herself," I said. "I'll wait here."

Ray took my keys and spun gravel as he left. I tumbled back down the hill to our picnic spot protecting the bottle but not caring how I got to the bottom. Kate lay awkwardly in the dirt so I rearranged her a bit, readjusted the bib overall strap that had slipped down, and covered her face the best I could with my handkerchief. Then I settled my ass at the base of a pine tree. "Here's to you, Kate." I swallowed some gin. She didn't say anything, but after a few more swigs from the bottle I became comfortable with her silence.

*

"He's drunk," George said.

"A snoot full," Doc Silverman agreed.

I cracked an eye. Too bright, it was too bright. "Not drunk enough. Anybody got another bottle?"

"A terrible thing, this," George said, "and with Kate lying here next to him."

"We'll have to get him back up the hill," Doc said. "We may have to carry him."

"You're both talking about me like I'm not here. Well, I'm right here. Talk to me." I tried to get up, but someone had greased my boots, and it took me a couple of tries to gain my feet.

"Calm down, Slim," George said, which didn't set too well with me.

"I don't need some stupid lug telling me what to do."

He just sighed and looked at me with a cow-chewing-cud look. That look burrowed under my skin like a tick in the summer grass, itching, burning, driving me crazy, so I took a poke at George. My feet slipped, and my fist whiffed past him. George slapped me upside the head with one of his big paws and knocked me on my keister. "Now what did you that for?" he asked.

"You stupid shit." I tried to push myself to my feet, but the ground rolled like the sea before a storm and I fell down again. "Stand still, and I'll kick your ass." I tried kicking George in the shins, but he and Doc jumped on me, rolled me over, and handcuffed my hands behind my back. I kept flailing with my feet, and Doc said, "Enough is enough," and stuck me in the shoulder with a needle. The dusty daylight dimmed.

"Is this the end of my days?" I asked.

"No such luck," Doc said. "You've got work to do." Then the son of a bitch turned off the lights.

Chapter 14

Someone kissed me in my dreams, wet, sloppy, foul-scented kisses, but welcome nonetheless. "Brush your teeth, Kate. You taste like a dog."

Kate woofed, and I awoke to find a hairy monster licking my chin and nuzzling me with his wet, icy nose. "Addison. You've come back to me."

"I found him running along Grimes Flat Road this morning," Doc said. "None the worse for wear." We seemed to have found our way to Doc's basement. He and George must have laid me on a cot down here. Addison pranced and capered.

Kate had been killed, but I scratched Addison's ears and tried to forget. "Any sign of the negro?"

"Not a hair," Doc replied, "but I did find this." He handed me Hoopie's missing steering wheel, sawed at the eight o'clock position by what appeared to be a hacksaw. I fingered the cut. "That's how the villain escaped," Doc added.

"Fuck, my head hurts. What did you give me?"

"It's your own fault," Doc said.

The basement was cool, too cool, and I shivered. "Where's Kate?"

"In the other room."

"I won't be attending the autopsy," I said.

"You aren't invited," Doc said.

"Head's killing me." I kept seeing Kate smiling at me in the seconds before the bullet tore into the side of her head. "Maybe a little nip, a little hair of the dog?" Addison whined and licked my fingers. "No offense intended." The booze would flush away the smell of her brains and blood.

"Not a chance," Doc said.

"You've never refused me before."

"You've never taken a poke at George before. He looks up to you, but take another poke at him and you'll end up with a pug nose." Doc had a point. I wasn't sure about looking up to me, but George didn't take guff from any man, even me. My whiskey buzz had already faded to a dull ache that pounded me right between the eyes.

"Grimes Flat, you said?" I asked.

"Yes, I found Addison on Grimes Flat Road near mile post seven and the steering wheel a few hundred yards to the east. I was headed out to the Sawyer ranch to talk to them about their kid, Tom. He's got the measles."

"Little red-headed guy, you've got him upstairs under quarantine." Something wasn't connecting that should be. Maybe if I could get rid of this headache, I could figure it out.

"I'll drive you home," Doc said.

My arms and legs felt heavy. I worried that my mind would break up into little pieces and drift away. "Where's Hoopie?" I asked. "I can drive myself, thank you. I've got to go up onto Twelve Mile Table and look for evidence."

"At the Courthouse, but you're in no condition to do anything. George and the State Police will take care of the murder investigation. I prescribe bed rest for you."

"Horse pucky." I pushed myself up from the cot. The room swayed to the right, and I plunked back down. "Okay, you can drive if it'll make you happy."

Doc loaded Addison and me into his coupe and hauled us back to my place. Suddenly, it had become night. Junipers, ancient and ignorant, loomed in the moonlight. A jackrabbit froze in the headlights, white on black, then skittered across the road. Addison tried to jump out the window, but I grabbed the ruff of his neck. "Not this time, my little buckaroo."

When we reached my place, Doc searched my rooms and confiscated all my booze. "Leave the beer," I said. "I'm mighty parched." But the old fart was resolute and packed everything into a wooden fruit box. "I want a receipt."

"I'll check on you in the morning," he said.

"Some friend you are." After he left, I fried up a can of Spam, half for me and half for Addison. He didn't seem to care for horseradish on his, so I scraped it off. He nibbled at the meat with dainty intensity. I sat in my one comfortable chair wanting to sleep but not finding peace. The sound of the bullet kept at me like a mosquito bite at the back of my knee. "Enough is enough," I said to Addison, and I hefted myself up into the attic where I'd stashed a bottle of champagne destined for some uncertain future prosperity. This seemed as prosperous a time as any.

I popped the top, spilled booze on my kitchen linoleum, and said, "What the fuck?" My stomach rumbled against the warm champagne but, after the third glass, the whirrs and thumps faded a bit. I slipped into sleep.

*

At six in the morning, Miriam hammered on the front door, perhaps expecting to find me dead to the world, but I was already up and frying more spam. "Sheriff, you look sucked dry this morning. You been drinking?"

"Not on my honor," I said.

"I brought you a casserole and some cookies. A man can't cook at a time like this."

"Spam casserole?"

She scratched Addison's back. "Tuna."

"That'll do," I said.

"A terrible shame about Kate," she said.

"I loved her."

"We'd figured that out a while back," she said. "George and I. Some other folks, too. Pretty obvious you had a serious case on her, and it's hard to lose someone you love. Hurt lasts a long time."

"Think Barnes knew?"

"That wouldn't surprise me," she said. "Stupidity isn't one of his faults."

"Why didn't he said anything?" Miriam slopped a large dose of tuna casserole on a plate, and put in on the table for me. My stomach shimmied like Jell-O. "I feel like shit."

"Eat up. You'll feel better." The first bite was better than expected. As I ate, my stomach calmed, but a little leprechaun jackhammered me right between the eyes.

I remembered that Hoopie was still at the courthouse. I had no desire to go to town just yet. "Buy me a bottle. Anything will do." I pulled my last fiver before payday from my pocket. Miriam ignored me and spooned some of her casserole into Addison's dish. He went at it as if I had been starving him.

"Eat up, my little pumpkin," she said.

"How's Barnes taking it?" I asked.

"Slightly worse than you are," she said.

"I'm in the grease now," I said.

"To say the least, but I have faith that you'll figure your way out of this mess." She patted me on the cheek and told me I'd live. "Feed the dog, and he won't run away again."

"I fed him regular," I said.

After she left, I tried to remember if I'd stashed another bottle somewhere. Maybe in the pump house, back behind a little used tool chest. "Come on, Addison. We've got to hunt down some important evidence." Intent on the tuna casserole, he ignored me.

The pump house turned up empty. My hands shook, but that had to be from losing Kate, not from being tossed willy-nilly onto the wagon. I made it as far as the porch before I had to sit down and rest a spell. Addison curled up next to me, content. I wanted to think about what to do next, but the fog in my brain seemed to absorb my rational thoughts, and my hands fluttered as if they had a life of their own. I decided to clean my gun to calm my nerves.

Addison tip-tapped behind me as I walked into the dining room and set a layer of newspapers on the kitchen table. My gun felt heavy in my hands as I ejected the shell from the chamber, dropped the magazine into my left hand, then unloaded it. I disassembled the gun, wiping and cleaning each part in turn, recoil spring, slide, and trigger assembly. The barrel deserved particular attention. I scrubbed it with a wire brush, then dried it with patches cut from an old T-shirt. At the end, I oiled each piece with gun oil and wiped them down with a rag. My hands felt steadier as I reloaded the magazine and racked a cartridge into the chamber.

My hands may have steadied, but a sharp ache still hammered me between the eyes. I wanted it to stop. What would happen between Barnes and me? I pictured us wrestling on the courthouse lawn, punching each other in the head and yelling, "Cocksucker!" while the townspeople gathered around and cheered, "Fight, fight, fight!" like kids gathered around combatants behind the high school. Barnes would punch me in the kidneys, and I'd bite his ear. We would trade "motherfuckers" and "fuck yous," furious, the winner able to keep his grief, but in my vision, neither one of us won.

I pulled back the hammer of my .45 and stuck the barrel in my mouth. The gun rested cold between my lips. It felt like something to hold onto, something solid in a world that swirled around me. I had done this before in New Guinea during the war, during the quiet time, shivering with jungle fever, so miserable, so sick of being shot at, killing other men, never seeing the end, I wanted to die, wanted to find a way out. The barrel of my .45 tasted just the same as the barrel of an M-1, except I didn't have to reach for the trigger with my toes. It was just a test, I'd always thought, testing myself, my resolve to live, my courage, my cowardice. Sometimes they came in the same frantic instant.

I touched the barrel with my tongue, tasted the acid tang, tasted my shame, my desires, my fear of dying alone. It was pretty fucking hard to think clearly while sucking on the barrel of a .45. It was as if I was standing on the lip of a volcano wondering if I could fly, but knowing deep down I couldn't. Maybe that was why I'd never pulled the trigger, I knew deep down I couldn't fly. I tasted the metal again. It tasted better this time, almost palatable.

Addison woofed and pulled me back to earth. He danced at the screen door, probably needing to piss. I wanted to ignore him, but tires crunched on gravel, and I realized that's what he'd heard, a visitor, someone coming up the drive. I slipped the .45 into my holster and looked out the screen door, smelled the aluminum and summer almost gone.

Ed Dilkes pulled up to my place in a dusty red Dodge. "Hail and well met."

"What the fuck is this?" I asked. "Grand Central Station?"

"This is a fine howdy-do when I came with good intentions to offer my condolences. Miriam called and said you might need some company. You'll be happy to know that Trooper Giovanni is hard at the investigation." I opened the door, and Addison, tail wagging, rushed out to meet him. He held up a covered dish so the dog couldn't get it. "Aren't you going to invite me in?"

"Is this visit official or off the record?"

"Off the record," he said.

"Bring a bottle?" I asked.

"You keep forgetting I'm on the wagon," he said. "We should talk about your drinking sometime. I'd like to help."

"Don't need your help," I said.

Dilkes shrugged as if he had expected my response. "My wife baked you a marionberry pie. We could each have a piece."

"Suit yourself," I said.

I held the door open for him. If he noticed the gun belt slung over the chair, he didn't mention it. "You keep a neat house." He set the pie on the kitchen table, and I rustled about finding a couple of clean plates and a pair of forks.

I found a quart of ice cream in the freezer. "Might as well do it up right. Right, Addison?"

"Dog eats ice cream?" Dilkes asked.

"That dog eats anything I put in front of him," I said.

"Thought he was lost," he said.

"Doc Silverman found him running along Grimes Flat Road. He must have escaped from the clutches of that villain, Thomas Stewart." I served the pie and spooned two scoops of vanilla ice cream for each of us, Addison included. The simple act calmed me; I stepped back from the volcano.

"Stewart didn't seem to be one to steal a man's dog."

"Maybe he went along willingly," I suggested, but I didn't believe it.

Dilkes made a noise in the back of his throat and thumbed through an old Police Gazette on the table. "Grimes Flat Road must be five miles from where he disappeared and not many places to hide on the way, 'cept maybe a barn or a pump house, but you'd think someone would have seen him out there. Curious. It's not like a negro blends in."

"Not like." I sighed. Still too hard to think, but the ache between my eyes had eased a bit, not enough for me to find clarity, but enough that I thought I might live to see the sun go down. Addison, a hacksawed steering wheel, and a prisoner that disappeared faster than Houdini. "How's Barnes taking things?" I'd already asked Miriam the same question, but with Barnes I needed all the opinions I could get.

"Somber at the moment," Dilkes said. "Is that tuna casserole?" I nodded and ladled some onto his plate. "You know Judge Barnes," he continued. "He holds his cards close, and this time they're closer than usual." He tasted the casserole and smiled. "Sad, angry, chain-smoking cigars. Looks pretty haggard."

"Say anything about me?" My stomach rumbled. Maybe it was the tuna casserole.

"We didn't get that far in the conversation," Dilkes said. "But if you want my opinion, Barnes knew about you and Kate for a long time."

"Why didn't he say anything?"

"Barnes has a reason," Dilkes said, "for everything he does."

True enough, I thought. That was how Barnes had reached the top of our little mountain. Sometimes I thought he liked me; sometimes he viewed me as a competitor. If Miriam and Dilkes were right and he knew about Kate and me, then he'd had to have held his tongue for a specific reason. As if I didn't have enough mysteries to deal with.

"Got an aspirin?" I asked.

"In the car."

I asked Dilkes if he'd give me a ride back to town. "I've got to pick up my truck." He asked what I planned on doing when I got there. Maybe he thought I was going to get drunk or try to kill someone. Maybe I would, but later. "I'm going to head up to Wasserman's Pillar and look for the sniper's nest, myself."

"Let the Staters handle it," Dilkes said. "You should take it easy and rest a spell."

"My case. My investigation." I didn't add 'my sweetheart.' Seemed my good uniform shirt was stained with blood, and my only other one was in the wash, so I put on a pearl-buttoned cowboy shirt and rolled up the sleeves.

"Could be conflict of interest," Dilkes said.

"Could be I'm going to catch this cocksucker." Maybe I'd kill him or them, but I couldn't tell Dilkes that. It would have to be during the arrest. Clean, neat, simple.

"Think this is connected with the other murders?"

"Hell yes," I said. "Three murders in a week out here next to nowhere. Last one was five years ago. They're connected." I buckled on my gun belt. The .45 slung on my hip kept me balanced, so I wouldn't list too far to the wrong side.

Dilkes helped me fill two olive-green surplus canteens. I figured I'd be hiking up into the rimrocks, though I wasn't too crazy about climbing the pillar. That would be my last option. "Come along, Addison," I said. "Let's hit the road."

When we got in the Dodge, Dilkes handed me a bottle of aspirin. I chewed three of them dry. The disgusting taste was poor penitence for my sins, but it was a start. I told myself I wouldn't take another drink until this was finished, but I had a habit of breaking my promises.

Chapter 15

The climb up to the rimrock was a hardscrabble affair, and I was thankful to be wearing combat boots; high heel cowboy shit-stompers would have made the task nearly impossible. Reluctant to see anyone I knew, especially Barnes, I'd bypassed my office and drove off in Hoopie without saying any 'howdy-dos.' For the same reason, I'd avoided the state bulls and Jackson, the forensics tech working on the crime scene at the base of the pillar. Instead, I climbed directly up to the rimrock. Somewhere up there, a sniper had set up camp and waited to shoot Kate down.

I sweated and grunted my way up the forty-five-degree slope toward the jumbled wall of stones at the top of the rim. The sun burned brilliant hot overhead, and the earth smelled of brimstone. My head felt as if it had swollen to about twice its normal size, and halfway up I stopped for a swig of water while Addison scared up a sage hen. It flew away low to the ground in a flurry of wings that startled both my dog and me. After that, the quiet hung oppressive and heavy until a dragonfly in its purple and blue iridescence buzzed by our heads, and the world moved again.

There was a level spot, a good enough place to rest, and I poured some water in the hollow of a red lava rock for Addison to drink. The dog lapped up the water, then wandered about sniffing at the sagebrush while I sat in the shade of a twisted juniper. Above, the rimrock lay in chiseled layers of basalt. Why Kate? Why not me? Did he miss his shot, or did he want me to suffer?

Addison woofed and scampered at a feather-leaved sagebrush, and a rattlesnake buzzed back at him. A full grown demon-red diamondback coiled in the shade of the bush, cocked back, ready to strike. Addison woofed again and made to snap at the rattler. I really didn't want to lose my girl and my dog in the same week, so without any thought, I jumped up, drew my .45, and blew the snake into two pieces. Addison yelped and ran off a bit. "Come back here, you stupid mutt," I said, but he crouched next to a copse of bunch grass and whined, probably more scared of the gunshot than the snake.

My ears rang from the blast and, once I realized what I'd done, I felt sorry for killing the snake. Unlike many folk in these parts, I didn't hate rattlers. Snakes weren't like people, they didn't kill for fun. They didn't kill unless they felt threatened. Was Kate a threat to the killer? Maybe her poking around with Betty McIntyre or at the high school had spooked him. By the same token, had Virginia or Joey been a threat? Virginia was fucking Dr. McIntyre. Someone fucked Joey in the ass. Was he killed to cover up the rape, or a series of rapes? Maybe. Other than a farm boy doing old Bossy from the top of a milking stool, folks in these parts didn't cotton to sodomy, or at least that was what they said. Then there was the matter of the letterman's sweater. I hadn't asked Margie Weekly about the sweater. I'd check with her again. I whistled for my dog, and he skittered over, ears laid back and tail tight between his legs. "It's okay, fella. Let's get this show on the road."

I was puffing like a steam train by the time we reached the bottom of the rimrock. Once upon a time, I was in decent shape, lifted weights before the war, had a waist like a schoolgirl, could run a couple of miles at double-time, but that had all dissipated over time due to coffin nails and cheap booze.

The top of the rim was at least thirty feet above us, maybe more, but the rust-colored basalt slabs had broken down enough over time that I could work my way up to the top with a rest spell here and there. I couldn't carry Addison and swing hand-to-hand among the rocks, so I told him to stay at the base of the rock and started climbing.

I fretted about another rattler hiding in the dark angles of the rocks, but my luck held, and I reached the top. The top of the rimrock opened out onto Twelve Mile Table, a sagebrush and ryegrass flat that I'd never visited before, it being mostly federal jurisdiction belonging to the Bureau of Land Management and almost impossible to reach. During the War, the Army Air Corps used the Table as a target range, dropping practice bombs and strafing the sizable pronghorn antelope herd up here into near oblivion.

I walked along the edge of the rim looking for signs that someone had been up there. A hundred yards to the north, the rim curved back towards Wasserman's Pillar, and I found signs of antelope, piles of round dark turds and hoof marks too small for mule deer. Out of the corner of my eye, I saw something twitch, dusty brown and white, and four antelope leaped away, silky muscles and simple grace. How could those flyboys shoot them down without remorse? The further away the victim, the easier the kill. Rage settled like a cold seed in my stomach.

A few yards further, I found the sniper's next. No shell casings on the ground, the bastard was smart enough to police his brass, but there were plenty of footprints, about size eleven, I figured, and a scuffed-out spot in the sandy soil where he'd taken his shot. It looked as if he hadn't proned out, but had sat with one knee as a brace, the other curled underneath him. I pictured a man sitting there peering through a scope at two lovers having a picnic at the base of the pillar. They ate beans and cake, laughed, shared intimacies like lovers do. The sniper wrapped the rifle sling around his arm to steady his shot. He'd done it before, both for animals and men, I figured. I looked hard, but couldn't see his face. Not yet. He'd let out half a breath, then held it without conscious thought to steady himself.

That time of day, there'd be a breeze from the east, not much of a breeze, but he'd make allowances for it. Acquired the sight picture through the scope, centered the crosshairs on Kate's head. How far would the bullet drop over a quarter-mile? Allowed for that, too. Squeezed, pulled the trigger steady-like, let the shot be a bit of a surprise. He'd have pressed the butt of the gun tight against his shoulder. The recoil would rock him back slightly, not painful, but reassuring. The scope would jump some with the recoil, and he'd have reacquired the scene in the scope. The shot was a good one, and he'd see some fool of a sheriff scrambling about trying to shovel his lover's brains back into her skull. The sheriff would have made another easy target, but 'not yet,' he must have thought. You should have finished me when you had the chance, I thought. That was your big mistake.

A fully loaded logging truck buzzed by on the road below, a rooster tail of dust kicking up in its wake. The crime scene folks still swarmed around our picnic spot. The sniper's footprints headed off toward the east. There was a dirt track that wound up onto the table from the back side of Barnes Butte. Were there others? I had no hankering to hike twelve miles or so following footprints. How'd the sniper get up here? Drove, I supposed. My county map was useless; I'd have to find a quad map at either the BLM or order one from Ochoco Stationery. Maybe the sniper had bought one there, too. I'd have to check.

I scrambled back down the rimrock on a straight line from the sniper's nest looking to find something he may have dropped. The sun was in full fire, and the hot rocks blistered my fingers. I invented a few new swear words as I swung down the rocks. In a narrow crevice, half-hidden by dried cheatgrass, I caught sight of a glimmer of gold, a brass shell casing. My legs trembled as I leaned against the rock, snatched up the casing, and examined it, trying not to handle it too much. I'd never been too fond of heights, although ladders seemed to spook me more than mountain peaks. The casing was a hand reload,

.30-06. The sniper had a reloading machine stuck away in his garage or tool shed. Not unusual in this county, but something.

I dropped the casing into my shirt pocket and worked my way back down to the base of the rimrock. Addison heard me coming and raced to greet me, all panting, wagging tail, and doggie slobber. As I sat on the ground to rest, he stood on his hind legs and licked my chin as if to say, "You're my man."

"You waited for me," I said. "Why didn't you do that before?" I realized Addison wouldn't have run off with Stewart on his own. He'd only leave with someone he knew, the same person who had used a hacksaw on my steering wheel. The trip down from the rimrock was easier than the trip up.

*

The stationery store smelled of fresh ink and clean white paper. Barnestown was a small town, and Len, the owner, tried to satisfy any need related to paper, not just stationery: school supplies, books, journals, ledgers, maps, canvas, and oil paints. There was a sweet little woodcarving kit I'd always wanted, but never had the money nor the gumption to buy. Maybe when I retired, if I made it that long.

"Hey, Sheriff," Len said. He had prematurely gray hair. "Those citations haven't come in yet, but I expect them any time."

"I'm looking for a map," I said. "Twelve Mile Table."

"Topo?" he asked. "We have a good county map."

"Something more detailed." I thumbed through some new books stacked in neat piles on a table. "Ride the Pink Horse, Dorothy Hughes. This good?"

"Dark, but suspenseful," Len said. "You want a set of quadrangle maps then. We don't stock them. You'll have to order them special."

"Didn't they make a movie of this?"

"Robert Montgomery," Len said. "Saw it at the Tower in Bend. I liked the book better. Usually, the book is better."

"You'd better order the maps," I said.

"Take six weeks, but you needn't bother. The county already has a set. Judge ordered them last year, said they were for the county assessor's office. Maybe you could check out his copies."

"Maybe so," I said. Miriam would know for sure if they made it to the assessor's office. "Anybody else?"

"Pardon?"

"Anybody else order a set?"

"Hold your horses. I'll check." He opened a file box and rustled around with canary yellow receipt copies. I thumbed through the novel about seeking revenge as told by a bad guy. This Hughes gal could write, I decided.

"Four sets in the last couple of years," Len said. "That's as far back as my records go."

"Far enough," I said.

"Library got one set, school district got another, the Desert Times Eagle got the third, and you know about the set at the Courthouse. Most folks just want the county-wide map, the quadrangle set costs ten dollars, pretty hefty price for working folks."

"Coach order the school set?" I asked.

Len shook his head. "Mrs. McCormack. I remember distinctly; she was working on a project for her geography class. Does this have something to do with the murders?"

"Mum's the word," I said.

"My lips are sealed," he said.

"You know the deceased?" I asked.

"Joey, not so much, but Virginia spent some time in here. Good girl, smart, liked to read. I gave her a discount on her journals."

"Do that with all the kids?" I asked.

"Just the ones without a pot to pee in," he said.

"I'll take this book." I held up the Hughes book. "But forget the maps. I'll track down the other sets."

Len wrapped up the book and gave me a two-bit professional discount on the purchase. Even though I figured I did have a pot to piss in, I wasn't too proud to take it.

Outside, as I stepped onto the sidewalk, Addison stuck his head out of Hoopie's window and woofed. I opened the door.

I didn't see Barnes coming until he grabbed my elbow. "Harkness, I've been looking for you." He had dark circles under his eyes and looked as if someone had beat him with a shit stick, though I supposed I didn't look much better.

"Fancy meeting you here."

"I'm in no mood for your bullshit," he said, showing the whites of his eyes. "My wife is dead because of you."

"Take your hand off me."

"It wasn't enough that you were fucking her, but you had to go and get her killed." His fingers squeezed my bicep enough to make me wince.

I grabbed his wrist and twisted against the grain. "Hands off!"

Addison hopped through the open window and skittered between us.

"You just can't keep your dick to yourself." Barnes's spittle sprayed across my nose and cheeks.

"I didn't shoot her." I twisted his wrist harder. His grip loosened.

"Your fault, dickhead." Barnes bumped up against me. He was built like a fireplug, and I stumbled back a step.

"Back off, cocksucker," I said.

Barnes swung from lowdown, somewhere around his knees, going up high, a slow roundhouse that only a man too pissed to know better would throw. I dodged and tossed a couple of quick shots into his short ribs, and then he was in against me, head pressed against my sternum, blows flailing against my sides. I wrapped an arm around the back of his head and flopped us both down onto the sidewalk. He landed beneath me, air whooshing from his lungs, and I took the opportunity to gleefully pop him around the ears with my right fist. He whacked me in the kidneys, which almost did me in. We flailed and grunted and swore and generally acted like idiots until someone pulled me off Barnes by the hair.

George, my deputy, held me in a bear hug, and Harley wrestled with Barnes while we 'motherfucker'-ed each other and made futile attempts to toss punches. "That's all, boys," George said. "Fight's over."

"I'm your boss," I said to George. "Kick his ass."

"Right now," George said, "you're within a whisker of going to the pokey. Both of you."

"Judge, Judge," Harley said all concerned-like and pressing his fingers against Barnes's bleeding brow. "You're hurt."

One piece dropped into place. I knew why Barnes hadn't said anything about me and his wife. "I get it," I said. "You and Harley..."

"You're fired," Barnes said.

"You've tried that before," I said. "I'm an elected official."

"Come along, Judge." Harley tugged at his arm. "Don't say anything you'll regret later."

"I'm not finished with you," Barnes said, but Harley was able to pull him away. The fight was done for the moment, and the pair zigzagged their way toward Harley's store.

"I guess I showed that asshole," I said.

"Sheriff, have you been drinking?" George asked.

"Not this morning." I took a moment to assess the damage. My good shirt had been ripped, and my hand hurt like a son of a bitch. "I think I broke a knuckle." I touched my face and came away with blood on my fingers. I wasn't sure if it was mine or Judge Barnes's.

"You know better than to hit a man in the head with a closed fist," George said.

"He tore up my go-to-town shirt," I said.

"You're both as dumb as fence posts," he said. Mrs. Adams and Mrs. Simmons approached us with looks of surprise and disgust frozen on their faces. Once they had passed, they whispered, biddy-like.

Goddamn, my hand stung. "Guilty, your honor."

I picked up the Hughes book and tried to get back into Hoopie, but George caught me by the shoulder. "Mighty big gash on your cheek. You're in no condition to drive. Let's go back to the office and wash your wounds, then we'll have Doc come over and stitch you up."

Chapter 16

Doc Silverman hovered above me slipping a curved needle in and out of the gash in my cheek. It didn't hurt. It should have hurt, but it didn't. I couldn't miss the series of numbers on the inside of the Doc's forearm, blue-gray ink on aging skin. Concentration camp numbers. *806978*.

"You never talk about the war."

"Some things are best not mentioned," he said. "Hold still."

The needle dipped and stung a bit. "Where?" I asked.

"Dachau. The Bosch needed a doctor for the guards, not the inmates. All the German physicians were shipped to the Eastern Front." The needle slipped in and out. "That's what kept me alive. That, and I let the commandant beat me at chess. He believed he was a civil man."

"Why didn't the Jews overpower the guards? You outnumbered them a hundred to one."

"At first we believed the world would save us." He sighed. "But our hopes were false. The world abandoned us. When they herded us into ghettos, my wife and I fled on a boat to Cyprus. The British sent us back to Germany. No room for refugees, no quarter for the oppressed. When no one is willing to help, you lose hope. Sometimes death is an option worth considering."

"Do you believe that?" I wanted to ask what happened to his wife, but I already knew the answer.

He clapped me on the shoulder. "No, of course not. Just an old man's meanderings. I'm done."

"Will there be a scar?" As if I needed another.

"You'll look dashing, like a pirate."

"Let's sit down tonight and shoot the shit about the war," I said. "I'll buy us a bottle. Maybe two."

"Not now," he said. "No drinking for you for two weeks at least. Doctor's orders."

I would have argued, but I kept thinking I might be ready for the wagon. I hustled him out of the office and headed upstairs to the County Assessor's office.

Miriam was flipping through a table-sized plat book and making notes on a steno pad. She fussed and bothered about my banged up face.

"Do you think I look like a pirate?" I asked.

"Judge Barnes did this to you?" she asked.

"He blames me for Kate's death." Hell, I blamed myself for Kate's death.

"He'll get over it in time," she said.

"Not likely," I said.

Miriam soaked a washcloth in cold water and slapped it on the knot over my right eye. She told me it would keep the swelling down. "You'll have a shiner," she said.

"I'll wear it like a badge of honor." I laughed.

"Quit it." She didn't laugh.

"Len Coleman said you have a set of quad maps up here for Twelve Mile Table."

Miriam nodded and pulled a sheaf of maps from one of the oak map cabinets. We spread them on the table. There was a jeep track going up onto Twelve Mile Table from the backside of Barnes Butte and the main road on the far side of Juniper Valley. Miriam traced a faint dotted line up the valley from Coach Conroy's place. "Looks like an abandoned road here."

"Could be," I said, but my money was on the route up from Barnes Butte. I put my finger on a small black square on the south rim of the Table. "Some sort of structure here. You got anything on it in your records?"

"Maybe," Miriam said. "Maybe not. That's federal land now, but there might be something in the old records. Hold on." She pulled another tax assessment book from the shelves and blew the dust off it.

"Barnes ordered this map," I said, while Miriam thumbed through the old records. "Did he pick it up at the stationery store?"

Miriam shook her head. "Orders are delivered here direct. Don't think Judge Barnes has ever seen these maps. Aha! Here it is. Gearhart homestead. Condemned by the county in 1932 for unpaid taxes and transferred to the BLM just before the war in a land swap."

"Gearhart," I said. "As in Sam?"

"As in his father, John."

"He lived there, though. He'd know the way up onto the Table."

"Who knew about your picnic with Kate?" Miriam asked.

"No one," I said. "I didn't tell anyone about the picnic. I'm not that stupid."

"No one? Someone had to have known you and Kate were headed up there." Miriam closed the plat book and returned it to the shelf.

"No..." I thought about it. "Cocksucker!"

"Matthew Harkness," Miriam said, "your French is showing."

"Sorry. I'm such a knucklehead."

"Only on Thursdays, dear." She patted my hand.

"I told the fellows at the barbershop I was going up to Wasserman's Pillar for an investigation. I didn't mention Kate, but they all knew I'd be up there that afternoon."

"Who's *they*?"

"Barnes and Harley...."

"Judge Barnes can be a real stinker when he wants," Miriam said. "But he wouldn't kill his wife."

I told her that Barnes and Harley were lovers, homosexuals. I said it more out of spite than anything else, I supposed.

Miriam appeared to chew on that a bit, swishing it around, trying it on for size. "Does that matter?"

"No," I admitted. "I guess it doesn't, but it doesn't rule either of them out. They're both still suspects."

"Who will you tell about Harley and Judge Barnes?"

I wanted to shout it to the world, but realized that I didn't have enough asshole in me. "Nobody, unless I have to."

"Who else knew about you going up to the Pillar?" she asked.

"Sam Gearhart, the Coach, and Eddie Dilkes. That's all I can remember. My mind was on other things, the funerals, Kate." Miriam nodded for me to continue. "I'll have to find out where they all were during the shooting. See if they have alibis." The Coach seemed to be thick with both Jeff McIntyre and Mike Barfield. Could he have told them I was headed up to the Pillar? Could he be in cahoots with one or both of them?

"Even Judge Barnes?" Miriam asked. "That will go over like a lead balloon."

"Fuck him if he can't take a joke."

"Isn't there another way?" she asked.

She had a point. I told her I could ask Herb, the barber, how long the game continued after I left. "Maybe I can eliminate some of my suspects if they were playing poker."

"Can you trust Herb?"

"He's a gossip, not a liar." I was anxious to talk with him. "Can I borrow the Twelve Mile Table quad maps?" I scooped them up without waiting for an answer and clamped them under my arm. "Oh, and can Addison stay here? I don't want to lose him again."

"You're the sheriff."

*

"Where's that cute dog of yours?" Herb asked.

"Serving his time in lockup for running off." I asked him what had happened with the poker game after I left that afternoon.

"Broke up no more than thirty minutes after you left," Herb said. "Most of the fellers went their ways, but Sam hung around and got a haircut. He's on the wagon, you know. Eddie Dilkes talked him into it."

"So I heard," I said. "See any of that crew after the game broke up?"

"Nope." He told me another game had fired up an hour or so after that. None of the earlier participants had returned for it, and Sam Gearhart had also left.

"This is just between you and me," I said. Herb said he swore to God he wouldn't tell a soul, but I knew our conversation would blaze across town in a couple of hours. Fair enough, that would put some pressure on my suspects, make them nervous. Nervous men made mistakes.

Next, I stopped by the Gearhart place. Sam and Ronnie idled in the shade of their porch sipping iced tea. The kid still had his shiner, almost as angry as mine. "You do that to your son?" I asked Sam, as I leaned my backside against the railing. Though they lived in a shabby house, it was almost too pleasant idling in the cool shade.

"Sit down and rest your bones, Harkness. Have some tea."

"He didn't hit me," Ronnie said. "I got in a fight at school."

"Bullshit," I said.

"Wouldn't shit a man like you," Sam said. "I'm still too stove up to swat anyone. 'Sides, this kid can kick my ass." The man was a little too proud, I thought.

"Where were you yesterday around two when Kate Barnes was murdered?"

Sam sipped his tea. Suddenly, I was thirsty, but I'd be damned before I'd accept anything from Gearhart. "Here," he said. "Me and my boy were jawboning. We haven't set and talked for a long spell."

"Liars burn in hell," I said.

"He was here," Ronnie said. "Scout's honor."

The kid didn't hold up his fingers, but I decided to let it go for the moment. "Tell me about your family's homestead, the one up on Twelve Mile Table."

Sam looked as if I'd spit in his tea. "Why you asking?"

"Kate Barnes's killer shot her from up on the rimrock at the hind-end of Twelve Mile Table. Your daddy's homestead is the only building up there."

"Our place is a fair piece from the edge of the rimrock." Sam stopped for a moment, but I told him to go ahead. "Daddy John lost the place to the bank back in the Depression. We couldn't make the payments on the mortgage." Sam had that faraway look in his eye that told me this hurt. "He tried everything short of cattle rustling to save the place. We sold the stock, the bull, and our Case tractor, but the deck was stacked against us."

"Stacked against most folks then," I said, remembering my family.

Sam nodded. "We loaded what we had left into the back of the wagon, and my uncle helped us haul it down into town."

"Ever been back there?" I asked.

"What's done is done," he said.

"And you, Ronnie? You been up there?"

"Family left before I was born," the kid said. That didn't exactly answer my question, and my gut told me he was hiding something. Kids were curious, and kids in this country explored. He'd been up there, but was lying. Maybe when I saw the place I'd know why.

I asked Sam who had been the first to leave the poker game. He told me it was Harley. He'd said he'd had to get back to the store. When Harley said he had to leave, Judge Barnes told them he was out, too. He had some county business to attend to. The coach had to get ready for Saturday's game with the Prineville team, the Crook County Cowboys. Everyone seemed to have something to do but Sam, so he had Herb cut his hair.

I shifted gears and turned back to Ron. "Joey had an appointment to get another letterman's sweater. Do you know what happened to his first one?"

Ronnie shrugged. "He told me he lost it, but as I recall he wasn't all that upset. He knew his dad could buy him a new one."

"Maybe he gave it to someone," I suggested. "Maybe Virginia or Margie."

"He wouldn't have given it to Virginia," he replied. "He didn't want the kids to know they were going steady. Margie? Nope, she'd have told me."

"Sure you don't want to sit a spell and have a glass of iced tea?" Sam asked.

"You're making my head spin," I said.

"See what A.A. will do for you?" Ronnie asked.

"I should have worn my hip boots," I said.

"Don't be hateful," Ronnie said. "Daddy's working as hard as can be to be a better man."

This conversation was getting too deep for me, so I said my goodbyes. Part of me was happy for Sam, and part of me wanted him to fail. There were some people you just disliked for who they were. Sam was like that for me. I just couldn't wish him well. Sometimes I could be a real shitheel.

*

For obvious reasons, I wasn't anxious to ask Barnes about his whereabouts when his wife was killed. Better to let that pot cool a bit before I picked it up. It was mid-afternoon, too hot for daily doubles to have started at the high school, but close enough that Coach Conroy might be there.

Mike Barfield was in the practice field; he was all sweaty and not at all as chubby as I had remembered. He worked at muscling a blocking sled off the field by himself. When I asked about Conroy, he pointed me in the direction of the gym. Conroy was there in shorts and a T-shirt shooting free throws. He used three balls, bounce, bounce, swish, bounce, bounce, swish, bounce, bounce, swish. Then he retrieved the balls and repeated the process. The tedium would have driven me nuts.

"Hey, Coach," I said. "You're pretty good at that."

"Practice," he said. "Practice. Why'd the dog drag you in?"

"Wanted to ask you where you were when Kate Barnes was killed. Just a routine question."

Conroy looked as if he was going to say something, but changed his mind. He shot another free throw. "I was here getting ready for practice. Barfield was here, too."

"He's your alibi?"

"Or I'm his." Swish.

"Joey lost his letterman's sweater," I said. The next shot clanked off the rim. "You know anything about it?"

"Nope," Conroy said. "Joey wouldn't tell me about it anyhow. He'd know there'd be twelve kinds of hell for him to pay if I found out he'd lost it, or more likely with him, given it away to some dame." Swish. He loped over to the basket and retrieved the balls.

"Margie Weekly?" I asked.

"I don't keep track of the kids' love lives," he said. "Got more important pots to stir. The game with Crook County is tomorrow."

"Might be tough without Joey," I said.

"I got a plan," he said. "A man's always got to have a plan." Swish.

"I'll talk with Barfield on the way out," I said.

"Suit yourself." The ball swished through the basket again as I left the gym and returned to the heat. Barfield had finished moving the blocking sled and started moving tires into a row for agility drills. He jumped as if spooked when I called his name.

"Mike." I closed the gap between us. "Where were you yesterday afternoon between one and three?"

He rolled another tire into place and rubbed his hands on his denim cutoffs. "I walked over here after lunch. Got here around one thirty. The second half of daily doubles starts at four. Coach wants me to have everything set up by the time the team arrives. You know, towels washed and folded, practice field arranged just so. Our opener is tomorrow. Coach says you win through preparation."

Barfield started to move another tire, but I told him to stand still. The sun seemed hotter now, full bore in the afternoon, when even rattlesnakes go into their holes. "Coach Conroy here when you arrived?"

"Sure," the kid said.

"Stay the whole time?"

"Yup." Sweat pooled at his hairline from the heat.

"You with him the whole time?"

"He was here," the kid said.

"With you?" I pressed.

"In and out," he said. Not good enough, but I decided to move onto something else.

"Joey McIntyre was set to order a new letterman's sweater. Know what happened to the old one?"

"Why? What's the big deal about a letterman's sweater?"

"Loose ends. I hate loose ends. Any idea where it got off to?"

Barfield shrugged. "Nope. Maybe someone stole it."

"Maybe he gave it to Virginia," I suggested.

The kid laughed for the first time since I'd known him, but the laugh was without humor. "Not a chance."

"How about Margie Weekly?"

"Doubtful." Barfield shaded his eyes with the palm of his hand. "Usually, a guy gives a girl his class ring first. She wears it around her neck on a chain. If it looks like things will pan out, then he'll let her wear his sweater. He and Margie never got that far along."

"How far they'd get?"

"Ask her," he said.

A new question popped into my head. "Do the kids have lockers where they store things?" Maybe the missing sweater had been stashed in his locker. Maybe the kid had put the flim-flam on his old man in an effort to get a new one.

"We don't get lockers assigned until school starts," Barfield said. "We store the practice gear here. I cleaned out Joey's basket myself. Jocks, socks, and t-shirts, nothing more personal that that."

"No sweater?" My stomach growled. I realized I hadn't had lunch.

"Nope," he said. "If that's all, I need to get back to work."

"Do that," I said. Being hungry was a good sign, wasn't it?

*

The stuffed jackalope head stared down with dull glass eyes from the wall as I entered the mostly empty café. Ruth Alexander had started up The Jackalope Grill shortly after the war in a surplus Quonset hut on South Main. My stomach was in full grumble, and not only was Ruth a good cook, but she'd let me carry a tab until payday.

Jackalopes were mythical beasts, half jackrabbit, half antelope, that old-timers swear roamed the Oregon high desert before the white man settled there. No one knows where they went. Maybe they fled with the Mayans. The other theory was that the old-timers were full of crap and were having fun with Californians that headed up this way for their summer vacations, much like snipe hunts.

I settled onto a stool at the counter, and Ruth slopped a load of beef hash on a plate for me. After a little wheedling, she also staked me a beer. "Just one," she said. I told her "just until payday," and she laughed like she knew full well that I'd be in Dutch with her again next month.

I spiced up the hash with some red pepper flakes and devoured it in massive gulps. "Some of your best, Ruth." Sweat dribbled down into my sideburns. I almost felt ashamed that I had an appetite after what had happened to Kate, but that didn't stop me from asking for a second helping.

The bell over the door tinkled, and I wiped my face with my handkerchief. Sven Sawyer slid onto the stool next to mine. "That stuff'll kill you," he said. "Ruth, flapjacks and eggs."

"I'll never understand why you Swedes eat breakfast at suppertime," I said.

"That's why we're so healthy," he said.

"Sorry to hear your kid is sick," I said.

Sven looked at me as if I were touched. "Tom's healthy as a horse."

"Doc told me he's got the measles."

"Tom's spending the summer with his uncle up at The Dalles bucking bales and working in the feed lot." He sipped his coffee. "Sounds like Doc's putting one over on you."

"Yeah," I said. "But I ain't laughing."

Chapter 17

A cricket chirped and an owl hooted. I jimmied the cellar door and slid inside. My two-cell flashlight illuminated Kate's body resting under a white sheet. She should have been off to the funeral parlor by now. Kate would hate it if she started to stink. I touched her head through the sheet. It felt cool and smooth and lifeless. Pain and remorse surged up my gullet, and I forced it back down. No time for mourning now, maybe later.

I'd left Addison in the truck alone, windows down enough for air. He'd whined when I left, but I didn't want Doc Silverman to hear. I snuck across the room, stumbled on a small stool, and cursed under my breath. The cricket and owl still made night sounds, then the big saw at the mill cranked up and subverted all other sounds.

No one was on the first floor. I should have known Doc would have had a hand in all this. Who else would take the risk to help a negro? The parlor still showed the hand of his long-dead wife, Edna. Maybe it was his loneliness that had driven him to this, or maybe his heart. Two men laughed upstairs. I realized a radio played up there, Amos and Andy scheming once again. I grimaced at the irony of the situation. Stupid. They may have heard me, but then they laughed again. I climbed the stairs, feet flat on each tread, pressure slow and even so they wouldn't creak.

I kicked open the door to the upstairs parlor. The jamb splintered, and the door ripped from the hinges and crashed to the floor. Stewart rose from a wingbacked chair, and I caught his neck with my right hand, stuck my gun in his ear, clicked back the hammer, and said, "It's been a bad week, you son of a bitch, so don't tempt me." Sometimes you bottled up your rage so long that you wanted to hurt someone, to see someone's brains splattered against the wall—if not yours, then some dumb luckless son of a bitch that wandered into your field of fire. Sometimes the world took a crap on your doorstep, and you were powerless to stop it. You wanted to kill someone, maybe then the pain would stop. I twisted the barrel of my .45 in Stewart's ear and watched his eyes pop and, God help me, it felt good. His fear smelled good, like bacon sizzling on a grandmother's stove.

"Stop it, Matthew," Doc said. "You've hurt the man." The sights of my gun had scraped Stewart's ear, and blood trickled down the side of his cheek.

"He's an escaped prisoner. I can shoot to kill." But the good feeling had already begun to ebb, and I shoved Stewart back down into the chair.

"He's the wrong man in the wrong place," Doc said, as he pressed his handkerchief against Stewart's ear.

"Aiding and abetting a fugitive," I said. "That's ten years at hard labor."

"Who will do this county's doctoring?" Doc took off the handkerchief, hummed at what he saw, and told Stewart to hold the handkerchief on his ear. "Have a ginger ale with us, and we'll discuss the situation."

"Kate's dead," I said. "Lying on a steel slab in your basement. She's wearing a fucking sheet." Amos cackled something about a taxi. My head hurt, and I switched off the radio.

"Thomas was here with me when Kate was killed," Doc said. "You know he didn't have anything to do with her death."

Yeah, I knew that, but I wasn't about to admit it just yet. A wave of nausea washed through my stomach, adrenaline unrequited, unneeded. I pointed my gun at the far wall and eased the hammer down. "What the hell am I going to do now?" I asked no one in particular.

"How's Addison?" Stewart asked. The blood had trickled down onto his white shirt.

I raised my gun again. "I promise to God, I'm going to murder you."

"Your dog hopped in Doc's car," Stewart said. "We didn't have time to get him out. He wanted to come along."

"That's your story," I said, but I holstered my weapon.

"How'd you know?" Doc asked.

"You lied about the Sawyer kid," I said. "I ran into his dad. He told me Tommy was up in The Dalles bucking hay. I should have figured it out sooner. The tattoo, the camps, storm troopers, racial extinction, you stood by once while your people were obliterated. You couldn't stand by and let it happen again. Could you?"

"Nor could you, I think," Doc said. "How about that ginger ale?"

I had a hankering for a short snort, but thought better of voicing it. "Fine, but don't do anything stupid."

Doc laughed. "We've passed that point." He walked back into the upstairs kitchen.

"Doc says he knows a good lawyer," Stewart said. "Says he'll be able to take care of everything."

"I'll bet," I said.

"A smart, slimy Jew," Doc said from the kitchen. "Up in Portland. Gentleman by the name of Cohen."

"Are you suggesting that I become an accessory after the fact?" I asked. Stewart checked his ear again. The bleeding had stopped.

"Precisely." Doc came back in the room carrying a silver tray bearing three tumblers containing ice and ginger ale. The tray was a legacy from his dead wife, I imagined. "Mr. Cohen tells us that Thomas had a reasonable fear for his life. There was talk in the community of lynching him. It's happened here before. We all know that."

As far as I knew, there was just some jabbering of lynching Stewart, not serious talk. "The last lynching was sixty years ago for horse theft, not a racial thing. That sheriff wasn't around to stop it. I am." The ginger ale tasted sweet, like flowers and sunshine.

"I didn't know that," Stewart said, "but I'm still scared." The ice in his glass clinked from the shaking of his hand.

"The original charges aren't mine," I said. "The D.A. or Barnes will have to dismiss them."

"I know the governor," Doc said. "He'll make a call for me."

"Why doesn't that surprise me?" What to do? The proper thing, the legal thing, was to throw them both in the slammer. Stewart would be breaking rocks for the next few years. Doc might dodge that fate, or he might die in prison. Nothing in this affair was certain. Even with the adrenaline pumping in my system, I felt sleepy. My bones ached. My butt ached. My heart ached, and I had reached the point where I didn't know what to do next.

"What's your call, Matthew?" Doc asked.

I mulled it over a bit more. "I'll lodge Stewart in the Deschutes County jail, where he'll be safe. Your Mister Cohen can do what he can to free him. I won't mention anything about your role in this, Doc."

Doc nodded. "Thomas has to say where he's been all this time."

"Hiding out in the old Gearhart homestead," I said. "It's abandoned and isolated enough that no one would think of checking it, except an intrepid and very perceptive sheriff." A thin story at best. It might work; if not, my ass would be hanging in the wind.

"I like it," Doc said.

"Me, too," Stewart agreed.

I didn't love it, but it was the best we had to work with. "Finish your soda, Stewart," I said. "We're going for a ride."

"Sure. Can I see Addison first?"

I sighed. "He's in the truck." Dog and man had a great reunion with much slobbering and wagging of tail. I lodged Stewart in the Redmond calaboose, a bigger and better jail than mine. They had fulltime jailers and a sally port. Hell, I was still trying to figure out what in the hell a sally port was.

That night at home, I worked my way through a short case of Blitz beer. I should have known better. Beer always made me piss, and I was up all night shooing the ducks off the porch. Addison slept through it all until six in the morning, when he jumped on my chest and whined for his breakfast. Luckily for him, my gun was across the room.

*

Margie Weekly held down a sales clerk job at Bank Drug. I wandered in, took her by the elbow, and sat her down on a red-upholstered stool at the soda fountain that ran along the front side of the drug store. "I'm buying," I said, as I lit up a smoke.

"Can I have one of those?" she asked.

"Smoking stunts your growth," I said.

"I think they make you look old," she said. Not older, old.

"Order," I corrected.

"Chocolate malt," she said to the tall, dour man behind the counter.

"Cherry coke," I said.

She laughed. "Tough guy like you, drinking cherry coke."

"Tell me how serious you and Joey had gotten," I said.

She shrugged. "It was a summer romance. He was a popular boy. I'm a popular girl. Most kids thought we were fated to be together."

"But you weren't?"

"I honestly didn't like him that much," she said. "He was really moody. He'd cry sometimes. Tough guys don't cry, do they?" The soda jerk put our drinks on the counter.

I thought about the nights that lay before me, alone without Kate. "Did Joey give you his letterman's sweater?"

She sipped her malt and looked at herself in the mirror behind the counter. "He didn't even give me his ring."

"Did he talk about losing it?" I asked.

"He wore it when we went to the drive-in in June," she said. "That's about when we broke up."

My coke tasted of all that had been denied me when I was a kid. That's why I liked them, but I wouldn't tell Margie that. "After Joey, you picked up on Ronnie Gearhart."

"He's much nicer than Joey. Too bad his dad isn't a dentist." Some folks would have been shocked by the sixteen-year-old's pragmatic attitude. Not me.

"Did Joey's dad make a pass at you?" Her eyes didn't wander from the mirror, but I thought I detected a curled lip of disgust. Maybe, maybe not, I thought. But he wouldn't have gotten anywhere; this girl was in control of her destiny. I shifted gears again. "Joey was moody. Know why?"

She leaned close. "He was scared of Coach Conroy."

"About the sweater?"

"I don't know why," she said.

"He wouldn't talk about it." "I heard that the Coach slapped Joey once," I said.

"I don't think he ever hit him, but Joey was scared of him. Nothing else seemed to scare him, but Coach Conroy did. He threatened to kick Joey off the team if he didn't straighten up and fly right," she said. "That's how the Coach put it to him. 'Fly right,' he told me."

"Does the Coach frighten you?" I asked.

She shrugged as if the question didn't make sense. I asked her if Joey had any connections with Barnes or Harley. "Nope."

"What about Sam Gearhart?" I asked. "Any friction between him and Joey?"

"Mr. Gearhart's going to A.A.," she told me, as if it was a piece of juicy gossip. "I think Ronnie's adopted."

"That wasn't my question." The world seemed a little sour. I sipped more of my cola.

"Mr. Gearhart flirts with me," she said, "but he doesn't mean it."

"As opposed to Mr. McIntyre, who meant it?"

She shrugged, and I took that as a yes. That was the extent of my questions, so I downed my cola and stood to leave.

She put a hand on my arm. "Do you think I should cut my hair?" She pulled back her blond curls with her free hand. "Would that make me look older?"

"Trust me, kid," I said. "Stay young as long as you can." She looked at me like I was nuts. Maybe I was.

*

When I walked into his office, Judge Barnes looked as if someone had crapped in his boots. His square face seemed to lengthen, and his eyes were as black as my grandmother's firebox. "Nice to see you're up and about, Judge," I said. Barnes's secretary had kept me in his anteroom for over an hour before granting an audience. At times, my ill humor translated into being overly polite.

"Make it quick; I'm a busy man." He lit a cigar and blew smoke in my direction.

I followed suit with a Chesterfield I'd bummed from George. I hacked when the harsh smoke hit my lungs. "Things'll be the death of me."

"Haven't you done enough damage?" Barnes asked.

"I need to know where you were when Kate was killed," I said.

"Go fuck yourself, Harkness."

"You can tell me now, or I can ask every swinging dick in this county where you were. Ask enough questions and people will get the idea you have something to hide," I said.

He went to the window and gazed at the valley. "You're a son of a bitch."

"Guilty as charged, Your Honor."

"And a smartass to boot." He slid both hands across his bald head. "You're going to fuck me, aren't you?"

"Only if you murdered Kate."

Barnes sighed and took a bottle of bourbon from his sideboard. He poured two stiff shots and handed me one. "I was with Harley. He'll vouch for me."

"Where?" The Chesterfield was getting to me, and I snubbed it out.

"My place. We were having a cup of joe."

"Your alibi is a little thin, considering your relationship with the man." He didn't say anything, just glared at me. He reminded me of a hot steam boiler with the safety valve wired shut. "But I believe you. I don't know why I should, but I do." The safety valve popped open, and Barnes seemed to shrink a bit.

"We're thinking of moving to Cuba," Barnes said. "Harley and me."

I reached over, opened his humidor, and took out a cigar. "For the smokes, right? Fine Cuban tobacco."

"Mucho grande opportunity for a man down there," he said. "President Batista wants more American involvement. Corporate America is jumping on the bandwagon."

"You couldn't give up your power here," I said.

"Sun, sand, dusky-colored young men, what could be better?"

"Kate's death has addled your brains."

"It's hard for you to understand," he said. "But in my own way, I loved her very much."

I nodded and sipped the bourbon, smooth with a long finish. Why couldn't I afford booze like this? "Kate loved you, too. We talked about her leaving you, but she couldn't bring herself to do it." A little lie to ease the man's pain—I wasn't sure why.

"After you blab my affairs to the county," he said. "I'll have to leave the country."

"You've always figured you were the most important man in these parts, but I don't give a shit about you and Harley. It's not police business, and as far as I'm concerned you two can bugger your brains out."

The safety valve slapped shut, and the pressure began to build, but then his political brain kicked in. "What will it cost me?"

I held up my glass. "A bottle of this bourbon and a handful of cigars for Christmas."

"That's it?"

"And on my birthday," I said. "I may be a son of a bitch, but I do have my scruples."

"Maybe you just don't have enough imagination," Barnes said.

"Maybe."

"Fine." He handed me the half-full bottle of bourbon. "Here's a deposit on account. What now?"

"I track down the man that murdered Kate and the kids and murder him."

"Your scruples are showing," he said.

I stood to leave, but Barnes stopped me with a raised hand. "Governor McKay called to say that he asked the DA to drop the charges on your negro. Seems he's taken an interest in the man's case."

"He isn't a murderer."

"I assured the governor we'd exercise all due caution in the matter. The DA won't charge Stewart with murder, but he has made the decision to hold onto him as a material witness until the matter is resolved. The governor and I concur." Barnes gave me the queer eye trying to figure me out. "I wasn't aware you had friends in high places."

"Governor Patterson knows me like shit from shinola," I said.

"You're a dangerous man," Barnes said. "You bear watching."
"As do you," I said.
"Take your bottle and get out," he said.
"As you wish, Your Honor," I said.

*

Addison whinnied, whined, and shimmied as we drove up the dirt road to the Conroy place. We'd already driven by the practice field to make sure that Coach Conroy would be occupied while I talked with his wife.

Addison and Tippy danced like only dogs can do, then disappeared around the corner of the barn. Roberta scooted out from under her Chevy coupe. She wore work coveralls a couple of sizes too large for her. "You'll get the litter if that wiener dog knocks up Tippy."

"He's just being friendly," I said.

"Sure, like most men," she said. "Glad you found him."

"Everybody know about that?" I asked.

"Seems so," she said. "A fella's got to have his dog." She invited me up onto the shady porch, and when we settled, she asked, "This about those missing kids?"

"Partly." Trying to ease into things, I asked her how she and Conroy had met. She told me at Syracuse University when they were students. "Syracuse?" I asked. "I thought your husband went to school in Alabama."

"The accent," she said.

"That and the sweatshirt."

From the back of the house, the two dogs yipped happily. "Nolan wants people to think he's from the South. The best coaches are from the South, he says. The affectation is a fault in his character."

"So you're an eastern girl."

"Born and bred," she said. "But it's not bad here. The climate suits me, and I have my horses, my garden, and my friends." Her friends? I never saw her with anyone in town. The dogs reappeared from behind the house, and Addison seriously sniffed Tippy's nether parts. "Your dog been fixed?"

"Addison, come here!" I ordered. "Sit." Roberta whistled for Tippy, and our dogs settled at our feet, calm for the moment, but eying each other with a certain yearning.

"You're right," I said. "This is about the kids. Did you know Joey McIntyre or Virginia Kelly?"

"Nolan brought the team up here during the summer to bring in the hay and dig out a spring. It got mudded over during the March rains. Joey was one of many. I never saw Virginia. A shame. I really do hope you catch whoever did this." She said it with such conviction that I tended to believe her.

"Anything about Joey stand out?" Addison tried to get up. I scratched him behind the ears and pushed him back down again.

"Do you think Nolan was involved somehow?" Her eyes were veiled. She'd had practice concealing her emotions.

"Of course not," I said. "I'm just trying to get a handle on Joey, talking with people that might have known him."

"Maybe he seemed a little more obnoxious than the rest of the boys."

"It sounds like you don't cotton to teenagers," I said.

"Just the boys," she said.

"Did any of them leave anything up here? Maybe clothing?" I asked, fishing about the letterman's sweater.

"No," she said.

I thought about lighting a smoke, but thought I'd better ask first. She told me to blow the smoke away from her. From her expression, it was obvious she didn't approve, so I decided not to smoke. I motioned up to Twelve Mile Table and told her that the person who'd shot Kate had done it from up there. I asked if she'd ever been up there.

"Nolan and I tried to drive up there last fall," she said. "Looking to get ourselves a buck, but the road had been washed out and was impassable. Nolan said it would be too much trouble to pack up there and back on horseback. Shame about Mrs. Barnes. We weren't friends, but she was always pleasant to me."

"She was pleasant with everyone." Talking about her made me ache again. "So if I wanted to get up onto the Table from this end, I wouldn't be able to drive up?"

"Fixing roads isn't high on priorities for the BLM," she said. "Do you ride? I could loan you a horse."

"Not much of a horseman," I said.

"Long hike to the top without a horse," she said. "Maybe you could use a jeep."

I laughed. "County won't spring for one. Is there a back way up to Barnes Butte from here, other than up and over the Table?"

"Up Camp Creek Road," Roberta said. "Ten miles of dust and washboard track, but a fellow could get through if he had a mind to."

"Do you hunt up there, too?"

She shook her head. “Redmond land. He’s not keen on giving permission to hunters. What kind of man would kill two kids?”

“Someone who has his own notion of right and wrong. Someone who believes he’s better than everyone else. Someone with more rage bottled up than we can imagine.” At odd moments, deep in the morning hours, I wondered if I had enough rage to murder someone without just cause.

“They’d be easy to spot,” she said.

“Not necessarily. Certain types of men are experts at hiding their emotions.”

“Some women, too,” she noted.

“Some women, too,” I said. We chit-chatted for a bit and watched the anvil-shaped clouds build in the south. Another big storm coming, I thought. Not today, but maybe tomorrow afternoon. I’d run out of questions, so I thanked Roberta for talking with me, and she saw Addison and me to my truck.

“Remember, you get the litter,” she said.

“They’ll look like movie stars,” I said.

“I really do hope you find whoever did this. People can be such beasts. Let me know if I can help.”

As we left, Addison cast longing glances out the window at Tippy. “In your dreams, my bucko.” But I couldn’t help envying him. He’d found someone he loved, and I was lonesome as a man could be. On the way back to my place, I cracked open the bottle Barnes had given me and tipped it up.

Chapter 18

Only half-full, Barnes's bottle didn't last long and, God help me, I wanted to be around people, so I slipped through the back door into the Spur Roadhouse. I figured Tony might be there chasing after the bank clerk or Catherine Steelhammer. I was wrong; he hadn't shown up yet.

As I walked through the crowd, folks avoided me as if a cloud of mustard gas surrounded me. I sidled up to the bar, and a couple of cowboys sidled away. Up on stage, the blond Olive Oyl dressed in buckskins yodeled her way through the latest Hank Williams song. Hank's song sounded awfully true to me at the moment.

Along about one in the morning, my fifth of whiskey was gone, and I realized I had a sweet buzz, but I stewed on Kate and my investigation enough that I didn't have the gumption to get stumbling drunk, so I'd decided to leave when someone touched my elbow. Tony, I thought, but it was the blond torch singer that I'd spent the entire night trying to ignore.

"My dear Olive," I said.

She'd obviously heard that one before and acted as if I'd shot her dog. "My name is Prudence," she said. "Prudence Knight."

"Of course it is." I doffed my imaginary hat. "Pardon my error." I told her I was the sheriff around these parts. "My friends call me Matt. Your singing is one of a kind."

She tee-heed, showing me all her teeth, and said, "My favorite uncle was a famous detective in Kansas City. I do admire men in uniform."

That may have included swabbies and jarheads, but she was starting to look better to me, so I held my tongue and signaled Jeanie for a couple more whiskeys. Prudence knocked the first one back neat as you please, and I signaled for another. "Would you like to hear about the time I caught a gang of bank robbers that had drifted up here from Kentucky on a crime spree?" I asked, and she cuddled up all warm and nice and said yes, so I ignored my conscience and spun my yarn.

We downed a couple more whiskeys and took a turn or two on the dance floor, whirling in our drunken way a passable Tennessee waltz. She told me I was a great dancer, and I told her she sang like a song sparrow. She went up on stage one last time, and sang "Long Gone

Lonesome Blues," which almost made me want to cry. When she came back, she suggested we go back to my place; I said, "Oh, yeah." How in the hell had I grown up into such a stupid son of a bitch?

*

"What do you take in your coffee, Sweetie?" Prudence called from the kitchen. Light beat feebly against the Venetian blinds barely bright enough to be called dawn.

"Don't settle in," I yelled. "I'm a solitary man." I didn't want to be mean, but my peter was chapped, I lay on a wet spot, and a strange woman knocked around my kitchen.

Prudence appeared at the bedroom doorway carrying two cups of coffee, a dish towel over her arm, and wearing nothing else. She was the skinniest woman I'd ever seen short of the pictures of dead Jews in the death camps. "My, aren't you Mr. Grumpy this morning," she said. I sipped her coffee and made a face. Sugar. "You didn't have any cream," she said, "so I put in a couple of extra lumps." She sat cross-legged on the bed next to me. She proved not to be a true blonde, but I was in no position to grumble. She picked up the book from my bedside table. Raymond Chandler. "You have more books than any man I've ever seen."

"Did you hear what I said? Don't settle in. My life is shit at the moment."

"Oh, sweetie. I'm not possessive. My band and I are off to Baker County this coming Monday, and we won't be back in this burg until next spring." Her face shifted, and the blank look disappeared. "I never expect much from a man like you."

"A man like me?" That hurt a bit. "What are you doing with a man like me?"

"Women have needs just like men."

At another time, that concept might bear more exploration, but at that moment, I only felt dirty and cynical. "The tee-hee stuff was an act."

"I do have an uncle in Kansas City." Addison, who had shown canine discretion and stayed in the kitchen during the night, poked his nose in the door, sniffed the wind, then promptly jumped on the bed and cuddled in Prudence's lap. She scratched under his chin. "Cute dog."

Fickle son of a bitch. "Don't get me started," I said.

"Terrible, all them murders," she said. "Those kids and Kate

Barnes all dead."

For a bit, I'd almost forgotten the dead: Virginia, Joey, and Kate, but now Prudence had brought them back. I wanted to hate her for it. "Terrible," I said.

"Matt." She rested her hand on my thigh. "You'll solve them. I have confidence in you." She looked so earnest, so sure of me with almost little girl admiration, that I realized the tee-hee girl wasn't all an act.

"How would your uncle in Kansas City have solved the case?"

"He was an asshole," she said.

"Not famous?"

"Yes, famous, too," she said sipping her coffee, "but still an asshole. He made a pass at me when I was thirteen. I told my Dad, but he didn't believe me. I ran away the next year, been on my own ever since."

I wasn't particularly interested in her life story, but it was too early in the a.m. to be rude. "Asshole, I've got," I said. "Why famous?"

"He solved the Crowley kidnapping case. It was on the front pages for months."

I dimly recalled the case. Baby girl disappeared from a rich meatpacking family, cryptic ransom note, daddy playing hide the weenie with the upstairs maid, mommy had the hots for the gardener. "If I remember correctly, didn't the brother-in-law and the gardener fry for that one?"

She nodded. "The little girl suffocated in the trunk of the brother-in-law's car. Uncle Dick told me that he had a hunch—a fair hunch, he said—that the gardener was in cahoots. The gardener knew where the boy was being held. Uncle Dick figured the gardener didn't have the stomach for the crime, so he lied to the guy and told him if he talked he wouldn't fry. When that didn't work, he beat on him until he told where they'd hidden the little girl. When they got there, it was too late."

"Sometimes you have to be an asshole to get the job done," I said.

"But you wouldn't make a pass at a thirteen-year-old girl." She uncrossed her legs and unfolded herself into a standing position. "I need a ride back to town." When she put on her buckskin dress, Addison looked stricken.

"Thanks." I pulled on my trousers.

"Don't give me money," she said.

"No, it was a great night, and I won't insult you. But you have given me an idea on how to attack my investigation."

"By beating someone up?" she asked.

"No, of course not," I said, wondering who I'd crack first.

"I'm sorry," she said.

"For what?"

"Your grim look means violence," she said.

"It's an occupational hazard," I said.

"I'm sorry about your lady friend, too."

"Don't forget your bag," I said.

Addison sat in Prudence's lap all the way to town. When I dropped her off at the Barnestown Inn, she told me she'd give me a call when she got back in the county. It was eighty-five degrees out and barely eight in the morning. Budding thunderheads built in the southern horizon.

*

My first stop of the day was the newspaper office. Ed Dilkes stood hunched over a table of type. He wore suspenders and an ink-stained undershirt that hadn't seen a washing machine for years. "Sheriff," he said when he saw me, "I've been aggrieved you haven't been by to question me."

"Aggrieved?"

"Yes, sir, aggrieved." He picked the one lit cigarette out from a thicket of snubbed butts in a white ashtray and stuck it between his lips. "I was wondering when you'd get around to asking me where I was when Kate was killed." Both of his cheeks were smudged with ink.

"You were, eh?"

"Seems only natural that you'd be checking up on the folks at the poker game that morning. Seems likely that whoever shot Kate was there. Someone went up on Twelve Mile Table with a purpose, and only a few of us knew where you were going."

"Maybe I told someone else," I said.

"Did you?"

"Nope."

"You're pretty particular about keeping things to yourself," he said. "Once I realized what was going on with you and Kate, I figured you wouldn't tell everyone about your assignation."

"It just came out," I said.

He nodded. "Want a cup of joe?"

"Pass. I've tasted your coffee." In truth, my stomach was sour. I sat on a high stool. "Where were you when she was killed?"

"Prineville," he said. "Covering the livestock auction. Feeder cattle are cheap. Hogs are overpriced."

"Lots of witnesses," I said.

"A whole slew." He stubbed out his cigarette and lit another.

"Refresh my memory," I said. "Who all was at the barbershop?"

"Me, you, Barnes, Harley, Sam, and Coach Conroy," Dilkes said. "Herb was out in front, but he didn't close up that afternoon."

"Someone said that Harley used to be a spy," I said. "Any truth to that?"

Dilkes shrugged. "Doubtful he was involved. He and Judge Barnes have a regular rendezvous most afternoons. They wouldn't do something that heinous to call attention to themselves."

"Might make a spicy headline," I said. That pretty much verified what Barnes had told me.

"Yellow journalism doesn't play well in these parts. Folks like their gossip over the back fence."

"And Sam?"

"The man took the pledge," Dilkes said. "He couldn't care a whit about you and Kate. He's completely taken up with his family life right now."

"That pledge business ain't gonna last," I said.

"Maybe so, maybe not. It's a hard road."

"His kid vouches for him," I said. "Wife, too."

"And so that leaves us..."

"With Coach Conroy," I finished. "But you knew that before I did."

"You weren't in your right mind," he said.

"That I wasn't." Still wasn't, but he knew that.

"You'll need proof," he said.

"Some kids know more than they're telling. I'm working on it."

He wished me luck and asked for an exclusive.

"Hell's sakes. Who else would I call?"

*

I wanted to wrap up all the loose ends, so I stopped by Okie town to speak with the Kellys next. Addison jumped from the truck and raced after a chattering chipmunk. Ethan had an old Buick transmission disassembled with the parts tumbled across the bare-scrabble back yard. I told him I had a couple more questions about his daughter, and we sat in the shadows and dust under an elm tree.

"Storm coming," he said. The thunderheads had built up to a considerable height, colored both fluffy white and dark purple and stretching across the southern horizon. "Looks she's gonna bust around late afternoon."

"Wanted to ask you about some folks that might have known your daughter."

He looked all sorrowful, and I thought maybe I was intruding on his grief, but he told me he wasn't home much and didn't know anything about Virginia's friends. "Faith would know," he said, referring to his oldest daughter. He called her name loud enough to make the dog in the next yard take up barking.

The girl opened the screen door and stepped out onto the stoop. She wore a mended and remended blue print cotton dress that looked too old for her. I figured it had been handed down from her mama, and one day had been destined for Virginia. She had a dull look in her eyes as if this life had already sapped her of her spark, or maybe it had never been there. Maybe Virginia had all the brains. "Come here," her daddy said. "Tell the sheriff what he needs to know, and don't you hold nothin' back."

The girl nodded, but wouldn't come too close or sit with me under the elm. I stood, but kept the distance between us. "Just me and her," I told Ethan. He nodded, none too pleased, but told Faith it would be fine.

I won't hurt you," I said after we were alone. "I need your help to find the man who hurt your sister. Do you understand that?"

She wrapped her arms around herself. "I'm scared."

"Did someone threaten you?" I asked.

"Just scared," she said.

"Are you scared of your father?" I asked.

She looked as if she had never considered that possibility before. "Just a little."

"Did he ever hurt your sister?"

Something flashed in her eyes, envy perhaps. "No, Virginia was his favorite." Addison trotted up to her, sniffed her feet, and settled on his haunches.

"He wants you to pet him," I said.

"Oh." She went down on one knee and slid her fingers across his long back.

"How about you or your mother? Does your father ever hit either of you?"

"Daddy works all the time; he's not home much." She said this as if the abandonment was as bad as being hit. "Have you been to Portland?"

"Sure," I said.

"Someone told me there's a hotel there just for women. That it's safe there. Maybe I could get a job in Portland and live in that hotel."

"Stay in school, graduate first," I advised. "These days, a high school diploma is important."

"Mama will miss me when I'm gone."

"She'll be proud of you," I said.

She nodded as if I had imparted a great kernel of wisdom. I motioned for her to sit under the elm, and she folded down with her legs tucked beneath her, and Addison curled up next to her.

"Do you know Margie Weekly?" I asked.

"She don't talk to me, or Virginia neither. We're Okies."

"What about Mike Barfield?"

"Mike has a crush on Virginia," she said.

I didn't correct her language. "How did she feel about him?"

"She thought he was sweet. They were best friends."

"Could he have hurt her?"

"I'm not scared of him," she said, as if that answered my question. Addison had fallen asleep and was snoring softly.

"Virginia was having an affair with Dr. McIntyre. Did you talk about that?"

"An affair?"

"They were seeing each other on the sly. Did you know she was seeing an older man?"

"I caught her sneaking out one night, and I knew she was seeing someone, but she wouldn't tell me who. She told me it was a secret."

"What about Coach Conroy? Did she mention anything about him?"

"Just that Joey was scared of him," she said.

"Joey McIntyre's letterman's sweater is missing. Did he give it to Virginia?"

She told me it wasn't in the house. I pointed to a small shed and asked if she would have hidden it in there. "Go ahead and see," she said. The shed was dark and musty, and Addison went in first. Someone had taken the trouble to sweep the hard-packed earth floor. Nails, lock washers, and bolts were sorted by size into small jars. The tools were old, almost ancient, but well-sharpened and oiled. I turned the place over as gently as I could and found nothing of interest other than a broken china-head doll hidden in a shoe box on a lower shelf.

Faith held it to her breast, and said, "She's mine. I didn't want to hand it down to my little sister. That's bad, isn't it?"

"No, honey. It's not a sin to want keep something for yourself."

Chapter 19

The clock ticked past noon, and Addison whined with hunger. "Just a moment, little guy. We need to talk to this kid first, then we'll rustle you up something to eat." He whined again. Why should I expect a dog to understand me?

Barfield wasn't at school, so I tracked him down at his house, a 1910 two-story saltbox near the center of town. His mother, a once-pretty woman just past forty, had one eye clouded with a cataract. She put her hand to her mouth when she recognized me.

"No worries," I said. "Your son isn't in any trouble. I just want to ask him some questions." I found him wearing cutoffs and a t-shirt and mowing the backyard. The newly mown grass smelled sweet.

"Looks good," I said.

The mower stopped, but the blades kept whirring for a few seconds. "I'll mow your lawn for a buck," Barfield said. "Trim the edges, too."

"I don't have a lawn," I said.

"Really?"

"No shit," I said. "But I'm not here about gardening. I want to know about the coach and Joey McIntyre."

"Sure," he said.

"Why did the Coach slap Joey the week before the murders?"

"I don't have a clue," Barfield said.

I stepped in closer. I wanted him to smell my bad breath. I wanted to taste his fear. "Don't shit a shitter. Tell me about Coach and Joey. Was it about football or something else?"

"I don't know what you mean," he said.

"You know." He made to turn away, but I balled up his t-shirt in my fist and pulled him close.

"Don't," he said.

"Coach ever slap you?" I asked.

"I'm just the manager," he said.

"Michael, two of your classmates are dead, some asshole splattered my girlfriend's brains on the rocks, Judge Barnes is pissed at me, and I'm really hung over. I'm through fucking around, and I feel a might bit crazy right now. You wouldn't fuck with a crazy man, would you?"

"He'll kill me," Barfield said.

I twisted the t-shirt, dug my fist into his neck, and slammed him into the side of the house. "Trust me. I'll protect you."

He laughed then, and I was so surprised that I let him go. "Something funny?" I asked.

"Kids tease me, kick me around every day," he said. "You don't protect me from them. The teachers don't protect me. You talk, and you get it worse."

"Kids piss you off, huh?"

His face reddened. "Sometimes I think about killing them."

"Joey?"

"Especially him."

"How would you do it?"

"Shotgun," he said. "In the face."

"And Virginia?"

"I'd never hurt her."

"You loved her?" I asked.

He pulled at his t-shirt, trying to straighten it out. "I didn't kill Joey, either. That's not something I could do."

"Do you think Coach Conroy killed Joey and Virginia?" He wanted to clam up, tried to turn away, so I caught him by the shoulder, spun him back around, and punched him in the sternum, gentle-like, no more than you'd do with a baby, just enough to give him a taste. That loosened him up.

"I walked into the locker room late after practice one evening. I was washing jocks and socks. Everyone was supposed to be gone, and I was supposed to be alone, but Coach Conroy was in there with Joey. They scrambled when I came in like they were doing something. Coach had a... a..."

"Hard-on?"

Barfield nodded. "Joey said he'd kill me if I told anyone."

"What did Conroy say?"

"He just smiled, patted me on the cheek, and told me it was time to go home. The look in his eyes scared me more than Joey's threats."

"Dead eyes?"

"No," he said. "Like fire. Like he was thrilled."

The kid shivered as if he was cold, but the afternoon was hot and humid. In the south, the thunderheads looked like giant anvils. They were headed north, and I already imagined I could hear the thunder, feel the crash of the lightning. "You did the right thing," I said.

"He'll kill me, won't he?"

I put my hand on his shoulder, and he winced. "No, he won't. I guarantee it."

The screen door screeched open behind me. "Honey," Mrs. Barfield said. "Are you okay?"

"Don't worry, ma'am," I said. "He's going to be just ducky." On the way to my truck, I spit on the grass trying to get the sour taste out of my mouth.

*

"Saddle up," I said to George when I entered the office. "We're going to get the bad guy."

"Who?" he asked.

"Coach Conroy."

"No shit," he said.

"I shit you not," I said.

"You have enough for the arrest?" he asked.

"I have enough to arrest him for molesting Joey McIntyre. Murder can't be far behind."

"We should raise the posse," George said.

"Not enough time, I'll call Tony," I said. "The three of us should be able to handle this." George nodded and set about gathering guns and ammo. When I called the State Police Office in Bend, they told me Tony was working an injury accident over by Culver. It would be an hour before he could join us. "He'll meet us up there," I told George. A little lie, I didn't want to wait. Tony would make it sooner or later.

"Shotgun or carbine?" George asked.

I took the Mossberg 12-gauge shotgun. "You're a finer shot than I am."

George settled for the lever action Winchester .30-30. "Suits me." He stuffed the extra ammo in a couple of army surplus bags and handed me the one with the shotgun shells. I called up to Miriam and told her we were headed up to the Conroy place. She worried on me a bit, then told us to be careful.

"Send in the troops if we're not back in a couple of hours," I said.

*

A lightning bolt cracked a telephone pole alongside the road splitting it from the crosstie to the base. My ears hummed, and for a moment I thought I was still in New Guinea head down in some muddy slit trench ducking Nip mortar rounds. Approaching Conroy's driveway, we saw the lightning jumping into the crowns of great junipers halfway up Twelve Mile Table. After I parked, George pulled up behind, and Addison jumped out from the pickup bed and skipped around me. "I thought I told you to leave that dog at the office," I said.

George shrugged. "He's your dog, not mine."

Roberta Conroy walked down the driveway to meet us. She was beat all to shit with a split lip and blackened eye. "Someone whupped your ass," George said, stating the obvious. Her nose canted off to the left.

"Fucker shot my dog," she said.

"Your husband?" I asked.

She handed me a piece of knitted blue cloth, a letterman's sweater. "It's Joey's," she said. "I got to thinking about what you told me, that the murderer could be anyone, could act normally. Nolan has his eccentricities, I have mine, but after you and I talked, I got to thinking. He has a footlocker out in the smoke shack. I jimmied the lock, found the boy's sweater and some guns inside. I was fixing to come into town to tell you when he discovered what I'd been up to. He punched me." She pushed up her chin to show me her black eye.

"He broke your nose," I said.

"Fair's fair," she said. "Duchess jumped him, and he threw her off him and shot her down. I hit him over the head with a shovel. While he was down, I ran and hid, stayed down by the creek 'til he left."

"Maybe you should have hit him again with the shovel when he was on the floor," I said. "Know which way he'll be headed? Maybe north on Camp Creek Road, it eventually meets up with the Burns Highway."

"Doubtful." She smiled an evil smile and tossed me a handful of wires. "Pulled the sparkplug wires on his truck while he was down."

"So he's somewhere around here?" George asked.

Roberta shook her head. "He took one of the horses."

I thought about it a bit. He'd already been up on Twelve Mile Table. The old Gearhart homestead was up there. A good place to spend the night. "He'll head for the high country. It won't be easy for us."

Roberta nodded in agreement. "There were hand grenades in the trunk, too. He brought them back from the war. Used some last fall for cleaning trash fish out of the pond."

I shifted gears and used her phone to call Dirk Redmond and have him bring the posse. Then I called the State Police and told them to have troopers stationed at the two roads down from Twelve Mile

Table.

"I'm going with you," she said when I came out.

"Nope, he could still be up there. Hiding in ambush. Pick us off one by one. Take my truck into town. Go see Doc and have him straighten out that nose."

Something yipped from the barn. When we got inside, I realized that I had to shoot the fucking dog. Not mine, but Duchess. The coach had gut-shot her and left her gasping on the hard-packed earth. She whined a bit when Roberta came close. The flies circled waiting for the end, and Addison whined and barked at her with wary concern. "I'll do it," I said to Roberta. "It has to be done. You understand that." She nodded, but I didn't tell her it was harder for me to kill an animal than a man. Killing men became too easy during a war.

George picked up Addison, placed his free arm around Roberta's shoulders, and gently guided them outside. When we were alone, Duchess looked at me. I didn't know what she was thinking, maybe she wanted to tell me it was alright. But maybe that was just my imagination, a requiem for a high-country sheriff. I knew my .45 would be too loud for this place, too loud for Duchess. Maybe she was one of those dogs that got spooked by gunshots. I stood back to avoid the blood splatter and pulled the trigger. The round entered behind her ear. "Good dog." I walked deeper into the barn. My ears rang, and I smelled ozone from the storm, the hay drying in the loft, and horse manure.

I went outside and circled to the front. "We can bury her for you," I said, not really wanting to waste the time, but she told me she'd do it. George and I decided to search the ranch just in case Conroy had doubled back. We leapfrogged from building to building, but it soon became apparent that Conroy had fled. In the smokehouse, we found the open footlocker containing a half-dozen pineapple grenades. Roberta came in and told us there had originally been twenty or more. Conroy had stashed some guns under some loose boards. The most notable was a water-cooled .30 caliber machine gun, the kind we used for perimeter defense in the jungle. Underneath it were coils of bright brass shells in belts, a few thousand rounds at least. I had killed more than one man with a gun like this. It was too heavy for Conroy to haul on horseback, just as it would be too heavy for George and me. Roberta told us that there had been a Thompson submachine gun in the footlocker; gone now, something else to worry on once we got close to him.

The corral was empty. Conroy must have scared off the rest. We kept looking, and Roberta found a couple of horses grazing on alfalfa in the back pasture. One was a swaybacked mare she called Daisy and the other a two-year-old gelding named Parker. The sun had sagged low on the horizon, and I felt like I was going to jump out of my skin.

"We're going to have to take your horses," I said to Roberta. "You should meet the posse on the way to town. Tell them we're headed up onto the Table, and that I'm figuring your husband will hole up in the old Gearhart homestead tonight."

"I'll help you saddle up," she said. "You'll have to ride Daisy. George is too big for her for a trip that long. He can ride the dapple gray."

"Can Daisy handle me?"

"She used to be quite saucy in her day," Roberta said. "Rather, the question is, can you handle her?"

Daisy and I stared each other down, neither of us willing to break off first. Finally, the horse whinnied and nuzzled Roberta. She patted her nose. "She'll be fine," she said. "She's not as mean as she seems."

"Why am I not reassured?"

At another time, Roberta might have laughed. Instead, she set about gathering her horses. I went back into the smokehouse, scooped up the rest of the grenades, and looked yearningly at the machine gun. Too heavy. Maybe the posse could haul it up the grade. If Conroy had indeed holed up at the old Gearhart homestead, we might have to lay siege to the place.

Chapter 20

"Your dog is still following us," George said.

Addison's little legs pumped hard as he scampered between the legs of the horses. Sooner or later one of them would kick him in the head.

"A man loves his dog," he said.

Addison skipped and yipped and dodged to avoid Daisy's hooves. "Fine, fine," I said to myself and reined in. I picked up Addison and slung him across my saddle horn. He'd made his point. The little guy woofed and looked up at me as if I was his personal god. What does a damned dog know?

Lightning hopped from cloud to cloud, the flashes highlighting the tops of the tall cumulus clouds. A rain shower engulfed us as we worked our way across the flats. Fat drops plopped on our heads like globs of pigeon shit falling in the big city. A moment after the rain ended, all traces of moisture sunk into the porous soil. Only the smell of ozone remained to remind us of the rain, that and the low rumble of thunder that sunk into our bones.

The land here rolled a bit, but was primarily flat, spotted with juniper, sage, and red volcanic rock that afforded us little cover. At one place, erosion and a dirt road battled. Erosion, as it always did, had won, and we had to pick our way up and down the new gully.

A half-cocked barbed-wire fence butted up against the north side of the road. The hand-cut juniper posts canted this way and that as if the makers hadn't bothered to sink their anchor postholes deep enough in the earth. Part of me wanted to stop and fix them with pick and shovel and sweat.

Lightning reached out and split a juniper on top of the ridge in front of us. The splintered trunk glowed in the purple light. George mentioned that the sun had sunk to a point where it would be difficult for us to work our way up the coming grade in the dark. We chewed it over a bit and decided we would hole up in a juniper copse near the base of the rimrock. We rode on.

"Ain't got no blankets," George said.

"You've got plenty of insulation." I swatted at a mosquito flitting around my nose. They pursued us with a determined hunger, whining around our heads. We were easier targets than the coyote and jackrabbits that normally roamed this part of the high desert. We should have stocked up on bug juice and rations before we left, but I was an impatient man.

"Why you think he did it?" George asked.

"Evil, sick, jealous," I said. "How in the hell should I know?"

"Jealous of Joey?"

"The other way around," I said. "Jealous of Virginia, jealous that she'd take the boy away from him."

"So he's a perverted homosexual." He stretched the final word out as if it had six syllables.

"Homosexuals aren't necessarily evil, nor are they necessarily perverts." I thought of Judge Barnes and Harley. "But Conroy, he's a man who preys on kids, for the power, not the sex, a sick, rabid animal..." Daisy snorted and tossed her head.

"Who should be shot like a dog," George finished. Addison yipped, and he added, "Present company excepted."

I thought about executing Roger back in the New Guinea jungle with a simple, quick round to the head. I wanted to tell George that we weren't executioners, just cops, but I wasn't sure I wanted to believe that. "Maybe," I said.

"Why Kate?" George asked.

"At first I thought it was because she was getting too close. She wanted to help out, and I let her talk with high school kids and the victims' mothers." My stomach felt tight. "Conroy probably heard from one of the kids that she was poking around. One of them had to know something rotten was going on. Maybe she did find out, but maybe she didn't know that she had uncovered something important. Maybe Conroy just wanted to make this a personal affair between us. Maybe for him this is all a game. I plan to ask him when I see him." I laughed, but wasn't sure why.

Addison whined, and I figured he was thirsty, so we pulled up a couple of hundred yards from the juniper copse and drank some water from our canteens. I formed a cup with my hands for Addison, and he lapped up the water. George and I discussed having a bite to eat, but we decided to wait until we reached camp. Dinner would consist of what we had scrounged from our trucks--venison jerky, white bread and candy bars. Compared to shit on a shingle or C-rations, what we had would be just fine by me.

We started up again and had almost reached the stand of juniper when Addison barked and flushed a magpie from a stand of sagebrush. The black-and-white bird burst out with an ugly squawk. Both horses snorted, and the big gray gelding George rode skittered sideways like horses did in the rodeo parade. The skitter probably saved George's life.

I didn't hear the whir this time, just saw George spin off his horse with blood spraying in an arc. His horse bumped Daisy, and the boom of the shot came next. Addison and I flew ass backward off Daisy. I tossed the dog to my left hoping he'd get clear of the falling bodies, then I thumped down flat on my back. My wind woofed out, and I lay there stunned for a moment.

A bullet pinged the red rock next to me, and I rolled behind it. The horses fled into the junipers with Addison in hot pursuit. I thought George was dead, but then he moaned. I stumbled over to him, grabbed him under his armpits, and pulled him to cover. "You could lose a couple of pounds," I said.

"I can walk," he said. Another round whizzed over our heads.

I helped him to his feet. "Run!" We half-sprinted, half-stumbled into the stand of junipers.

George slumped against a rough-barked juniper trunk while I tried to staunch the blood with the palm of my hand. The shot had gone through his shoulder. Conroy was using steel-jacketed military ammo.

"A fine mess you've gotten us into," George said. His face was pasty. God, don't let him go into shock.

"You'll live," I said. He was right about the mess. My eagerness to capture Conroy had overcome my good sense.

"You may regret that," he said, laughing.

I surveyed our situation. The Conroy place lay three-hours walk behind us. Our horses were gone, no food and no water. George's bleeding had slowed, but he needed to see Doc soon. Oh yeah, my damned dog had scampered off again.

"What now?" George asked.

"We'll have to wait until dark to move. We can't stay here. Conroy knows where we are. Maybe a half-hour until we go, maybe less."

George coughed. "I can't go far."

"I'll figure something out." But I wasn't sure what. I could stash George somewhere and walk out for help, stash him and go after Conroy, or hunker down somewhere and wait for the posse. They'd be along a couple hours after daybreak, I figured. Long night in any case, I wasn't looking forward to it.

The darkness crept over us, and we gathered ourselves to move. Something rustled at the far side of the thicket. I pulled my .45 and hoped that George wouldn't feel the need to moan.

Something rustled again, and something big moved through the darkness. Maybe a mule deer, maybe a man. I waited, wanting to be sure of my target. A branched cracked. I aimed my .45, and Addison barked. He nipped at Daisy's heels, pushing her before him. She kicked at his head with her hind hooves, and he skittered away. When Daisy came close, I grabbed her reins. She whinnied and nuzzled me as if glad to see me. The food was gone, but one canteen still hung over the saddle horn. The 12-gauge shotgun rested snug in the scabbard, and the saddlebags with the grenades were still there. I smiled and stroked Daisy's sleek neck. My little game with Conroy wasn't done, after all.

Addison sniffed George, whined, and licked his hand. Even in the dim light, George seemed to be looking better. I patted Addison's head, and said, "Good dog." I asked George if he could ride. He said yes, so I told him that he should ride Daisy back down the road toward the Conroy ranch, meet up with posse, and send them back to me. I'd make sure that Conroy didn't double-back down this way.

"You'll wait for reinforcements, then?" George asked.

"Sure," I rummaged through the saddlebags and found a couple of bandanas. They'd work for bandages.

"Bullshit."

"Get up on the horse," I said.

"Roberta said she's too small for me." I secured the bandanas with his belt. They'd hold until he reached the Conroy ranch.

"She'll make it back," I said. "She's as tough as you are."

"You could walk with me," he said.

"I'll slow you up."

"But—" he said.

"Orders." I felt guilty for wanting to get rid of him and be the first one at the Gearhart homestead. "You'll need to get moving. The moon will rise in a while. Light everything up. Big lug like you'd make a jim-dandy target."

"You're the sheriff," he said.

"And don't you forget it." I placed his foot into the stirrup and, with some grunting from both of us, he crawled onto Daisy's back.

I watched George's hulking form fade in the darkness. "It's just you and me, boy," I said to Addison. I couldn't see him, but I heard his tail swishing back and forth on the sandy ground. I considered hiking up the road, but realized I'd break a leg in the dark. Better to wait for moonrise or dawn. Finding comfort with all the rock on the ground was near impossible, but I did the best I could, scraping out a bare spot in the earth behind an ancient juniper. A few stubborn sharp stones poked up, but we could work around those.

Once we were settled, I lit a cigarette. Cover was good enough that Conroy wouldn't get a bead on us. Addison's eyes reflected green in the light of my match. He looked at me with such blind trust that I felt inadequate. "We'll wait here a bit," I said. "Sorry to say, we can't have a fire. We'll have to dry camp and save our water for the morning." Addison didn't seem to mind. He clambered into my lap, circled three times, and settled down. In a trice, he was asleep.

I awoke twice during the night. I'd expected to dream, a dream full of portents and omens, or a nightmare perhaps, but my sleep was dreamless. The first time I awoke, the moon had risen and shone directly in my eyes. I scooted us around to the far side of the juniper. A fair ways to the east an animal howled. My imagination wanted to believe it was a wolf, but they'd been hunted out of this country by the turn of the century. Must have been a coyote or a feral dog.

The second time I awoke, the chill of the desert night tugged me from my sleep. My teeth chattered, and I lay on the ground in a fetal position surrounding Addison's warm little body. False dawn lay on the eastern horizon, so it must have been around four o'clock. To the south, there was another glow, a rosy one that silhouetted Twelve Mile Table. There wasn't moon nor sun in that direction. It could have been the faraway lights of a town, maybe Prineville. But in my gut I knew it wasn't. I lay awake until the real dawn, fretting about what lay ahead.

Chapter 21

Nighthawks, silent and daring, wheeled through the junipers. They were sleek black birds with a white spot on the tip of each wing. I walked among them, and they paid me no heed, just zoomed past me, banking in tight turns like nimble fighters. I remembered that the old-timers called them mosquito hawks. There must have been a hundred of them diving and wheeling through the trees, a sight a city person wasn't likely to see. Didn't these hawks usually do this dance in the evenings? Then I smelled wood smoke, juniper, and sage, pungent and acrid.

The rosy glow of early morning had become a dense red haze. Twelve Mile Table was aflame, or at least part of it. Lightning-caused blazes, I supposed. No man up on the Table this morning to start a fire except for Conroy, and he was killer crazy, not stupid.

I'd helped fight a few fires in my time as sheriff, usually a single ridge-top tree snag struck by lightning or some rancher's haystack up in flames. It was hot, dirty work that I didn't enjoy. The BLM boys usually let fires like this run unless they threatened structures or private property.

Addison quivered as he watched the nighthawks dance through the dawn, but he didn't bark. Maybe like me, he was too amazed. "Come on, boy," I said. "Let's get cracking." He snapped out of his trance and capered to and fro chasing the silent birds until I called his name. We were off.

The road up to the Table wound through the junipers for a while before climbing the final grade. We paralleled the road, staying low and in the cover of the trees as much as possible. Back when I'd been elected, I had decided to put slings on all our long guns, including the twelve gauge I carried now. That made the trek easier, gun and saddle bags slung over my shoulder, a mostly-empty canteen bumping my hip. Addison stayed by my side, a game little guy, but I held back my pace a bit, and we stopped for water more than I would have liked.

We'd already crossed a couple of washouts on the road, but we finally reached the big mama of all washouts. A dry gulch cut across what was left of the road, making a small canyon fourteen feet deep. The sides were steep and difficult, but not impossible. I carried Addison in one hand and used the other to hold onto roots as I eased myself down, digging footholds in the flaky earth with my clodhoppers. I slipped and had to jump the last few feet, landing awkwardly on my ass. Addison barked as if this was all great fun. "No comments from the peanut gallery," I said.

We rested for a moment in the protection of the gulley. I smoked a cigarette while Addison explored upstream. I thought about Kate and how useless her death had been. Though she had only been gone a couple of days, the loss felt eternal. I was a solitary man, mostly by choice, but being solitary meant that when there was no one in your life, you dealt with the constant ache of loneliness. Being a cynic, I'd always thought I'd prefer that constant ache to the sudden sharp pains that could come when you loved someone, but now I knew I'd been wrong. Sitting in this giant trench, squatting among the rocks and the dust, I felt a tightening in my stomach and behind my eyes. Blood throbbed in my ears. It would have been easy to push down my feelings, but this time I examined them as if they were objects in a box, hidden, secret, wrapped away. I pulled back the wrapping paper, exposed the object to the air, and felt it open like a black flower. I felt the guilt of killing men, the shame of surviving battles, the hole in my guts from losing Kate. I stubbed out my cigarette. Would it be worse for me if I killed one more man?

Addison barked from the bank above me. He must have found an easy way up to the far side of the gulch. I wiped off my tears and headed upstream.

After about fifty yards of skipping across rocks, I came to a place where the bank had caved in, creating an easy route up to the road. When I caught up with Addison, the glow of the sun was bumping up against the horizon. Dawn would come soon enough. The road switchbacked up the grade to the top of Twelve Mile Table, but going that way would be fatal. Conroy would be watching.

A game trail took off straight up the hill. Mule deer didn't climb rock like mountain goats, so I assumed that they had discovered an easy way up through the rimrock. "Sorry, buddy," I said to Addison. "We're going up the trail, and it ain't gonna be easy. I want to sneak up on Conroy."

The climb was steep, steeper than I expected, and I stopped often. I wanted to tell myself it was Addison, but I knew full well the stops were for me, too. We finished the last of our water about halfway up. I hoped that Conroy had brought enough for all of us.

The sun had cleared the horizon when we reached the base of the rimrock. My thought was correct; a crude trail wound up through the rocks. I helped Addison past the rough spots, places where he couldn't or wouldn't jump with his stumpy legs, but he faired well enough, and we gained the crest in short order.

The top of the Table was as flat as if the hand of a god had scraped off the top of a mountain. We emerged about a hundred and fifty yards east of the Gearhart homestead. The smoke was thick, and the sky ranged in color from yellow to red to dark gray. In the distance, flames hopped from sage to juniper, but as far as I could figure, the wind quartered from our right, pushing the fire away from us.

Old man Gearhart had built his home on the edge of the rimrock. City folks would think it was for the view, but I figured Gearhart wanted to maximize his farmland. The whole affair leaned to the right with the prevailing wind, and the family had planted a stand of poplars on the windward side. The house had one main story with a high-peaked room and a small attic window. Maybe that's where Sam had his room in the attic. Time had not been kind to the exterior; the clapboards were warped, gray, and split. The house may have been white at one time, but any paint had been stripped by time, wind, and the harsh desert winters. No glass in the windows that I could see, but I imagined old Mrs. Gearhart had fashioned curtains out of checked gingham and hung them on home-fashioned curtain rods. How they must have grieved when the bank took the place from them.

The floor plan would be simple: kitchen, parlor, a bedroom, maybe two if the Gearharts had planned on a big family, maybe a small pantry off the kitchen. No basement, bedrock on the Table would be no more than a couple of feet beneath the sandy earth. There might be a crawlspace underneath if they had been ambitious and planned on putting in running water someday. One shack out back, mostly fallen down, the remnants no more than a ramshackle lean-to. A pile of lumber told me where the outhouse had been. Did they use an old Sears's catalog? As a kid, we had one, almost like we lived a cliché. Kate would have liked this house when it was built. We could have raised some kids, been happy.

Much of war was waiting, waiting to be fed, to smoke, march or go on or off duty. Sometimes you waited for the enemy to attack or you hid in ambush, the mosquitoes feeding off the tender parts of your neck while you're unable to swat them away. You counted the days until you got off the troopship, then counted the days until you went to the front. You lost count then, hunkering down in the jungle, time stretched and you could only dream of rotating out, back to Australia, back to flush toilets, cold beer, and women.

Addison and I reached a large pile of lava rocks that old man Gearhart must have stacked after clearing them from his field. We crouched behind them and waited, waited and watched. Addison lifted his leg and peed on a clump of sagebrush; I did the same. The house was silent, cocked, sinister. I couldn't see him, but I felt Conroy was there.

When I was a kid, my dad, my real dad, took me hunting once. I was five, and it was my first time. Dad hunted birds, ducks, and chucker mostly. We got up before dawn; he cooked bacon and eggs when things were still plentiful, before the bottom dropped out. I could still smell the bacon. We took his dog and drove to a farmer's pond at the base of Powell Butte. The temperature was in the teens, and I pranced to keep warm until Dad told me to be quiet and still. For warmth he gave me his gloves, huge, woolen, and fragrant. I pressed them to my ears and peeked between the reeds as he fired his shotgun. I'd never heard anything so loud.

I didn't get to shoot that day, just take the wet, dead ducks and place them in the bag when Dad's dog brought them to us. The ducks were limp, sleek, and beautiful. I didn't tell Dad I didn't want to shoot, that the sharp violence, the blood, scared me. But I was happy to be with my dad, proud that he had let me come along. We never went hunting again, never seemed to have the time before he died. When I grew up, I hunted birds just like my dad, but gave it up after the war, telling myself I'd killed enough. Maybe I never did enjoy the sharp violence and just lacked the excuse to let it all go. What I did miss was the smell of frying bacon, the tan color of reeds around the pond, the sight of the ducks reeling by in formation, and the weak sun shining on my head trying to break the chill grip of a winter morning.

No ducks flying overhead this morning, no clear sky or sun, and the only smell was of burning juniper. A pair of chipmunks, brown and white, hastened by, running from the flames. Addison barked, and I shushed him with a hand on top of his head. I stroked his soft ears. "I'm thirsty," I whispered. "And you are, too, I expect. It's time for me to move, but I want you to stay here. Understand?" He looked at me as if he did.

"Stay." I held my hand toward him, palm out. I took a step, and he followed. I picked him up and put him back in place. "Stay!" That time he did, quivering with anticipation, but he stayed, and I crawled on my belly toward the house.

In basic training, they made us crawl through the mud on our bellies while a trigger-happy corporal fired live rounds from a .50

caliber over our heads. Short of true combat, that was the most scared I'd ever been. This crawl was a little longer and no bullets flew over my head, but I'd be a liar if I said I wasn't scared.

I found cover behind the pile of shredded boards that had once been the outhouse. Nothing left smelled bad there, only smoke and dusty wood. A clothesline post leaned half-cocked next to the outhouse. I imagined old lady Gearhart, maybe a young woman then, hanging white sheets on a blustery, sunny Monday morning. Did Sam remember his mother scrubbing the wash by hand and hanging the laundry? I didn't know her name. She'd passed before I arrived in these parts, but I decided to call her Sarah. Good name, Sarah.

I would have liked to stay there for the rest of the morning lying in the cool dirt, but the wind shifted into my face, and the smoke came with it. My eyes itched and filled with tears. The range fire leaned in my direction, and I knew I had to get this show on the road.

I decided to do it the easy way, run around the house tossing grenades into the windows. Conroy would either be killed outright or forced into the open. I picked my point of initial attack, a back bedroom window. My tongue had swollen from thirst. Did that old hand pump work? Pointing the shotgun at the window, I crept to the side of the house, placed my back to the wall, and listened. All I heard was the rush of the wind, the distant crackle of flames and, somewhere overhead, a bird squawking.

Pulling the pin on the grenade, I tensed myself to toss it through the window. Before I released the spoon to ignite the fuse, something rustled and pattered nearby, but not inside the house. A black and brown streak hurtled across the yard.

"Addison," I whispered. "Stop!"

Heedless, he ran with all four legs churning and scooted into the crawl space beneath the house. I searched the dusty ground, found the pin, and slipped it back into the grenade. The fuse hadn't been ignited, so the grenade was safe.

What the fuck could I do now? I could crawl under the house to find Addison. Conroy might not expect an attack from below, but black widow spiders love dark, cozy places, not that I was especially scared of spiders, but I was a prudent man. Addison could fend for himself. I listened again. Wind and fire whistled and cracked, but the house was silent. Maybe I heard Addison rooting around underneath, maybe it was my imagination.

Pineapple grenades didn't make as big a bang as in the movies with John Wayne killing Japs, but they threw out enough shrapnel to clear out a good-sized room. Given the state of the Gearhart house, the explosions might collapse the place in on itself, crushing Addison. I sighed. Damned dog. Time to do things the hard way; clear the house room by room.

The back bedroom seemed a decent enough point of entry. If I was lucky, the coach might be napping in the front room. He might not know about the fire or my being here. I peeked into the window; the bedroom seemed almost empty. I peeked again, then leaned back against the wall picturing what I'd seen. Some floorboards were missing beneath the window. I'd have to avoid the hole as I entered. A wisp of a curtain fluttering in the wind hung from another window. Muslin, probably. Why hadn't Sarah taken it with her? Bits of trash here and there on the floor, but not as much as I'd expected. The closet door in one corner was askew, the interior dark and cobwebbed. I'd have to check that first. The Gearharts had tacked newspapers to the walls for insulation. Someone, maybe Conroy, had removed the door that led to the rest of the house. I snuck a longer look. 'Sorry, Sarah, for the violence I am about to inflict on your home,' I said to myself as I slipped through the window.

Chapter 22

I felt quite pleased with myself, sneaking around the Gearhart back bedroom like some little boy poking around in his parent's dresser drawers, except this time, the blood pounded so hard in my ears I was sure Conroy would hear me. The newspapers tacked to the walls were from the turn of the century. Teddy Roosevelt and the Bull Moose Party, fear of the Huns, and ads for bicycles and heroin—guaranteed to help kick that opium habit. The back closet contained a single button-up woman's boot without a sole. The house's timbers creaked as the wind increased, and the smell of abandonment was almost overwhelmed by the smoke.

A short hall led to the second, smaller bedroom, the children's. I imagined Sam Gearhart, the child, not the asshole, playing with a wooden top, spinning it on the floorboards. There were bits of clothing, boy's pants and shirts and a single sneaker. Too new for Sam, I figured they might have belonged to Joey—Conroy's trophies of conquest. A letterman's sweater had been carefully folded and placed on a wooden apple crate, almost as if in reverence. If not Joey's—Roberta had found that one—then whose? I examined it closely. There was a student's name written on the label. How many silent victims walked the halls of our high school?

Someone had drawn pictures in pen and ink—pictures of boys and young women, faces filled with fear and terror—and tacked them on the wall. The artist was good, someone whose skill had been refined both by practice and imagination. Maybe the coach, but he seemed too brutish to have this talent. I figured he must have a partner or maybe a pawn in this enterprise. I wanted to feel sick, repulsed, even angry, but all I felt was the need to be quiet, to find my enemy and kill him. The shotgun felt solid, just right in my hands.

I snuck to the door and pressed my back to the wall listening and waiting. Crackles and creaks, but no sounds of man. Something sounded underneath, damned Addison searching underneath the house, looking for mice or rats perhaps. I hoped he'd be okay.

I peeked into the parlor, then slid around the corner. Conroy had slept here for sure; a bedroll had been stretched out and smoothed carefully in one corner of the room. A half-full knapsack rested at the foot of the makeshift bed. Neat, nothing out of place. Conroy was an orderly man, what I'd expect from a squared-away Marine.

The north half of the parlor had caved in upon itself. A ceiling rafter had tumbled into the floorboards creating a gaping hole in the floor. I knelt and looked into the crawlspace, seeking Addison, but only seeing tiny pale things crawling in the darkness. A breeze, dusty and dry, blew into my face. This was where bad dreams lived, a place of children's nightmares. Stupid, fucking dog. I wanted to call to him, but that would be suicide. I'd already marched down that road and found it not to my liking.

Something skittered from the direction of the kitchen, and I honest-to-God got spooked. It was the last room. I crossed to the parlor in two giant steps and spun around the corner, my finger tight on the trigger, my shoulder tensed for the jolt of the recoil, but the room was empty. Completely empty, no stove, icebox, or kitchen table. Did Conroy cook outside in a fire ring?

My stomach twisted and ached with nausea from unrequited adrenaline. The smoke from the range fire was almost overwhelming, and tears ran from my eyes without sorrow. I repressed a sneeze. Conroy should have been here. The fucking attic, I thought too late.

Something clumped behind me in the living room, and I acted without thought. I leaped into the living room and cut loose with the twelve gauge; five hard jerks pounded against my shoulder. The double-ought buckshot blasted holes in the walls of the house. Wood splintered, and more smoke flooded through the gaps. The room quickly became shrouded, confusing. As happened in combat, I hadn't consciously heard the shots, but my ears rang. Another timber had fallen into the living room. Stupid, I thought. Stupid.

The ceiling over my head opened like the devil's door, and boards, dust, and something heavier, something leaden, came crashing down on me, knocking me off my feet. I tried to scramble away, and Conroy hit the side of my head with a glancing blow, not enough to put me out, but enough to queer me. I crawled on my hands and knees until I reached the wall and pulled myself to my feet.

Conroy stood bare-chested, legs spread, in the center of room. He was clad only in stained sweat pants and sneakers. He held a revolver in his right hand and as he brought it to bear, I leapt at him, driving my shoulder into his gut. He oofed backwards onto his ass, and his gun slid across the floor. We grappled, rolling over. First I was on top, throwing short rights into his side, then he rolled on top. His weight pushed the air from my lungs. He punched me hard in the face and grabbed my throat. I dug my fingers in his eyes; his eyeball shifted under my fingernails. He barked, and the pressure on my throat was gone.

Conroy disappeared toward the back bedrooms. I hopped up and ran after him. I caught him trying to climb out the back window and grabbed him by the shoulders. He whirled with a knife in his hand, and I stumbled back, my shirt and the flesh of my chest sliced and gaping. He tackled me, and I went down beneath him, his knees pressed on my shoulders like a schoolyard bully's. He twisted the blade of the knife against my throat. Blood seeped from his right eye.

"You don't give up, do you?" he asked.

"You killed the kids. Virginia first," I said.

"A complication," he said.

"And Joey?"

"Chicken-shit pussy," he said.

"And Kate?"

"She was getting too close for comfort," he said. "And to fuck with you."

"Mistake," I said.

"No," he said. "I'll win. I'll always win."

He dug the point of the knife into the side of my neck and laughed, fully insane. I arched my back to push him off. No luck, he'd balanced himself well. "You hurt me," he said, touching his bloody eye. "I want payback." The blade hovered over my eye, and I struggled to push him off. Never give up, I thought.

Just as the blade kissed my eye, a black blur flew at Conroy's neck, and he screamed, twisting off of me. Addison had sunk his teeth into the Coach's neck and hung on with grim resolve. Conroy ripped the dog from his neck and hurled him against the wall. Addison yelped as he hit and lay motionless. I jumped to my feet, and Conroy dived through the bedroom window. "Fucker," I said, and followed him, no time to check on Addison at the moment.

Fire had encircled the house, and smoke swirled thicker than February fog. I blinked my eyes to clear the tears. Snot ran from my nose, and I wiped it with the back of my hand. Blood covered my hands. Mostly mine, I supposed, but maybe some of Conroy's. The noise and heat of the fire engulfed me, and I had to pause for a moment to reorient myself. My head hammered, and I felt as if I was back in the war.

Conroy had already disappeared into the smoke. Flames jumped from cheatgrass to sage, closing off escape on three sides. He'd head for the rimrock, the only logical escape. I drew my .45 and ran around the house to the cliff.

The vertical drop from the rimrock to the start of the hillside had to be at least seventy feet. If the drop didn't kill you, the tumble down the sixty-percent grade into the valley below would. At first glance, I didn't see him. He crouched behind a dense sage. When he moved, I popped off a round without bothering to aim, my second mistake. It flew high and wide, and he ran back toward the house.

I ran to the corner of the house, tugged a grenade from my pocket and pulled the pin. I counted to five and flipped it around the corner. The boom was sharper than I remembered. I swung around the corner. Shrapnel had scored the side of the house, but Conroy wasn't there. Out of the corner of my eye, I caught movement by the outhouse. I played dumb, scratched my head as if confused, peeked in the bedroom window, then walked around the house as if I thought Conroy was inside.

Suddenly, I spun and ran toward the outhouse. Conroy tried to run, but I caught him hard in the side with my shoulder. He crashed down, and I jumped on top of him. I cracked him alongside the head with the Colt. "Bastard," I grunted, and hit him again. He lay quiet, and I considered killing him. No one would know. No one would care. Barnes would back my play. He'd loved Kate in his own way.

"Okay, pal," I said. "This is how it's going to be."

"No," he said. "This is how it's going to be." He stabbed me in the back and intense pain radiated from the back of my shoulder. Conroy bucked me off, and my gun flew out of my hand. I lay on my side trying to reach the knife. Don't go into shock, I thought. Don't give up.

Conroy leaned down and jerked the knife from my body. The range fire was only yards away. I screamed. No shame for screaming in battle. I kicked out at his feet, and he stumbled while I reached in my back pocket searching for my sap. In a flash, he was at me again, laying the blade across my neck. No laughing for either of us now.

He took it slow, enjoying his work. The knife sliced my skin, not quite deep enough to reach an artery. My sap, where was it? My fingers touched the handle. I grabbed the sap and swung in desperation, hitting Conroy in the mouth. Blood and chunks of teeth exploded, and he rolled off me. Tears ran down my face, either from the pain or the smoke. It didn't matter. Conroy lifted up his body, blood covering his face and bare chest. On my knees, I slapped him alongside the head, and he sagged, stunned. I tried to stand, but my legs wobbled and I collapsed.

I crawled to my .45. The fire almost upon us, Conroy jumped to his feet and ran into the flames. "Stop!" I cried. The fool, I thought. Then I remembered a story of a man jumping through a grass fire to save his life. I still thought the story was nuts, but I had no other options, so I ran along the facing edge of the flames. At first I thought I was sunk, then I found a narrow gap in the fire no bigger than a man's body and, without further internal debate, jumped through it. Heat whipped around me encasing me like a cocoon, and my head felt as if my hair caught fire. I hit the ground and rolled, patting my body and head to make sure any flames had gone out. I touched my eyebrows. Fire had singed them off. The wind blew in my face, pushing the smoke and flames away from me. I staggered to my feet. The world had turned black while we had fought.

The fire had reduced junipers to smoking stumps and sagebrush to piles of white ash. Sudden pain shot up from my feet. White-hot embers lay underneath the black ash, and the heat had radiated up through the soles of my combat boots. I hopped and danced like a New Guinea tribesman. I ran deeper into the blackened landscape until I reached cooler ground. I was alone—no animals, no birds, no sound except for the white noise of the flames at my back. I dropped to my knees and ash drifted up and over my head. The noon sun felt cool compared to what I'd gone through.

"No time for prayer." Conroy stood twenty feet away.

I aimed my .45 at the center of his torso. "You're done."

"Not yet." He held his knife in his right hand. The fire hadn't been kind to him. His left arm was burned, and blood and goo oozed through the cracked black skin. His white eyes stared through the soot covering his face, and the effect was that of a minstrel wearing blackface. Hot cinders had burned holes in his sweatpants, and the soles of his sneakers smoked.

I could have said something cheesy like, "Don't be a fool," or "Reach for the sky." Instead, I said, "I could kill you, and no one would know."

"You would," he said. We stood there looking at each other, held in place by the white noise of the flames, then something stung me on the side of the neck. "Ouch," I said, and instinctively slapped my neck with my free hand.

Conroy screamed and rushed me. I backpedaled and fired one round just as he reached me. The heavy slug tore off the business end of Conroy's left foot and he tumbled onto the ground. "Fucking grunt," he said. "You girls never could shoot straight." He struggled onto one knee and tried to lever himself up to come at me again. He looked like some primitive with half his teeth knocked out and his face stained red and black with blood and ash.

I shot the son of a bitch again, this time in the right kneecap. He collapsed screaming, and I said, "Oh God, that felt good."

He screamed and yelled for me to finish him, but his pain didn't taste as sweet as I had imagined. He'd bleed to death sooner rather than later if I didn't so something, so I cracked him alongside the head with my .45, and he quieted down. Okay, that part felt sweet enough.

I used Conroy's shoelaces to fashion tourniquets to stem the bleeding. The shoelaces were too narrow to make good tourniquets, and I figured the prolonged constriction might cost him his legs. I rooted around on the ground, found a couple of sticks, and used them to cinch up the laces. I whistled while I worked and imagined Conroy, legless in prison, living the rest of his life with a large sex-starved cellmate named Bluto.

I dug through my pockets, found my lighter and a crumpled pack of smokes, and lit up. The flames chewed through what was left of the Gearhart homestead. Help would be arriving soon. After a while, Conroy started keening like an old woman. This man had taken children from Esther Kelly and Betty McIntyre. He had taken my Kate. I slapped him as hard as I could, and said, "Buck up, candy ass." He sniveled louder so I sapped him back into unconsciousness.

*

The morning bloomed bright and sunny, but there was no shade for Conroy or me, not up here on the Table. I sat Indian style in the ash and watched wisps of smoke twist up into the still skies from what remained of the Gearhart chimney. A dozen antelope meandered by on the distant horizon, and I imagined them jumping and running before the range fire. I felt about as lonely as a man could feel.

"Addison!" I called with little hope.

"Fuck your dog," Conroy said from his half-stupor.

I considered laying my sap into the man's ball sack. "Let's examine your possible futures, cupcake. First, they'll convict you of murder, and they'll gas you like a mad dog. That thought makes my toes curl. Second, you may get life cracking rocks at the State Pen. With your bad pins, you won't last long. Third, you'll plead insanity and end up at the loony bin in Pendleton. Trust me, I've seen the place. You'd do better in prison. And if you get off, I'll hunt you down and kill you."

"Know what I regret?" he asked. "Killing them horses. Flehardy had some fine horseflesh there, but I just couldn't turn them loose."

"How about your wife's dog? Do you regret that, too?"

"Never did cotton to that dog, too fucking independent." He lapsed back into unconsciousness.

The posse arrived an hour later. "You're late," I said to Dirk Redmond.

He handed me a canteen, and I gulped half of it. The water was warm and metallic, but still tasted sweet. "Looks like you had a little tussle," Dirk said.

"Can't say I've had worse," I said. "How's George?"

"Doc says he'll be fine. Right now, he's flourishing under Miriam's tender care," Redmond said.

"Conroy will need the doc soon enough," I said. "I figure he'll lose one leg. Maybe both."

"Shame," Redmond said without conviction. "Doc's on his way up. The National Guard loaned us a jeep. They're coming up the back way. Should be here sooner rather than later."

Conroy mumbled something, and I made to sap him again, but Redmond stayed my hand. "Might want to lighten up on that," he said. "You don't want to kill the son of a bitch."

I told him he was right and sheltered myself on the shady side of his horse while Redmond looked after Conroy. The other men in the posse sidled away from me as if I frightened them somehow.

We heard the jeep whining up the grade before we saw it. The engine noise covered the sound of barking, and I didn't see Addison until he leaped on my lap and started licking my face. "Great days!" I said.

"We found him running down the road, barking like Rin Tin Tin," Doc said. "We figured he was looking for help."

I scratched Addison behind the ears. "Let's not give the son of a bitch too much credit." I wasn't sure who was happier to see whom. Doc checked my knife wound first, but the blood was barely oozing out of my shoulder by now, so he slapped a bandage on it and said he'd stitch me up back in town.

Conroy whined about having to wait, but Doc said, "Hold your water. Not much I can do for you up here. That right leg will have to come off and most of your other foot, too. Other than that, you'll be just ducky."

"If that's supposed to be funny," Conroy said, "I ain't laughing."

Doc smiled. "Me either."

Chapter 23

Margie Weekly waved, and yelled, "Hiya, Sheriff," as I limped across the football field. She and the rest of the rally squad practiced their cheers, kicking tanned legs and flipping pleated skirts to an imaginary crowd. Addison barked and ran among them, dodging their feet and dancing on hind legs until the girls called for a break and gathered around my wiener dog, petting him and telling me what a cutie pie he was. I can't say I didn't envy him.

The rodeo grounds had been converted into a football stadium, horse shit scooped and hauled away, green turf laid down in anticipation of the first big game. Mike Barfield pushed a four-wheeled machine in straight lines across the field, laying chalk and creating the yard markers that would define the field. I said, "Hold up there, Mike." He stopped and waited with wary suspicion until I reached him. "No game tonight," I told him. "It's been cancelled. Coach Conroy is under arrest."

"Really?" He shaded his eyes with the palm of his hand.

"Don't bullshit a bullshitter," I said. "You already knew that he murdered Joey and Virginia. You drew the pictures up at the Gearhart homestead. I'm not sure when you were there, but you left your letterman's sweater."

"I don't know what you're talking about," he said.

"The sweater had your name written on the label. Kid's proud of a letterman's sweater, the first thing he'd do is write his name in it," I said. "I've got you cold. The question is, did you help Conroy with the murders?"

"Shit," he said, and half-sat, half-fell onto the grass.

"Better to tell me all about it. Better to get it off your chest."

Sweat dripped off the end of his nose. "I didn't know he was going to kill anyone. I didn't know until afterward, but I couldn't say anything. He said he'd kill me."

"But he did tell you afterward?"

"I think he wanted to brag," Barfield said.

"Guys like that need an audience," I said. "If you had said something, you'd have saved Kate Barnes's life. You're responsible for her death." The kid cried then, big silent sobs. He hid his eyes with his forearm trying to conceal the tears. In that moment, I hated him, hated his silence, hated his acquiescence. I looked into myself for forgiveness and found only despair. I sat there for a long time, waiting for him to finish, listening to the cheerleaders play with my dog.

"I'm sorry," he said finally. "So sorry."

"What about Dr. McIntyre? He and Conroy were cozy. What was his involvement?"

"Coach knew that Dr. McIntyre was having sex with Virginia, and he was blackmailing him. He laughed and told me that McIntyre was going to keep him flush. That's the word he used, *flush*. Said he'd be able to buy a new pickup pretty soon."

"Why'd Conroy kill Virginia?"

"Joey was his favorite. There were others. We were all scared of him, what he'd do to us, but Joey was his favorite. Joey told Coach he was in love with Virginia and that he wanted it to stop. Coach got pissed. *Really* pissed. I guess he killed Virginia because he was jealous. He didn't say so in so many words. That's just what I figured. He told Joey that he'd be blamed for the murder and that he'd have to hide out for a while until things got sorted out." The kid shrugged. "I don't know why he killed Joey. He didn't tell me that part."

"Was Ronnie Gearhart involved?" I asked.

Barfield shook his head. "Not that I know. Coach didn't screw with Ronnie for some reason." Maybe Conroy knew that Gearhart wouldn't brook the bullshit and would fight back or tell someone.

"But Conroy did abuse other boys?" I asked.

"Will I go to jail?" he said.

"The circuit judge is driving down from The Dalles. He'll decide what will happen to you." Barfield wouldn't see any significant jail time, but I wanted him to swing in the wind a bit. "You will need to tell him and the D.A. exactly what happened and who was involved. No lying anymore. Understand?"

The kid nodded, and I hauled him to his feet. I considered handcuffing him, but figured what would be overkill. The ride down to the courthouse would be long enough. He was guilty of not telling what he knew earlier, guilty of being a scared kid, but with our D.A., I figured he wouldn't end up doing any time.

I collected my dog and told the girls the game had been cancelled. They said, "Ah gee, that's too bad," but didn't seem all that concerned. For them it was only a game.

*

The funeral procession filed into Pioneer Cemetery, Tony

Giovanni first in his almost-new Ford police car, red light flashing, Barnes next in his pearl-white Caddy convertible, Harley and his family further back in line. I'd taken a pass on the funeral service at the Baptist Church. My mom was a hardcore Baptist, and that shit got old for me. Kate would have understood my absence at the church. She was an understanding woman. Instead of listening to the preacher talk of redemption, I'd swung by the McIntyre house and snapped up Jeff McIntyre. When he asked, "What for?" I told him he was charged with statutory rape. Betty, his wife, didn't cry when I clicked the cuffs on her husband. Maybe she knew he was guilty, or maybe she was just all cried out. After I locked up McIntyre, I hurried to the cemetery. It wouldn't be right for me to miss the arrival of my sweetie.

Addison frolicked among the junipers chasing chipmunks but being silent as if he knew the gravity of the affair. The day should have been sunny, but hadn't turned out that way. Smoke from range fires on the high desert and forest fires in the Ochocos had created a translucent haze that dampened the sun, and the light reminded me of the rose-colored cloud cover we might get before the first snow of the season.

Somewhere further up the valley, the mill's big saw whined—no rest for progress—and a sage hen waddled across the grass and ducked under the fence into the alfalfa field next door. Luckily, Addison didn't see the sage hen and run after her barking and disrupting the ceremony.

Folks gathered by the grave while the preacher said some words. If Kate had been here, I would have told her that I loved her, always loved her, even when I was in San Francisco. I'd always wanted to tell her why I'd stayed in San Francisco after the war instead of going back to her and getting married. I'd always wanted to tell her that I was scared, scared of the sharp violence in me, scared that I'd turn out just like my Mom, let that violence well up and beat my kids with a strap.

I was a man who had become accustomed to violence, but as I stood there under pink skies and reflected on what had happened over the past few days, I realized that violence could come easy to me, but that I could control my urges, that I wouldn't hurt my kith and kin, that I wasn't like my mother. My great regret was that I would never be able to share my feelings, my revelations, with Kate. I hoped wherever she was, that she would forgive me.

I was so caught up in my own misery that I didn't notice Doc sidle up next to me until he cleared his throat, and said, "Care for a little jab after she's in the ground?"

"How's Stewart doing?" I asked.

"Should be up in Portland by now," Doc said. "He'll be just fine." When I told him I was glad, he asked me again if I wanted a drink.

"You can buy me a cup of coffee down at the cafe," I said.

"Great day for a wake," he said.

"Just too early for me," I said. "That's all."

"Coffee it is," he said.

Addison was playing tag with an old tomcat, and I had to whistle twice to get his attention. "Come here, you damned dog." When we got home from work that evening, I set up a wooden orange crate by the stove and stuffed an old torn army blanket in it. Addison pawed at the blanket a bit, climbed into the crate, circled three times, and settled down looking at me with sad brown eyes. "Okay, fine," I said. "You can stay, for now at least."

The End

About the Author

Michael Bigham has worked in a lumber mill, fought range fires in the Ochoco Mountains and spent many years as a police officer. He graduated from the Vermont College of Fine Arts with an MFA in Creative Writing. Michael lives in Portland,Oregon with his wife, daughter and a puppy named Pumpkin. Harkness is his first novel.

Author Michael Bigham

www.ingramcontent.com/pod-product-compliance
Lightning Source LLC
LaVergne TN
LVHW050638100826
845148LV00011B/1900

* 9 7 8 0 6 1 5 7 2 1 9 7 2 *